Hard Truth

***Also by Mariah Stewart
in Large Print:***

Cold Truth
Dead End
Dead Certain
Dead Even
Dead Wrong

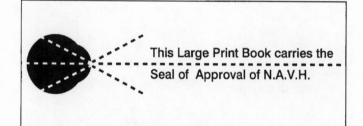

This Large Print Book carries the
Seal of Approval of N.A.V.H.

Hard Truth

MARIAH STEWART

WHEELER
PUBLISHING

Published in 2006 by arrangement with The Ballantine Publishing Group, a division of Random House, Inc.

Wheeler Large Print Romance.

The text of this Large Print edition is unabridged.
Other aspects of the book may vary from the original edition.

Set in 16 pt. Plantin by Myrna S. Raven.

Printed in the United States on permanent paper.

Library of Congress Cataloging-in-Publication Data

Stewart, Mariah.
    Hard truth / by Mariah Stewart. — Large print ed.
        p. cm. — (Wheeler Publishing large print romance)
    ISBN 1-59722-170-8 (lg. print : hc : alk. paper)
    1. Missing children — Fiction.   2. Private investigators
— Pennsylvania — Fiction.   3. Pennsylvania — Fiction
4. Large type books.   I. Title.   II. Wheeler large print
romance series.
    PS3569.T4653H53 2006
    813′.54—dc22   2005031100

For Carole, who left us way too soon.
I think of you and miss you every day —
love you still.

As the Founder/CEO of NAVH, the only national health agency solely devoted to those who, although not totally blind, have an eye disease which could lead to serious visual impairment, I am pleased to recognize Thorndike Press* as one of the leading publishers in the large print field.

Founded in 1954 in San Francisco to prepare large print textbooks for partially seeing children, NAVH became the pioneer and standard setting agency in the preparation of large type.

Today, those publishers who meet our standards carry the prestigious "Seal of Approval" indicating high quality large print. We are delighted that Thorndike Press is one of the publishers whose titles meet these standards. We are also pleased to recognize the significant contribution Thorndike Press is making in this important and growing field.

Lorraine H. Marchi, L.H.D.
Founder/CEO
NAVH

* Thorndike Press encompasses the following imprints: Thorndike, Wheeler, Walker and Large Print Press.

Three things cannot be long hidden: the sun, the moon, and the truth.
— SIDDHARTHA

With much gratitude to Nicole Morley, Esq., Assistant District Attorney, Chester County, Pennsylvania, who cheerfully let me pester her;

and

District Justice Christopher R. Mattox, Esq., Upper Darby, Pennsylvania, who freely offered his wealth of judicial wisdom and legal expertise, thereby saving me from looking extremely foolish.

It goes without saying that any and all goofs are mine.

Prologue

Callen, Pennsylvania
October 9, 1980

"I thought your mother said you weren't allowed to wear that dress until your birthday party." Nine-year-old Lorna Stiles watched her friend Melinda slip the pretty yellow-and-white dress over her head.

"She did, but today is my birthday, and I want to wear it." Melinda struggled to zip up the back of the dress before turning her back to Lorna. "Here. See if you can get it."

"You're just trying it on, though, right? To show me?" Lorna persisted even as she fastened the dress. She knew Melinda's mother had a hot temper. Nothing provoked her more than having Melinda do what she was specifically told not to do.

"I'm going to wear it to your house. It's sort of like a party, right?" Melinda twirled in front of the mirror.

"Just birthday cake that my mom made for you. It's not really a party, Mel. Maybe you shouldn't —"

"I like it. I'm going to wear it. What good is having a pretty dress if you can only wear it one time?"

"You can wear it again after your birthday." Lorna paused, then lowered her voice, as if afraid of being overheard. "You know what your mom will do if she finds out, Mellie."

"She won't find out." Melinda pulled a brown paper bag from under her bed, and stuffed her play clothes in. "See? I'll change before I come home, and I'll put the dress in the bag. You can help me fold it real good, and she'll never know."

Melinda beamed, pleased with her plan.

"Come on, Lori," she said, calling her friend by her nickname, and tugging on her hand. "Let's go. I can't wait to see my cake! Did your mom get candles, too?"

"I think so." Lorna nodded glumly, an uneasy feeling spreading through her insides. In the experiences of her short life, she'd discovered that truth always outs. If Melinda wasn't afraid of her mother, Lorna was, not for herself, but for what Billie Eagan would do to her daughter.

The last time Melinda had disobeyed her mother, she'd lost three days of school. Oh, she'd never told Lorna exactly what her mother had done to punish her, but Lorna had seen the bruises on her friend's arms and legs.

Once, when Mellie's long sleeves had ridden up to display the fresh welts on her arms, Lorna had suggested gently that she tell someone. But Melinda had quickly pulled the sleeves down and asked, "Tell someone what?" with that defiant look she got sometimes, and Lorna had let it go. When Lorna had mentioned to her own mother that sometimes Melinda's mom might be a little strict — without mentioning the bruises — her mom said that the Eagans had had things tough since Mellie's father ran off with that woman from the flower shop and Mrs. Eagan had to work two jobs just to keep food on the table for her two kids and a roof over their heads.

"And God knows she has her hands full with that boy of hers." Mary Beth Stiles had shaken her blond head. "You'd think at fourteen he'd understand the situation his mother is in and try to give her a hand, instead of causing more problems for her. He's old enough to help her out once in a while."

"Jason's mean, Mom," Lorna had told her mother. "He is just plain mean. He's mean to Mel and he's mean to me."

"He hasn't ever done anything to you, has he?" Her father, who'd been half listening while he skimmed the headlines, put the newspaper down.

"No, he just gives us dirty looks and talks mean to us. He's never done anything bad," Lorna denied. *Unless you call talking dirty to us and chasing us with snakes — really big snakes — doing something to me.*

Of course, he hadn't done the snake thing in a while. Now he mostly stared. It had gotten so she almost hated to go to the Eagans', because if Jason was there, he'd stare at her and Mellie and it scared the daylights out of her and she didn't know why.

Lorna never told her parents how scary she thought Jason was. There was something about him that gave her the creeps, more and more, something she didn't have words to explain. All she knew was that the older he got, the creepier he got. She and Melinda never discussed it, but she knew that Jason rattled his sister even more than he rattled her.

"Let's go, Lori. If we don't go now, my brother will be home and he'll tell Mom about the dress. Besides, I can't wait for cake." Melinda turned the light off in her

12

room and ran down the steps, the yellow skirt of her party dress billowing around her legs.

Lorna followed behind, happy to leave the dark little house and the threat of Jason's imminent arrival behind her.

"Let's take the shortcut through the field." Melinda ran toward the wheat field that ran behind her house, and started along the side where the ground had been plowed but not planted.

"It's too muddy," Lorna protested. "We'll get our shoes all dirty."

"We'll clean them when we get to your house. Come on." Melinda took off, and Lorna followed, trying her best to avoid the ruts the plow had made when it turned around. This morning's rain had left little puddles here and there, and she knew her mother would not be pleased if she came home with her new sneakers all mud-stained.

They were halfway across the field to Lorna's, when somehow Melinda slipped and went down on her knees.

"I knew it, I knew something was going to happen . . ." Lorna gasped. "My grandmother says every time you do what you know you're not supposed to do, you get —"

"Shut up." Melinda pulled herself up and looked down with horror at the front of her dress, where brown smears marked the places where her knees had hit the ground. "Oh, shit. Look at my dress. Look at my dress."

"You're not supposed to say curse words."

Melinda spun around and looked at Lorna with wide eyes.

"What the hell do you think I should say?" Her hands were beginning to shake. "What the hell am I supposed to do?"

Her bravado crumbling, Melinda began to cry.

"She's gonna kill me. She's gonna beat me but good."

"Okay, look, my mom is home, she'll know what to do." Lorna took Melinda by the hand and started to pull her along. "The longer we stand here talking about it, the harder it's going to be to get the mud out. Come on, Mellie, let's run."

She tugged on Melinda's hand.

"You don't understand, Lori, she's gonna really hurt me." Melinda's voice was filled with true fear.

"Not if she doesn't know. Come on."

Lorna dragged Melinda along the bumpy field until they reached the Stiles' property. They ran around the back of the barn and across the yard and straight up the back steps.

"Mom! Mom!" Lorna called from the door.

"Lorna?" Her mother came out of the kitchen and saw the two girls panting, Melinda muddy and obviously in distress. "What on earth —"

"Mellie fell in the field, we have to get her dress cleaned before she goes home. She wasn't supposed to wear it, but today's her birthday and . . ." Lorna gasped.

"Slow down," her mother demanded. "Mellie, let me take a look at that dress."

Mary Beth knelt down in front of Melinda and studied the muddy mess. She looked up at the crying child and said, "I think I can get it all out, but if it's going to be dry in time for you to take it home with you, we have to hurry. Your mother didn't want you to wear this today?"

Melinda nodded tearfully.

"Go on into the laundry room and take it off. Lori, run upstairs and get Mel something to put on."

"I have stuff." Melinda held up the bag.

"Then go change and give me the dress. Let me see what I can do. And in the meantime, I want you to stop crying, wash your face and hands, and get ready to blow out the candles on that birthday cake, okay?"

Melinda had nodded gratefully, the tears beginning to dry.

"Lorna, go find the matches so we can light the candles. The cake is in the dining room," Mary Beth whispered after Melinda disappeared into the laundry room.

"Mom," Lorna whispered back, "do you think you can get the dress cleaned up in time?"

"I'm pretty sure I can. Why was she wearing it, if getting it dirty was going to be such a big deal?"

"I think it's because it's her birthday dress and today is her birthday. You can do it, can't you, Mom?"

"I'll give it my best. Now go get the ice cream out of the freezer. I'll be in to light the candles in a few minutes."

Melinda had blown out all ten candles — nine for her years, and one to grow on — with one big breath.

"My wish will come true now." She smiled at Lorna. "Everything is going to be all right."

Mary Beth cut the cake and served the girls ice cream — cherry vanilla, Melinda's favorite — then disappeared back into the laundry room. When five o'clock came and Melinda had to leave, Mary Beth handed her the dress, all clean and pressed, looking as good as new.

"Mrs. Stiles, you did it. You did it!" Melinda squealed and jumped up and down, clapping her hands, her smile lighting the room. "Thank you, thank you."

"You're welcome. Now, the next time your mother says not to wear the dress, do us all a favor and don't wear the dress," Mary Beth said as she handed her a bag holding leftover cake. "This is for your mother and brother. And there's a little extra for you, for a snack."

"Mrs. Stiles, you're the best." Melinda hesitated, then threw her arms around Mary Beth's neck, and shared a whispered secret. "My wish came true. Thank you."

A rudely loud knock on the back door startled them all.

Lorna opened it to find Jason's dark eyes staring at her.

"My mom wants Mel to come home now."

"I'll drive her, Jason, and you, too," Mary Beth offered, looking for her keys. "It's starting to get dark."

"My mom said for me to walk her."
Jason looked beyond Mary Beth to where
Melinda stood. "Come on, Mel. Now."

"Thank you, Mrs. Stiles, for everything."
Melinda's voice held a solemnity beyond
her years. The smiles were gone, the happy
glow had disappeared. She ran out the
back door, a bag in each hand, calling over
her shoulder to Lorna, "Thank you, Lorna.
That was the best birthday ever."

Lorna waved good-bye from the back
porch.

It was the last time she ever saw
Melinda.

One

Callen, Pennsylvania
August 2005

The two-lane road meandered languidly through a countryside alive with the colors of late summer. The sun was still uncomfortably hot at four in the afternoon, hot enough that the jacket Lorna Stiles had worn when she set out that morning from Woodboro — forty miles south of Pittsburgh — had long since been removed and tossed into the backseat. At some point while traveling the Pennsylvania Turnpike, it had slid onto the floor behind the driver's seat, but Lorna had failed to notice. There'd been plenty to think about during the drive east across the state, to her hometown of Callen. A soiled jacket was the least of her worries.

Change had been slow to come in this southernmost tip of eastern Pennsylvania, where Amish and Mennonite farms were interspersed with pricey new housing developments. The one gas station in town was now pump-your-own and was attached to a convenience store, but the stores in the little strip mall on the corner still remained closed on Sundays. While the facades remained the same, the once ramshackle old house on the opposite corner — boarded up as little as three years ago — now housed a day spa and a boutique, while its counterpart across the street had been spiffed up and turned into apartments, with the first floor converted into a bakery and coffee shop. And most noticeably, a housing development was growing in a field where corn once grew a half mile from the intersection that served as the center of town.

A sign of the times. Lorna sighed, and wondered how many other farmers had been approached by developers who wielded huge sums of cash, much more than the farms were pulling in from crops these days. Hadn't her own mother sold off thirty acres of their land sixteen months ago to pay her medical bills?

A horn sounded behind her, urging her to make up her mind. Turn or go straight.

Lorna went straight, then pulled to the side of the road, waving the impatient driver behind her to go on his merry way. She sat for a moment and read the names on the mailboxes: Hammond, Taylor, Keeler. All names she knew well.

Veronica Hammond had been best friends with Lorna's grandmother, Alice Palmer, and would be in her eighties now. Corrie Taylor had been one of Lorna's field hockey teammates, and Mike Keeler had been her first love. His brother, Fritz, had taught her how to drive a pickup. Over the past month, she'd received a card or letter from each of the families, following the death of her mother.

Mrs. Hammond, in particular, had written a touching note, remembering Lorna's mother as a young girl. "She was a lovely child, your mother was. I can still see her chasing the baby rabbits in your grandmother's garden, holding out lettuce leaves, hoping to entice them closer. How disappointed Mary Beth would be when they ran from her — she'd only wanted to play. She was certainly Alice's pride and joy . . ."

Making a mental note to pay a visit to the Hammond home before she left Callen for good, Lorna checked her mirrors for traffic before pulling out onto the road again. She drove another three-quarters of a mile, then slowed, her turn signal clicking away as she made a right into the wide drive.

The red brick house she'd grown up in

21

never changed, for all of its one hundred fifty–plus years. The door was painted dark green, the shutters black. The magnolia tree she'd climbed as a child still stood in the backyard, though a lightning strike two years ago had resulted in an ugly split down the middle. Her mother would have had the tree taken down had her focus not been on other things. Like putting up a fierce fight against the disease that, in the end, took her in spite of her bravado and her most valiant efforts.

Lorna parked under the magnolia and looked through the open windows to the fields beyond the barn, which long ago had been painted white but now was weathered to a pale gray. The parcel of land her mother had sold to the developer sat at the far end of the property, so the new homes would not be visible from the farmhouse, except from the second or third floors. She wondered how many homes were being built on the land where several generations of Palmer farmers had planted every spring and harvested every fall. Maybe tomorrow she'd take a walk across the back field and see just what was what.

Her last correspondence from anyone in Callen who'd mentioned the development was a short note from Gene Enderle, who graduated from the local regional high school a few years before Lorna. He'd written her hoping she could do something to override her mother's decision to sell the land, citing everything from concern for the wetlands to the potential for over-crowding and too many cars clogging the local roads. Lorna had called him after receiving his note, a call that had left her with the distinct impression that Gene just didn't like change in general, and change in and around Callen in particular. Some people didn't, but she'd been surprised to find that sort of resistance in someone so young.

Lorna was well aware that if circumstances had been different, none of the Palmer farm would have been sold. If her father hadn't died of that heart attack eighteen years ago, for example, leaving her mother to raise and educate three kids alone. As it was, with her mother's expenses already in excess of her insurance to the tune of one hundred thirty thousand dollars, the family really hadn't had much choice. It was sell off some land, or her mother went without the radiation and chemotherapy her doctors had recommended.

Put in that context, no discussion had

been necessary among Mary Beth's children, other than how much land to sell off at any given time. Lorna's younger sister, Andrea, married, the mother of two young children — she was now expecting her third — and living in Oklahoma, had left it all up to Lorna. Rob, the youngest and only boy, an aspiring actor who had left for Los Angeles the day he turned eighteen and had never come back, hadn't bothered to respond to the several messages Lorna had left on his answering machine, which really hadn't surprised her at all, though he'd had plenty to say about it when he came home for the small, private memorial. Once he found out how much the land could be worth, that is.

In the end, Lorna did what she felt was best for their mother. The money from the sale had given Mary Beth fifteen months of treatment in a fine hospital thirty minutes from Lorna's house. Lorna wouldn't have traded those fifteen months for all the Palmer land. In the end, her mother had lost the fight anyway, and the loss of a few acres was totally irrelevant, as far as Lorna was concerned.

She got out of the car, marveling at how quiet it was even for a Sunday afternoon in late summer. She inhaled deeply, recog-

24

nizing the familiar smells of earth after a rain — wild roses and ripe grapes. A few daylilies were still in bloom along the fence that surrounded the field across the drive from the house, and Lorna wondered if someone had been tending them. When Lorna first moved Mary Beth to Woodboro, where Lorna's home and business were located, she'd asked Gil Compton, a neighboring farmer, to keep an eye on the property and let her know when things needed to be done, and had offered to pay his son to mow the grass. Mr. Compton had kept the property as neat as Lorna's father had, made sure the heating oil in the tank never ran out and the timer never failed to turn the lights on inside the house every night, but he refused every attempt she'd made to pay him for his troubles.

"No trouble at all, Lorna," he'd insisted. "Your mother was a godsend when our oldest was in that car accident a few years back, driving my wife down to Wilmington three times a week to the hospital. If it weren't for her, neither of us would have been there when Kevin died. Thanks to Mary Beth, at least Kim was with him at the end. So you just go on and do what you have to do for your mother, and don't you give a second thought to what's going on down here. I'll take care of the farm as if it were my own."

And he had, bless him. From looking at the farm, no one would ever guess it had been uninhabited for almost a year and a half.

Lorna stuffed her hands in her pockets and shuffled up to the front door. An old habit had her checking the mailbox, but of course it was empty. They'd been having mail forwarded to Lorna's house ever since Mary Beth had moved in with her.

The key slid into the old lock and stuck in the same place it always had. She had to pull the doorknob toward her and hold it while she turned the key again. She pushed on the door and stepped inside, and immediately punched in the code to disarm the security system her mother had had installed six years ago. The foyer was dark, the afternoon sun having moved to the other side of the house, leaving the front in shadow. Lorna closed the door behind her and looked around.

Virtually nothing had changed since Lorna's childhood. Her grandmother's upright piano still stood along the back wall of the living room, a faded shawl of burgundy velvet tossed over its top. The dining room furniture was the same her grandparents had purchased as a wedding gift to each other. The old oriental carpets were worn in spots, but the colors hadn't faded too much over time. The china cupboard was bare — Mary Beth had packed up its contents and had insisted on taking everything with her to Lorna's — china, silver, and crystal that had been in the family for generations — just in case the burglar-alarm system failed.

The house was as dry and stuffy as a tomb. In spite of the heat and the high humidity, Lorna pushed open all the windows on the first floor. Out with the bad air, in with the good air — Lorna's CPR instructor's favorite chant, she recalled as she ran her fingers through the thick layer of dust on the hall table on her way back out to the car.

One of the barn cats came running toward her, and though it wasn't one she recognized, she welcomed it, enough to offer entrance to the house, but the cat declined after Lorna'd scratched it behind the ears for a minute or two. She brought her bags in and dropped them all in the foyer, then went back to the car and returned with the staples she'd picked up at the new supermarket ten minutes down the road, and spent the next half hour putting things away and making iced tea. She wanted to sit on one of the old rocking chairs that used to line the front porch, but they'd been stored someplace, so she had to content herself with a seat on the front steps. Tomorrow she'd look for the rockers.

The air was heavy with moisture and the smell of steamy August. Nostalgia washed over her and she ached with the need to cry, but no tears came. She drank her tea and watched the occasional car pass by. When her stomach told her it was time for dinner, she went inside and settled on the rest of the sandwich she'd picked up at a deli earlier in the day. She had bought lettuce, tomatoes, and cucumbers from a Mennonite farm she'd passed on the way into Callen, but was too weary to make a salad. She poured another glass of iced tea and ate the sandwich standing up, looking out the kitchen window.

When she finished, she went back outside, the local phone book under her arm. She thought of looking up some high school classmates, but decided against it after locating several names. She'd lost track of so many people over the years, she felt foolish just calling out of the blue.

Hi, I'm home for a while . . . No, don't

*know how long, probably not too, though.
I'm only here because my mother wanted
her ashes divided between the family plot,
her garden, and the pond on the other
side of the woods.*

In typical Mary Beth fashion, she had
wanted to be everywhere.

"You want a third here, a third there . . . ?"
Lorna had asked. "You're kidding, right?"

"No, I'm not kidding." Her mother had
smiled weakly. "You can divide them up
any way you want, doesn't have to be in
thirds. And if you want to keep some, you
know, a tiny bit in a cute little box, that's
okay, too. I think in the cartons we brought
from Callen there are a few of those
Limoge boxes that Gran used to collect."

"I'll do the pond and the garden and the
plot," Lorna had replied, forcing herself to
smile back, as if they were discussing
nothing more important than what stores
to stop at on their next shopping trip.
"We'll hold off on the Limoges."

"It's up to you, sweetheart." Mary Beth
had closed her eyes and added, as she
nodded off, "But we used to have a porce-
lain box shaped like a fancy little shoe. I
think that would be highly appropriate,
don't you?"

Lorna had smiled in spite of herself. Her

29

mother's love of shoes was legendary.

The phone rang, startling her. She went inside and picked up the kitchen extension, but by the time she got there, the caller had hung up.

"Probably a wrong number, anyway," she muttered as she replaced the receiver.

She walked from room to room, wondering what to do with herself. The television she'd brought with her was in the back of her SUV, but there was nothing she felt like watching. She'd been debating whether to go to the expense of having the cable connected, since she wasn't sure how long she'd be staying, but decided that was just one more decision to put off until tomorrow.

In the meantime, she'd bring in her laptop, check her email to make sure there was nothing from a client that needed to be handled immediately, and then she'd turn in early. She was tired from driving and from the emotional ordeal of coming home for the first time since her mother had moved in with her. So far she'd been okay — a little unsettled, but okay. She wasn't sure how the rest of the night would play out, though. She'd never slept alone in this house that she and her siblings had long ago accepted as having unseen occupants.

"You still here, Uncle Will?" Lorna called from the front hall. " 'Cause I'm going to be around for a while and I'd appreciate you letting me get some sleep, okay? I'll mind my business if you mind yours . . ."

She was grinning as she went outside to bring in her computer and a few other items, the television included, just in case she was unable to sleep and needed an electronic diversion. The entire family had long recognized that her great-uncle Will Palmer had remained in the house since his passing in the 1940s. His was a benign if sometimes disconcerting spirit, and over the years they'd all come to accept his presence. Actually, for the most part, they ignored it. Though it had been such fun as a teenager to tell the stories about his sightings. Invitations to sleepovers at the Stiles' house were prized by Lorna's and Andrea's friends — especially slumber parties where there was safety in numbers. There were those who even today would swear to having encountered Uncle Will in the upstairs hall or in one of the bedrooms, but whether such sightings had really taken place had not seemed to matter. Uncle Will's ghost had found a place in local legend.

The phone started to ring again while Lorna was setting the television onto a kitchen counter, and she grabbed it on the second ring.

"Hello?"

"So how is it?" True to form, Lorna's sister, Andrea, didn't bother to identify herself, but jumped immediately into conversation. "What's it like there?"

"Quiet."

"Where's Mom?"

"Still in the back of the car."

"You haven't scattered the ashes yet?"

"Christ, Andi, I've only been here a few hours." Lorna was grateful that her sister couldn't see her face at that moment. "Let me get unpacked, okay?"

"Well, I'd have thought that would have been the priority."

Easy for you to say, since you're there and I'm here.

"My priority was unlocking the front door, getting something to eat and something cold to drink. There's no air-conditioning here, you might recall, and the temperature is —"

"Okay, okay, so you'll take care of it tomorrow. I don't know how you can stand having them just sit there. The whole idea makes my skin crawl. I wish she had wanted to be buried, like Dad did."

"Well, she didn't, so we have to respect that, don't we?" Lorna replied tersely.

"I suppose." Andrea sighed as if somehow she'd made a huge concession on Lorna's behalf. "Where are you sleeping tonight?"

"I haven't decided yet."

"Is Uncle Will still there?"

"I don't know. I haven't been here long enough to find out."

"Let me know if he prowls around tonight. He might not like anyone being in the house, now that he's had it to himself all this time."

"I doubt he'll notice."

"Are you all right there by yourself?"

"Sure. I'll be fine."

"Is there anything I can do for you while you're there?"

"I don't know what you could do from Oklahoma, Andi."

"What do the new houses look like?" Andrea said, changing the subject abruptly.

"I haven't seen them yet. I thought I'd walk across the field tomorrow and take a look."

"I hope they're not tacky boxes."

"I doubt they are. The builder told Mom

they'd be selling for a lot of money."

"That's good. How was the ride to Callen?"

"Long and hot. I'd forgotten how far a drive it is."

"You figure out yet how long you're going to stay?"

"I have no idea. Andi, we talked about all this. I don't know what's the best thing to do with the farm. I hate to sell it, but none of us wants to live here. You have your home and your family out there in Oklahoma, and Rob has his life in L.A. I have my business out in the western part of the state —"

"Which you can run from Callen. You do it from home, as it is. Why can't you run it from Callen?"

"I can, and I will, for a while. But just because I don't have a husband and family in Woodboro, or because I don't have to go into an office every day, doesn't mean I don't have a life there. I have friends, I have a social life, and I'd appreciate it if you'd respect that."

"I do respect that," Andrea soothed. "I just meant that right now, you're the logical one to deal with all this. Neither Rob nor I are in a position to take off for a few weeks. We're lucky that your accounting business is such that you can work from anywhere."

"Oh, the wonders of technology and computer systems that interface."

"That's exactly what I'm talking about. You said your computer hooks into your clients', so you can travel back and forth. When was the last time you went into any of your clients' offices?"

"I do an in-house audit twice a year for each client."

"And you have how many clients?"

"Twenty-two."

"Well, there you go, then. Your business is a success, you only have about a month and a half when you need to be on-site. The rest of the time, you can work from Callen."

"I don't plan on being here long enough to worry about it. You wouldn't be having second thoughts about selling the farm, would you?"

Andrea's hesitation spoke volumes.

"I just want what's best for everyone," she said. "Maybe we could keep the house and a few acres."

"I thought we already agreed that it would be best for everyone if we sold the entire property."

"I think we need to discuss it a little more."

"If you were undecided, you should have said something before I drove across the state to get the ball rolling on the sale."

"I simply think we shouldn't be too hasty."

"Andrea, I will stay here long enough to take care of our business and to carry out Mom's last wishes. But I have a life in Woodboro, and I intend to return to it. This is a temporary stop for me. If you want to hold on to the farm, I suggest you and Jerry find a way to buy both my and Rob's shares and move yourselves out here."

"You know we're not in a position to do that."

"Well, neither am I."

"But —"

"Enough, Andrea. I'm exhausted. I'm not going to continue this discussion anymore tonight."

"Well, fine, Lorna. We'll talk about it after you've had a few days to rest up from your trip. Maybe you'll feel differently after being there. Let me know when you've put Mom to rest."

Andrea hung up before Lorna could respond.

"And thanks for your support," Lorna muttered as she dropped the receiver in its cradle.

What had gotten into Andrea, she wondered. Two weeks ago she thought selling the property was the best thing to do. She and Rob had both agreed that, with no one in the family interested in running the farm, the smart thing would be to sell it off, pay the taxes, and split the proceeds three ways, as Mom's will had decreed they should do if and when they decided to sell. Why the sudden change of heart on Andrea's part?

"Well, no change of heart for me," Lorna said, reminding herself to call a Realtor tomorrow and make an appointment to have the property appraised. She had no idea what it was worth, but she suspected it would be quite substantial.

She started to lock the front door, then remembered the three urns in the back of the car. She went outside and lifted the box gently, carefully carrying it up the front steps and setting it down on the top of her grandmother's piano. She didn't know what to do with it overnight, though, so she locked the front door, turned out all but the hall lights, and carried the box holding her mother's ashes up to the second floor. She placed it beside her mother's favorite chair.

"Sorry, Mom. I don't have much experience with this sort of thing." Somehow, she knew her mother would be amused.

But when it came time to sleep, Lorna lay on her old bed in the room she'd shared with Andrea from the time they were little until Lorna had left for college. The pillow felt like a rock, the mattress like a bed of nails. After an hour of tossing and turning, she went down the hall in the dark to her mother's room, and climbed into her mother's bed.

You are ridiculous, she told herself. *Thirty-four years old, and you're curled up clutching your momma's pillow.*

But in spite of her best efforts to shame herself into returning to her own bed, somehow it felt right. Within minutes, Lorna was sound asleep, and if Uncle Will was on the prowl, he didn't bother to disturb her.

Two

Lorna woke to the sound of voices being carried from a distance. She roused herself and went to the window and leaned out. At the far end of the property — the parcel that had been sold — three police cars were lined up along the side of the field.

The builder must have forgotten to apply for his permits, she thought. God knows, anything passes for high drama in Callen.

She pulled on a pair of gray knit shorts and a red tank top, and tried to brush her light brown hair into submission. Finally she pulled it back into a ponytail and searched her suitcase for her flip-flops. Before she went downstairs, she peered out the window again. An ambulance was just pulling up beside the cruisers.

One of the workmen at the development must have gotten injured somehow was her first thought. She took the stairs two at a time and went into the kitchen to look for coffee, but came up empty. The convenience store a mile down the road sold coffee, she recalled from her last trip home, so she grabbed her purse and headed out the front door. She could deal with just about anything if she had her coffee first.

Twelve minutes later, Lorna was returning home, a twenty-ounce cup of coffee in hand, when a black car bearing the words *County Medical Examiner* on the door sped by. She pulled over to the side of the road and watched the car turn right onto Conway Road, the road that ran behind the farm. The road one took to reach the new development that was growing across the field.

She hesitated only a moment before heading toward Conway. If there had been an accident of some sort on her property — on what had once been her property — she wanted to know. She made the right turn, then followed the narrow two lanes around to the entrance of the development.

Welcome to the Estates at Palmers Woods.

Ugh, she thought. She wished they hadn't done that. Then again, the builder had bought and paid for it. He could call it anything he wanted. She slowed at the foot of the service road and watched the county car disappear in a cloud of dust on the unpaved road.

"Sorry, miss, you can't — Hey, Lorna, that you? Lorna Stiles?" The police officer walking toward her car removed his sunglasses as he drew near.

"Brad Walker, a cop?" She grinned. "I'd heard the rumors, but of course I didn't believe them."

"Yeah, well, it's sort of the family business."

"Your dad still chief of police?"

"Still chief." He nodded and leaned into the car window. "How you doing, Lori?"

"It's been a long time since anyone outside the family has called me that," she told him.

"Seems like a long time since you've been back." He patted her on the arm. "Hey, I was sorry to hear about your mom. She was a real nice lady."

"Thanks, Brad. I appreciate that."

"Guess you're home to settle up things?"

She nodded and tried to be subtle about the fact that she was trying to look over and behind him.

"Oh, you're wondering what's going on back there?" He turned in the direction of the field.

"Well, yeah. I saw the cruisers out by the field, then the ambulance. But when I saw the medical examiner fly past, I got really concerned. This being our old property and all." She took a sip of the coffee. Still too hot. She put it back in the cup holder. "Please tell me that no one's been killed."

"No, no — well, not recently, anyway. The guy operating the backhoe found a bunch of bones, and he —"

"Bones? Out here?" She frowned. "Human bones?"

He nodded confidently. "Yeah. I saw them myself. They're definitely human. They've been there awhile, though. The clothes are just about disintegrated."

"How could bones . . . ?" Lorna was still frowning. "There's a family burial plot on the farm, but that's way over on the other side, I doubt the bones could be from there."

She pointed to the opposite end of the field. "And it has a fence around it. As far as I know, no one's ever been buried outside the fence."

"No telling how old they are just by looking at them, but the medical examiner is going to take the bones back to the morgue and he'll look them over."

"But you took pictures, right? Before the bones were taken out of the ground?"

Before she could prod further, he said,

"Oh, wait. Let me guess. You're a graduate of the CSI School of Forensics. And here I thought you were still an accountant."

She colored slightly. "Ouch. I deserved that. And you're right. I watch entirely too much TV. I'm sure you know what you're doing. Sorry."

"Apology accepted." He turned back to the field, where someone from the county was trying to slip the skeleton onto a large piece of plastic. "I think I need to check on what's what back there. Good seeing you, Lori. Maybe I'll get a chance to see you again while you're in town."

"I'll be around for a while. Don't forget to give my best to Liz. I'll try to run over and visit with her while I'm home. I still haven't met your baby."

"The baby isn't a baby anymore. She's five, going to kindergarten already. I'll tell Liz you'll be giving her a call."

Lorna waved as he walked away, then sat for another minute, craning her neck, trying to see over the crowd of law enforcement and county personnel who'd gathered around the remains of . . . *Who?* she wondered.

She drove back to the house, still wondering. How long had the bones been buried on the Palmer farm? Whose bones were they, and how did they get there?

Lorna parked in her drive and emptied the rest of her belongings from the back of the car. She stacked everything near the front door, then took her coffee and walked to the edge of the field. From this vantage point, she couldn't see across to the Conway Road side, though years ago she could have. Over the past decade, a small grove of trees had sprouted up along the right-side property line, and in order to see past them, she had to walk out into the field.

The weeds were waist-high, and the dirt was dry from lack of rain. She stumbled in the rutted furrows, bumpy reminders of the last tractor to have plowed over the field. After the death of her father, her mother and grandmother had agreed to lease out the back fields to a farmer down the road to put in corn, a popular cash crop. They'd been happy to see the fields productive again, and had welcomed the extra money at a time when money had been tight. Back then, when her grandmother had been alive, there had been no talk of selling off any of the Palmer land.

Lorna paused at the top of a rise and looked down to her left, to where the field sloped gently and row after row after row of white trellises lined up like headstones in an unkempt graveyard. A mass of vines and weeds overgrew all, making Uncle Will's fabled attempt at establishing a vineyard one big wild tangle.

Lorna had heard the story of the vineyard from her grandmother, Will's sister, about how a young Will Palmer served in France during World War II, where after having been injured and taken to a nearby farm to recover, he had met the love of his life. The daughter of the owner of a vineyard, the equally young Marie-Terese Boulard, had agreed to marry her suitor and come to the States after the war. Before Will left to return home, Marie-Terese's father had given him cuttings from several of his prized grapevines, having talked his future son-in-law into trying to establish vineyards of his own on American soil.

It hadn't been so far-fetched an idea, Will had told his parents upon his arrival back in Callen. He'd done some research, and he'd found that the first commercial vineyards in America had been in Pennsylvania. "Why not now, why not here, in Callen?" he'd asked.

Grateful that their son had survived his injuries, and delighted that the once wild child was not only willing to settle down, but to settle down there on the farm, his father gave Will his blessing and offered him thirty acres to experiment with. Will returned to France to make Marie-Terese his bride, and while he was gone, his father built them a cottage overlooking the future vineyard. Will spent almost two years in France, learning all his in-laws could teach him about grapes and winemaking. When he and Marie-Terese came back to Callen, they brought with them more cuttings and their infant son. The grapes flourished in the southeastern Pennsylvania climate, but in 1948, Marie-Terese and their son were stricken with a dreaded virus that had been making a lot of news. Before the year came to a close, both Marie-Terese and the child succumbed to polio. A broken Will lost all interest in his grapes, and late in the summer of 1949, he lay down on his wife's grave and shot himself in the head. The would-be vineyard was forgotten, and the thirty acres of grapes soon grew wild.

Lorna wondered what her great-uncle would think of the decision to sell it all.

It can't be helped. There's nothing else to do, Lorna reminded herself.

All the same, it still bothered her, still made her feel guilty, as if somehow she'd let down generations of Palmers who must be, at this moment, frowning down upon her and wringing their hands.

She hoped Uncle Will wasn't one of them.

That afternoon, Lorna sat on one of the rockers she'd found in the barn. After she'd cleaned it up and dragged it to the front porch, she had sat and rocked mindlessly for a while, listening to the birds chatter in the hedge and wishing she hadn't made the trip to Callen alone. Why hadn't she insisted on Andrea or Rob taking a week off from their lives to come home with her? Why had it all fallen to her to make the decisions and tend to the family business?

She knew the answer. She was the oldest. She had the most flexible life — no husband, no babies, no budding career on the opposite side of the country. Andrea had been totally appalled at their mother's decision to be cremated and had wanted nothing to do with the ashes. Rob, self-centered and spoiled, had left home years ago and had never looked back. He'd already told her to just mail him a check once the property was sold. He wouldn't be coming back to the East Coast anytime soon.

The soothing back-and-forth motion of the chair served as a reminder of why rockers were so popular. She went back to the barn and brought out the other one, hosed it down, and set it in the sun to dry. If anyone ever stopped by, it would be nice to be able to invite them to sit for a while. It was certainly way too hot to invite someone inside the house.

If anyone ever stopped by.

Out on the road, a police car went past, and she thought again of the bones that had been found that morning. She wondered how long before the bones would be identified. She wished she'd asked whether they appeared to be those of a child or those of an adult.

What if it turned out to be Melinda, she wondered. Melinda Eagan, her best friend in fourth grade, who had disappeared in the blink of an eye on her way home from Lorna's house after celebrating her ninth birthday. Melinda, who hadn't been at the bus stop the following morning, or any other morning.

It didn't take much to recall the shock and sense of the surreal she'd felt when, as a child, she'd been told that Melinda had disappeared. Just thinking about that night brought back the fist-to-the-gut feeling you get when something is too terrible to be true.

Melinda's mother had called the Stiles' house around six-thirty that night, looking for her daughter. Lorna was in the dining room clearing the dinner table when the phone rang, and her mother answered it. She walked toward the kitchen, and heard her mother say, "Jason stopped by for her around five. I offered to drive them, but he said . . . Are you saying she hasn't arrived there yet?"

Lorna went into the kitchen. Her mother stood at the back door, looking out into the growing darkness.

"What did Jason say?"

Lorna set the dishes on the counter and watched her mother's face. "Billie, I'm going outside to take a look around. Maybe she forgot something and doubled back and got disoriented in the dark. I'll bring her home if I find her."

Mary Beth hung up the phone, a very worried look on her face.

"What happened to Mellie, Mom?" Lorna had asked.

"She must have gotten distracted by something, someplace between here and there, because her mother says she hasn't gotten home yet. She said that Jason told her Mellie ran ahead of him through the field and he thought she went straight home, so he stopped off behind the Conrads' house to talk to his friend Matt. But when he got home, she wasn't there."

"Did he go look for her?"

"Billie — Mrs. Eagan — says they looked over on their side of the field, but she wasn't there. Or maybe she's there and just doesn't want to be found."

Lorna watched her mother grab a jacket from a hook near the back door.

"Maybe it has something to do with the dress . . . maybe Mellie's trying to hide the bag so her mother won't know she took the dress out of the house. Who knows what that child is thinking?" She turned in the doorway and looked at Lorna. "Can you think of any place she might have gone? Any place she likes to hide, or someplace she goes when she wants to be alone?"

Right then, Lorna's father came into the kitchen.

"Mary Beth, where are you going?" he asked.

"Melinda hasn't arrived home and her mother is worried. I thought I'd take a look around the barn."

He glanced at his watch.

"She left around five, right?" He

frowned. "It's been an hour and a half already. Billie's just looking for her now?"

"She's been looking on their side of the field." Lorna's mother opened the door and went outside. "I'm thinking maybe she's hiding here, on our property. I won't be long."

"I'll come with you. And here, Mary Beth, we need light." Lorna's father took two flashlights from the closet and followed her mother outside.

Lorna had leaned against the windowpane and watched the twin yellow circles of light from the flashlights glide across the yard and disappear into the barn. All the while, she was biting her bottom lip, wondering if she should tell about the secret place where she and Mellie sometimes went to read or to be alone and talk. If she told now, and Mellie wasn't there, then everyone would always know their secret, and if Mellie came back, she'd be mad that now everyone knew and she'd have to look for a new hiding place.

But if Mellie was there, she needed to come out and go home.

No doubt Mrs. Eagan was going to be loaded for bear. Lorna had heard her grandmother say that, and while she wasn't exactly sure she understood what bears had to do with anything, she understood the sentiment perfectly.

But they hadn't found Melinda that night, or any other night. It would be years before Lorna dropped the "and please bring Mellie home" from her prayers. The thought that Melinda could have been right there, on the Palmer land, all this time, twisted Lorna's stomach into knots.

I would have known, wouldn't I, if my best friend had been murdered and buried in a place I could see from my bedroom window? Wouldn't I?

Only in books, or in movies, she told herself, slapping at the mosquito that had landed on her leg. *Not in real life.*

But if it was Melinda, and she had been buried out there at the far end of the farm, it would go a long way toward easing that little twinge of guilt that bit at Lorna every time she thought of how she'd not given up the secret hiding place.

Thunder rumbled from somewhere over toward West Grove, and Lorna stood to watch the darkening sky. The clouds were low hanging and fast moving. The storm would hit within the next twenty minutes or so, she figured, but wouldn't last too long. Above the rain clouds, the sky was lighter and held promise. Maybe after the rain passed, she'd walk down to the family plot and sprinkle some of her mother's ashes, as she was bound to do.

Or maybe she would just sit there on the porch, and wonder what had become of her friend all those years ago.

Three

At eight forty-five on Wednesday morning, Lorna was seated at the dining room table, eating dry cereal from a small blue plastic bowl and preparing a profit-and-loss statement on her computer for one of her clients. To access the Internet, she'd had to plug into the house phone and go the dial-up route. It had been a long time since she'd done that, and the squawk through the phone line sounded like fingernails on a chalkboard.

She made a mental note to look into broadband service while she was there. Even if it took her a month to finalize things in Callen, it would be worth the connection fee to have cable brought into the house.

She'd set up the laptop at the far end of the table, so that her back would be to the china cupboard. Empty of its contents, it reminded her of a mouth without teeth. Each piece of china or crystal had left its footprint on the dusty shelves, ghostly reminders of holiday dinners and birthday parties long past.

Stone crunched under the tires of a car

in the driveway, and she went to the front door, arriving just in time to see Chief Walker get out of his cruiser.

"Hi, Chief," she called as she unlocked the screen door and stepped outside.

"Hey, Lorna." He walked toward her, one hand resting on the holstered gun that sat on his right hip.

"What's going on?"

"Just thought I'd stop by and see how you're doing, make sure everything is all right."

"Everything's fine, thank you."

"Wanted to talk to you a bit about the bones we found out in the field on Monday."

"Want to come in? Or have a seat on the porch? It's probably cooler out here."

"The porch will do just fine."

He walked up the steps and sat in one of the rockers.

"Can I get you something?" She paused beside the second rocker.

"I'd love a cup of coffee, but I've already surpassed my daily limit."

"Just as well, then." She sat in the rocker nearest the door. "I've been buying mine at the mini-mart up the road. I did find Gran's old percolator, so I'll probably pick up some coffee on my next trip to the market. Maybe I'll get up there later today."

"We were all sorry to hear about Mary Beth. She was a good woman, your mother was. We'll all miss her."

"Thank you, Chief. We appreciated the card you and your wife sent. Please thank her for us."

"Least we could do." He rocked for another moment, then said, "About those bones . . ."

"Any idea yet who it might have been?"

"Actually, it looks as if they've been identified." He stopped rocking and leaned forward a bit, his elbows resting on the arms of the chair. "Looks like we might have found Jason Eagan, after all these years."

"Jason!" She stopped rocking, too. "Are you serious?"

"Absolutely. The medical examiner estimated we were looking at a young adult male who'd been dead about twenty-five years. We went back through the files and found there were only two men reported missing around here from that time period. One was Alvin Hawkins, who was in his late forties, the other was Jason. He was only fourteen but he was tall for his age. We brought his mother down, she identified the shirt we found with the remains as belonging to Jason. It did match the description she'd given back then of what he was wearing the last time she saw him. The ME is looking at the dental records that Dr. Pollock dropped off, but we're pretty sure it's him."

"How 'bout that, after all these years," she murmured.

"Well, here's the thing." He started rocking again, but with more deliberateness. "The bones showed signs of old abuse. Like both arms having been broken in more than one place, and not at the same time, according to the medical examiner. Looks like that boy took a lot as a child."

Lorna took a deep breath and exhaled slowly.

"My wife remembered that you were good friends with the sister, the girl who disappeared, said you used to come into the library together all the time. I was wondering if you knew whether or not she was roughed up, too."

"I know that Mrs. Eagan had a temper, and that Melinda was afraid of her." Lorna chose her words carefully. "I never saw her mother hit her, but I did see bruises on Mellie. On her arms, on her legs. I never asked her how she got them. I figured if she wanted to talk about it, she'd tell me. She never did."

Chief Walker tapped on the arms of the chair with the fingers of both hands.

"That's pretty much what I thought. I'd heard Billie Eagan had a reputation for being tough with her kids." He pushed himself out of the chair and stood up. "I just wanted to know if you had any first-hand knowledge of that."

"I can't swear that Mel's bruises were caused by her mother, but I strongly suspected that they were. I had heard her say things like 'My mother is going to give it to me when I get home,' things of that nature."

"Ever hear her say, 'My mother said she'd kill me if I did . . .' whatever?"

"Yes, but all kids say stuff like that." Lorna stood and followed the chief to the porch railing. "I remember times when I did something stupid, or maybe got a C on a test I should have gotten an A on, and said, 'My mother will kill me for this.' It's just something kids say."

"Your mother ever hit you hard enough to leave a mark, or grab you hard enough to leave a bruise?"

"Are you kidding?" She shook her head.

"My mother never raised a hand to anyone, as far as I know."

"Billie Eagan did. I can't help but wonder if that was all she did."

"Wait a minute, you're not suggesting that she killed either Melinda or Jason?"

He turned and looked at her. "When the girl went missing, I really thought the brother had killed her. He was the last person that we could prove had been with her. Then, right before we go to arrest him, he disappears. We figured he ran. Now it looks like if he did, he didn't get very far."

"I can't believe Mrs. Eagan had anything to do with what happened to either Melinda or Jason. Yes, she was rough with them, I know that, but I can't believe she would have gone that far."

"Who knows where the line is drawn?" he said. "If you can lose it enough to break your kid's arm, can you lose it enough to go one step further? Where does it end?"

Lorna frowned. "But why would she have done that?"

"Maybe the boy did kill the sister," he said, shrugging. "Maybe she found out that he did it, maybe he even told her he had, and she hit him. Could have been accidental, but could have killed him, all the same."

"Does the medical examiner know what killed him?"

"A blow to the head with something heavy. One blow to the front, one crushing blow to the back. Either one could have killed him."

"That's horrible." She shivered. "Poor Jason." Even though she hadn't liked him, had even feared him, he hadn't deserved that. No one did.

"Anyway, I just thought I'd let you know what was going on, since you were friends with the girl, and the remains were found on your property."

"Not mine anymore."

"It was when the body was buried. And, like I said, you were friends. In any case, I should probably get going. You take care, now, Lorna." He walked to the police car and got in the still-open door. "We've been keeping an eye on the place while you were gone. We'll continue to check on you when we do our rounds at night."

"I appreciate that, but I've been fine."

"All the same, you're by yourself here." He waved and then slammed the car door.

"Thanks," she called to him and returned the wave.

She walked after the retreating car and watched as it disappeared a few hundred yards up the road to the left. Then she walked back to the house and stepped inside and poured herself a glass of iced tea. The temperature was already well into the eighties, and it was barely nine-thirty in the morning.

She returned outside and sat on the top step, wondering if Billie Eagan had had a hand in the disappearance of either or both of her kids. It had made Lorna uncomfortable to admit that she'd known that Melinda had been abused by her mother but had pretended not to. All these years later, Lorna still felt guilty that she'd been too much of a coward to have confronted Mellie with it.

But how do you make someone talk about something they don't want to talk about, or confront something they're not ready to deal with? she asked herself, not for the first time. Mellie had angrily brushed aside the few feeble attempts Lorna had made. How could she have forced her friend to admit that her mother had hurt her, when maybe Mellie didn't want to admit it to herself?

There had been times Lorna had wanted to talk to her own mother about it, but she'd always rationalized her way out of it. What if she was wrong? What if Melinda really had fallen down the steps that time she'd broken her arm? What if Melinda got really mad and stopped talking to her? And what if her mother had said something to Melinda's mother and Mrs. Eagan got mad and really hurt Mellie? It would have been Lorna's fault. The list of what-ifs and possible consequences seemed endless. As a child, Lorna had hid behind excuses for her silence. As an adult, she was ashamed that she had, but still wasn't sure what she could have done differently back then.

What if Chief Walker was right? What if Mrs. Eagan had killed Melinda, even by accident? And what if she had killed Jason, too?

What, Lorna wondered, could she have done — should she have done — that would have made a difference, all those years ago?

The question stayed with her, nagged at her. It followed her to the family burial site that afternoon when she took one of the urns holding her mother's ashes, as she had promised she would do.

"Okay, Mom, we're here," she said aloud as she went through the black iron gate into the enclosed area that sat by itself on a slight rise. She held the silver-colored urn to her chest as if it were a child. "I'm not really sure how to do this, but I'll give it a shot."

She walked among the graves, some of them ancient, the engraving on several of the markers now little more than faint scratches on stone. The air was heavy with the sounds and scents of August, the ZZZZZ of the cicadas only barely drowning out the buzz of the yellow jackets as they fed on the season's first fallen apples rotting on the ground on the other side of the fence.

"Guess you'd want some here, by Gran, and some over there, by your aunt Emily." Lorna removed the lid and tilted the urn slightly, letting the breeze catch the coarse gray dust and carry it. "Maybe a little by Grampa . . . and the rest over here by Dad."

Lorna stood behind her father's headstone and sprinkled the ashes, watching them disperse on the ground around her. He'd been gone for so long, it was hard sometimes to remember all the things she'd thought she'd never forget. She could recall his laughter and the sound of his voice, and the way his eyes narrowed when something displeased him, and the look on his face when her mother came into the room. Mary Beth had been his life; the children had often seemed to be afterthoughts, as far as he'd been concerned. He had loved them in his own way, Lorna felt certain, but he'd always somehow looked upon them as belonging more to his wife than to him. She was his. The children were hers. They had never held the importance in his life that she had, and all three children had instinctively known.

When Lorna was growing up, her mother had always been the dominant force in her life, her father's absence felt more than his presence had been. The one thing she could never forget was the way they had all grieved when he died so unexpectedly, the anger that first year after his passing, how Rob had withdrawn and for a long time after been awakened nightly by nightmares, and the way her mother had never been quite the same.

Well, she thought, tears coming for the first time since she'd stepped through the iron gate, they were together again, wherever they were. *She's all yours again, Dad.*

When the container was empty, she set it on the ground. She had thought it would have been more difficult. Then again, she'd shared her mother's last days, watching the life fade away, mystified by the way it had drained from her in stages. The end had come quickly, mercifully, and having held her mother in her arms as she'd breathed her last, for Lorna, watching the ashes scatter was almost anticlimactic. She did it because she'd promised to, but she felt no more or no less of her mother's presence once the urn was empty.

"There you go, Mom. One down, two to go."

The graves were untidy, so Lorna spent a half hour pulling weeds. She'd come back later in the afternoon, or tomorrow, if it was cooler, and bring that hand-mower she'd seen in the barn, to cut the grass. Overgrown graveyards always made her sad, as if those laid to rest had all been forgotten.

Well, I guess for the most part they have been, Lorna conceded. *At least since Mom came out to Woodboro.*

Before she left town, Lorna would ask around to see about having someone tend to the graveyard, after the property was sold. Her grandmother — who had kept such a tidy and immaculate house — would definitely not be pleased to have her final resting place such a tangle of weeds. Lorna owed her that much.

She finished weeding, tucked the urn

under her arm, and set out for the house. She worked for a few hours on the monthly billing for a boutique in Woodboro, then turned off the computer. She was just about to open the refrigerator door when the phone rang.

"Lorna? Chief Walker."

"Hi, Chief."

"Lorna, I have Billie Eagan down here at the station with me. She's asking to speak with you, and I was wondering if —"

"To me?" Lorna frowned. "Why would she want to talk to me?"

"Well, I asked her if she wanted to make any calls, and she said the only person she'd want to talk to was Mary Beth Stiles, but she knew she'd passed on. I told her you were back, and she asked to talk to you instead."

"You're not holding her, are you?"

"Actually, we are."

"Then she should be talking to a lawyer," Lorna protested. "I'm not a lawyer."

"I'm well aware of that. I already told her we'd recommend to the court that she be given a public defender. No question she qualifies. But she still wants to talk to you."

The chief fell silent for a moment, then

said, "You're her one call, Lorna. What do you want me to tell her?"

He lowered his voice. "You coming down here or what?"

Four

The Callen Police Department was housed in the back of a small, one-story, redbrick building, the front section of which served as the municipal offices. The library was in the basement, and the jail — such as it was — was in the annex, a low-slung square of gray block and mortar that connected to the main building through a short corridor.

Lorna parked behind the building and went to the side door, which led directly into a small lobby. Through the glass, Lorna saw Brad Walker leaning against the wall, talking to his father, and when Lorna knocked, he nodded in her direction. Chief Walker stood and waved to her.

"Come on in," he told her. "Just give that door a push — it sticks in hot weather. Here, let me do that."

He went to the door and gave it a shove. "Don't want the air-conditioning to escape. It's hot as hell out there."

Lorna pushed a strand of hair back off her forehead. "It is that."

"You ready to talk to Billie Eagan?" he asked.

"Sure. I'm still not certain why she wants to see me, but sure, I'll talk to her."

"She's in here, in the conference room. Normally, we'd have her in a holding cell while we wait for the sheriff to drive her out to the prison, but the air conditioner out there hasn't been working, and it's just too damned hot for man or beast. Joel Morgan, of the PD's office, was in on another matter, and the judge asked him to handle Ms. Eagan's case, at least through the preliminary hearing, which won't be until next week. He'll be by in a minute to talk to her."

"She's been charged?"

"Charged, arraigned, and has a room reserved at the county prison."

"Can't she get bail?"

"That's up to her, I guess, if she can post bail. You can discuss that with her, makes your visit sort of official."

The chief gestured in Lorna's direction and she followed him through a door at the end of the room. Billie Eagan sat at the head of a rectangular table, her hands folded in front of her, her pale, thin arms stark against the dark wood. Her hair was straight, stringy, gray, no longer the thick, dark strawberry blond Lorna remembered from her childhood. She wore a sleeveless cotton blouse that was stained on one side. When she looked up at Lorna, it was through watery blue eyes set deep into a gaunt face.

"Hello, Mrs. Eagan," Lorna said from the doorway.

"Lorna." Billie's voice was as flat and low-pitched as Lorna remembered.

"Chief Walker said you wanted to see me."

Billie nodded. "I do."

"Lorna," the chief touched her on the arm, "I'll be right outside here, if you need me."

He closed the door behind him, leaving the two women alone. Lorna moved farther into the room, taking a seat across the table from Billie.

"I just wanted to tell you how sorry I am about your momma." Billie's voice still held a trace of the West Virginia hills where she'd been born. "She was as near to being a friend as anyone I ever knew. She was a good woman, through and through. I just wanted you to know."

Lorna hesitated. She hadn't recalled her mother speaking of any particular friendship with Billie Eagan.

"Surprised, are you?" Billie looked faintly amused.

"I didn't know that you and my mother were . . . friends," Lorna said awkwardly.

Billie nodded.

"Well, I appreciate you thinking of her."

"I think about her every day."

"You do?"

"She used to stop by once or so a week. Drop off a bag of groceries. Sometimes something she might'a baked. She made these little lemon muffins with poppy seeds . . ."

Lorna nodded. Her grandmother's recipe.

Her mother used to make muffins for Billie Eagan?

"She always took me to my doctors appointments, stopped at the drugstore on the way home to pick up my prescriptions. She even made sure I got to my meetings at night, said I needed the support if I was to overcome my addictions," Billie continued. "Every once in a while, she'd bring me a pack of cigarettes."

"My mother bought you cigarettes?" Lorna's jaw dropped.

"Oh, she didn't like doing it, I know she didn't. But she knew how hard it was for me to quit, especially on top of everything else I was trying to quit at the time. Said she'd gone through that once with cigarettes herself, and she knew how tough it was, so she —"

"My mother never smoked," Lorna said flatly.

"She tell you that?"

"Well, no, I never asked her, but she hated cigarettes. Hated smoking."

"Yes, she did. Said she'd been real happy none of you kids ever picked 'em up. But back when she was younger, she did. Stopped when she found out she was pregnant with you and never picked 'em up again." Billie leaned back in her chair. "Or so she said."

"I'm stunned. I never knew that about her."

"I guess there's lots of things you didn't know."

Lorna stared at Billie, not sure what to say. Billie stared back.

"Like what?" Lorna finally asked.

"Your mother never believed that I had anything to do with whatever happened to Melinda." Billie's face hardened. "I know everyone else around here thought I did, but she believed me. Even after Jason ran away — at least, back then, that's what we thought happened to him. Now they tell me they found him there in the field."

Billie's lips tightened. "Can you imagine

that? All these years, I thought he'd run away, maybe to the city someplace. And there he was, just a couple'a acres away from where I lay my head every night."

"No, Mrs. Eagan. They found Jason at the back of our farm, over where the new houses are being built. Your house is over on Conway Road."

"I lost that house long ago. After all that craziness, after the police started questioning me when Jason went away and they needed someone to blame, I lost my job. I lost my house. I got sick. I lost everything . . ." For a moment, her eyes seemed to cloud over, and her lips shook slightly.

"Where have you been living, then, all these years?" Lorna asked.

"Here and there, moved around for a long time. I guess I should'a gone home to my family, but I always thought Jason would come back, maybe Melinda, too. Then, a few years ago, when I got really sick, your mother let me move into that cottage out there near the grapes." Billie glanced up and saw the look of surprise on Lorna's face. "Oh, I guess that was something else you didn't know."

"No. No, she never mentioned it."

"Maybe she thought you wouldn't have approved," Billie said softly.

"It was her property, her cottage. She didn't need my approval."

"Well, by then, you were over there near Pittsburgh and setting up your business — she was real proud of that, that you had your own business, but I'm sure you knew that — and your sister and brother had both moved away. I guess maybe she got a little lonely sometimes."

Billie smiled for the first time since Lorna entered the room. "Or maybe it was that goodness of hers, coming through. She was such a kind soul."

Lorna's throat tightened unexpectedly.

"Anyway, I just wanted you to know how much I miss her. Not only the things she did for me, you know? I miss talking to her, miss having her company." When Billie looked at Lorna this time, there were tears in the corners of her eyes. "I never knew anyone else like her."

"Neither did I," Lorna whispered.

The door opened, and Brad stuck his head in.

"The public defender is here to see Mrs. Eagan, Lorna. You about finished?"

"Oh. Sure. I'll just be a minute." Lorna nodded, then turned back to Billie after Brad closed the door. "Mrs. Eagan, I have to ask you something."

Billie looked up, waiting.

"Did you kill Melinda?"

"No. No, I did not." The answer was quick, and sure. "I do not know what happened to that child, I swear on her life."

"What about Jason? Did you kill Jason?"

"No." Billie shook her head firmly. "I thought he'd run away. I wouldn't have blamed him for that."

She looked Lorna directly in the eyes and told her bluntly, "I do not deny that I was harder on my kids than I should have been. There were times when I hurt them bad, and I will have to face God with that. He knows how sorry I am for any pain I caused them when I had them. I guess maybe that's why He took them away from me. Mary Beth always said she didn't believe that God did things like that, but still. If you don't take care of what you have, you lose it, that's what my momma always used to say." She cleared her throat. "I think about the times I hurt them, and the times I had them so scared, they could hardly breathe. I was a different person back then. I drank too much and I worked too much and I slept too little. I had two jobs and I still had no money and no life. I was fifteen years old when I had Jason, twenty when Melinda was born. And their father left me here with them when she was just a year old. I was left high and dry with two small kids, barely old enough to legally buy a drink."

Billie took a deep breath.

"I was a lousy mother, I'd be the first to admit that. But I didn't kill my kids." She paused, then added, "I swear it on Mary Beth's memory. I did not kill my kids."

Brad opened the door again, and this time stepped into the room. "Lorna, I have to ask you to —"

"Yes, yes. I'm leaving." Lorna stood up. "May I come back to see you?"

"I don't know where they're going to take me from here," Billie told her.

"I'll find you." Lorna turned to leave, then looked back over her shoulder. "Thank you. For . . . for all the things you said."

Billie nodded, then turned her face to the door, where her lawyer stood. Lorna walked past him into the hallway.

"You were in there a long time," Chief Walker noted as she passed. "What did you talk about?"

"A lot of things." Lorna paused, then said, "You don't really believe she killed Jason, do you?"

His eyes narrowed. "Did she tell you she didn't?"

"Yes, she told me she didn't. Didn't she tell you the same?"

He waved his hand. "Everyone says they didn't do whatever it is they've been arrested for. I never expect anyone to admit to anything anymore."

The phone was ringing in his office, and he went in to answer it. A second later, he closed the door behind him.

"She didn't kill him," Lorna said to Brad when they reached the lobby.

"She convinced you of that?"

"What evidence do you have?"

He raised his eyebrows almost to his hairline. "I'm sorry, I thought that was business school you went to, not law school."

"Is that your way of saying it's none of my business?" she asked softly, trying not to sound as if she was challenging him, which she had no right to do.

"We know that she was physical with her kids. She didn't deny that she'd been the cause of those broken bones he'd had. We know that she did think he killed his sister, and that she had questioned him about it on more than one occasion. She told me that. So what would stop her from trying to beat it out of him? She'd beaten him before, she said she did. Maybe that last time, things just got out of hand. I think it was an accident, I'll give you that. I don't think she intended to kill him, but I think she killed him, all the same."

She started to say something, and he cut her off.

"The last time they questioned her, years ago, they felt very strongly, my dad and the DA did, that she had a hand in whatever it was that had happened to her kids. Back then, they didn't even have a body. Now we do. It shows signs of abuse that she admits to. The night that Jason Eagan disappeared, he'd been drinking with a couple of guys out at White Marsh Park. He was dropped off at three in the morning and was seen walking up his front steps. No one has reported having seen him since that moment."

"That doesn't mean his mother killed him."

"She admits she got into an argument with him that night after he came home. She admits everything, except the actual murder." Brad folded his arms over his chest. "It's good enough for the DA, Lorna. I'd think it would be good enough for you, especially since Melinda was your friend."

"I don't know, Brad. I just don't see it."

"Well, I guess we'll have to agree to disagree."

His radio squawked and he responded.

"Accident out there at the intersection." He started to the door. "It's gonna cause a major traffic jam. You might want to take one of the back roads home."

Lorna stood in the lobby for a long minute, then followed him outside. She got into her car and fished around in the bottom of her bag for her keys, then remembered they were in her jeans pocket. When she started the ignition, the radio came on. She snapped it off, wanting silence, and drove home mechanically, without thinking where she was going, and got caught in the traffic jam Brad had warned her about.

Lorna sat behind a dark red pickup while the injured were loaded onto gurneys, her mind still trying to process everything Billie Eagan had told her.

That Billie and her mother had, over the years, become friends.

That Mary Beth had taken Billie in and given her a place to live. That she'd made sure Billie had food to eat and medical care, and the support she'd needed to overcome her addictions.

That Mary Beth had believed in Billie's innocence.

Had she? Or was Billie just trying to find a sympathetic ear?

She was still debating that point when Brad waved her through the intersection.

Five

When Lorna was in line to pay for her coffee at the mini-mart the next morning, a hand reached past her from behind and plunked down two quarters.

"*County Herald.*" The man attached to the hand held up the newspaper for the clerk to see and turned to go on his way, but not before Lorna caught the headline.

"One large coffee?" the clerk asked.

"And one *Herald*," Lorna said.

She picked up the paper on the way out of the store and folded it, carrying it under one arm till she reached the car. Once behind the wheel, she opened the paper and scanned the front page.

Callen Cops Catch Killer! screamed the caption over the picture that sat right on the fold. In it, Billie Eagan was being led from her house in handcuffs, looking confused and tired. The story reiterated the disappearances of both of her children and the "facts" that led to her arrest.

This isn't right, Lorna told herself as she pulled out of the parking lot. *It just doesn't feel right.*

She read through the item again when she got home. She'd thought about Billie for much of last night, and had come to the conclusion that if her mother had been convinced of Billie's innocence, there must be something there. But how to convince Chief Walker of that, without any evidence to the contrary?

And how to begin going about looking for something that could help Billie? Lorna wasn't a lawyer, as Brad Walker had pointed out, and all she knew about investigating crime she'd learned from watching *CSI* and *Law & Order,* and her newest favorite, *Medium.* There were no psychics in Callen, that she was aware of, and she knew no sleuths to call upon for advice.

Not quite true, she reminded herself as she sipped her coffee. *There is Regan Landry . . .*

Regan, who had shared a flat in London with Lorna and six other girls one summer long ago, and who, following in the footsteps of her famous father, was making a name for herself as a major writer of true crime fiction.

While it had been years since the two women had seen each other, they had stayed in touch. Most recently, Lorna had written a letter of condolence when

Regan's father had been murdered last September. Regan had responded with a note and had sent her business card with her phone numbers . . . Where had Lorna put that?

Lorna went through the business cards in her wallet, then through the electronic phone book on her computer. She finally found Regan's card stuck in the back of her Day-Timer. She debated with herself whether to call.

Maybe first talk to the public defender, she thought. *See what he's thinking. Maybe there are motions he can file, something he can do to get Billie out on bail, if nothing else.* At nine a.m. she called information for the county courthouse, and when she got through to the switchboard at the number given, she asked to be connected to the PD's office. After a series of transfers, Joel Morgan answered his extension.

"This is Lorna Stiles," she told him. "I'm a . . . a friend of Billie Eagan's. I was there at the police station yesterday, when you went to speak with her."

"What can I do for you, Ms. Stiles?" His voice was curt and crisp.

"Well, I was wondering what's going to happen next, for one thing. Is Mrs. Eagan going to be transferred to the county prison, is she —"

"She's already there. They moved her last night."

"Oh." Lorna was taken aback by the news, though she didn't know why she would be. She knew there weren't facilities at the Callen police station to hold a prisoner overnight.

"Was there something else?"

"Is she going to stay in prison? I mean, don't you usually arrange for bail, or file something to protest the charges?"

"I can't get her bail, because she has no guarantor for the funds. As far as 'protesting the charges,' I'm not sure what that means, frankly."

"I mean she's innocent. What are you doing to prove that?"

There was silence, then a chuckle.

"Everyone is innocent, until proven guilty." The sarcasm was blatant.

She decided to ignore it.

"My point exactly. What are you doing to prove her innocence?"

"I spoke with Mrs. Eagan at length last night. She has no alibi for the night her son disappeared, the night the police assume he was killed. She has admitted to me and to the police that she and her son argued that night, that the argument turned violent. She stopped short of an out-and-out confession, but that might come, who knows?"

"Are you serious? She didn't kill Jason."

"And you know this how?"

"She told me."

"She told me as well. But I don't know that there isn't more she's not saying, frankly."

"You're her lawyer. Aren't you supposed to believe in her?"

There was silence on the line for a long moment, then he said, "I'll be getting copies of the original police documents — the reports that were filed following the disappearance of her daughter, and those that were made after the son disappeared as well. I'll look over the statements that were taken at the time, and then I'll decide where to go from there. Now, unless you have some information that might be relevant to her defense . . ."

"How much is her bail?"

"What?"

"Her bail. What was it set at?"

"One hundred thousand dollars."

"Isn't that a lot of money?"

"She's a suspect in a murder case."

"How much money has to be put up?"

"Seven to ten percent. It's basically a guarantee that the bail will be paid if she skips."

"So if I can guarantee that she won't skip, they'll let her out?"

"I can talk to the bail bondsman." He paused. "You're willing to bet that she won't run?"

"Yes. Can you arrange that?"

"Give me a number where I can reach you."

Lorna gave him the numbers for her cell phone and the house.

"I'll wait to hear from you," she said, then hung up.

She walked outside, wondering where she'd get the money from, if in fact Billie Eagan decided to leave town.

She wondered, too, how hard the public defender was going to work on Billie's behalf. He hadn't sounded that interested, frankly, in proving her innocence. He'd actually sounded as if he believed in her guilt.

Lorna didn't have enough money in cash. Maybe they'd take something in collateral. Her eyes fell on her SUV. A shiny black eight-month-old BMW — her first new car in over seven years.

What do you think, Mom? What would you do?

The phone rang, and she ran back into

the house to grab it. It was Joel Morgan, telling her where and how to post the bail for Billie Eagan. She took the information, called the bail bondsman, and made the arrangements.

Then, before she changed her mind, she called the number on Regan Landry's card. She was just about to leave a voice message when Regan picked up.

"Hello?"

"Regan, it's Lorna Stiles."

"Lorna! How are you?" Regan sounded genuinely pleased to hear her voice. "I almost didn't pick up, the caller ID has another name on it."

"Palmer. My grandmother's phone. I guess my mother never took Gran's name off the listing. I don't know that I was even aware of that."

"Oh, you're at your mother's?"

"I'm at the farm, yes. My mother passed away last month, and I'm here to try to get things in order."

"Oh, Lorna. I am so sorry. Had she been ill?"

"Yes, for almost two years."

"I am so very sorry. I know what it's like to lose a parent at this stage of your life. It's hard, isn't it?"

"Very."

"I appreciated the letter you sent after my dad died. I wish I'd known about your mother."

"Thanks, Regan."

"But you aren't calling to tell me about that, are you?" Regan asked gently.

"No, actually, I called to ask you for some advice."

"Anything. Shoot."

Lorna told her about Billie Eagan's situation.

"So, you believe this woman is innocent?"

"I do." Lorna heard the conviction in her voice, and added, "Apparently my mother believed it, too."

"Are you sure? You have only Mrs. Eagan's word for that, right?"

"True enough. But I think Mom would have. I doubt she'd have done so much to help this woman if she believed Billie had murdered her son."

"That makes sense."

"I need to find the truth." Lorna took a deep breath. She hated asking for favors, especially from an old friend she hadn't seen in years. But she could think of no one else with experience in this area. "I guess I need some guidance, Regan. I know that you investigate old crimes, and then write about them. I'm wondering if maybe this is the type of thing you look into."

"Actually, it would be, under normal circumstances. Right now, though, I'm working on a tight deadline and running late on a book that I should have finished a week ago. If I weren't tied up, I'd be more than happy to delve into this for you. I am so sorry I'm not in a position to help you out right now."

Lorna felt her heart sink. "That's all right, Regan. I knew it was a long shot. I just couldn't think of anyone else to talk to."

"Well, let's think this through for a minute. What you want is an investigation, right? You need to look into the old case. You need to find out what happened that night this woman's son disappeared."

"I suppose I'd have to start there, yes."

"Have you considered a private investigator?"

"No, I haven't. But I could." Lorna frowned. "How would you go about finding one that's reputable?"

"I have a friend who's in the FBI. Maybe he knows someone. Would you like me to ask?"

"Regan, I hate to put you to all that trouble."

"Oh, no trouble at all." Regan laughed. "Actually, I was trying to think of an excuse to call him. You've given me one."

"Anything to help a friend."

"If I hang up right now, I might even get him before he leaves for lunch. Can I call you back at this number?"

"Yes, but let me give you my cell number as well." Lorna waited while Regan found a pen, then gave her the number.

"Great. Let me see if I can get in touch with Mitch. I'll call you back."

"Regan, I really appreciate this. Thanks so much."

"Don't thank me yet. Talk to you later."

Lorna hung up and slid Regan's card into her wallet, which was, she decided, a better place to keep it. It was a miracle she hadn't lost it, a miracle that she had stuck her Day-Timer in the car. She still wasn't sure why she had, or when, for that matter.

Serendipity, her mother would have said.

She pulled the elastic band from her hair and then swept it up into a ponytail again, securing the loose ends tightly to keep them off her neck. It was another hot day. The ancient window air conditioner she'd found in the attic barely worked, but it cooled enough so that she could sit in the dining room and work. And for now, that was all she needed. She poured herself a cold drink, set it on the table next to her laptop, and went to work on a billing statement. She was midway through it when the phone rang.

"Lorna, Regan. Listen, Mitch has a friend who might be able to help you. He's a PI — Mitch knows he's licensed in Maryland, he's not sure about Pennsylvania, though. The PI's a former FBI agent who went out on his own a few years back, formed his own agency. Anyway, Mitch thinks he's still in business. I took the liberty of giving Mitch your name and phone number, I hope that's okay. If Mitch can get in touch with his friend, he'll ask him to contact you. So if some strange man calls, just ask him if he's a friend of Mitch Peyton."

"What's his name? The investigator."

"Oh, it's Dawson. T. J. Dawson. Let me know if he calls, okay, so I can tell Mitch?"

"Will do. Regan, I can't thank you enough."

"Thank me after you find the information that you need," Regan said. "Thank me after you've proven that this woman did not kill her son."

Six

"Lorna Stiles?"

"Yes?" Lorna was out of breath from running to answer the phone before her mother's old message came on the answering machine. She made a mental note to change it.

"T. J. Dawson. Mitch Peyton asked me to call."

"Who?" She frowned, then remembered yesterday's conversation with Regan. "Oh. Regan Landry's friend."

"Friend of a friend, right. I thought you were expecting my call."

"Regan said she'd ask her friend — your friend Mitch — to speak with you, but I didn't expect to hear from you this quickly. I appreciate you calling so soon."

"Mitch said it was important."

"Well, where would you like me to start?" Lorna tried to stretch the phone cord into the dining room, where she'd left her handbag. She wanted to write down his name and phone number but couldn't quite reach the pen and paper. She started opening and closing the kitchen drawers, hoping to get lucky.

"You have a friend who's been arrested on murder charges?"

"Yes. I believe she's innocent, but the police —"

"What were the charges?'

"That she killed her son."

"I mean, first degree, second . . . manslaughter . . ."

"Oh. I don't know." She felt her cheeks twinge with color. How could she not know? "I didn't think to ask. I should have."

"I can find that out."

"When do you think you can start working on this?"

"In about three hours."

"What?"

"I'm on my way from southern New Jersey to Baltimore. I'll be driving along Interstate 95. Mitch said you're in southern Pennsylvania."

"Right. I'm about thirty-five minutes off of I-95, actually."

"Would it be all right if I swung by on my way through the area? I can get all the information from you, we can talk about the case, my fee, see how much time you want to invest in this."

"Fine." She gave him directions from the highway, then hung up, and gulped. How much did private investigators charge? She had no idea, but figured them to be fairly expensive.

And just how much did she want to invest in Billie Eagan?

She'd been having second thoughts since volunteering to post the woman's bail. That was one thing, since the money would be returned to her. But offering to take on the expense of a private investigator was something else. That had been a strictly emotional response to the situation, she had finally acknowledged to herself as she had lain awake the night before, questioning her sanity. She'd wanted to do what she thought her mother would have done under the circumstances to help her friend. However, as Regan had said, Lorna had only Billie's word that she and Mary Beth had been friends. What were the chances Billie was playing on Lorna's sympathy? She had never been what one might consider an upright citizen. For all Lorna knew, Billie could have fabricated the whole friendship story to get Lorna on her side, where she could take advantage of her. Like by having Lorna post bail to get her out of prison.

Well, she'd deal with that later. Right now, she hadn't paid anyone anything, so no harm, no foul. Besides, at the moment, she had a client waiting for his monthly accounts receivable number, and she had another hour's worth of work before she could send it to him. She pushed Billie Eagan from her mind, and went back to work.

She finished the receivables and went on to the payables report for the same company, pausing only to heat up a frozen pizza, which she ate sitting on the front porch. At one point, Brad Walker's wife, Liz, passed by — at least, Lorna had been pretty sure it was Liz — but she hadn't stopped and hadn't returned Lorna's wave. Maybe it hadn't been her.

Lorna was still working when the doorbell rang at two-fifteen, startling her. She hadn't realized how late it was.

The man standing on the front porch was tall — almost a foot taller than Lorna's five feet six inches — and sported a baseball cap over curly blond hair. He wore dark glasses, and a beige T-shirt over deeply tanned arms, and cut-off denims over legs that were long and muscular. She knew he had to be the PI, but wished she could see the look on her face. She'd been expecting Barnaby Jones. What she got was more like a fair-haired Magnum, PI.

"Mr. Dawson?" She opened the inside door, leaving the screen door locked. Just in case.

"It's T.J., yes. You're Lorna Stiles?"

"Yes. Come in." She opened the screen door and he stepped into the foyer and pretty much filled it. She took a step back unconsciously. The man looked as if he was feeling the heat as much as she was. "We can talk in here, or out on the porch. It might be cooler out there, though."

"Then the porch gets my vote."

"Can I get you something cold to drink first? Iced tea?"

"That would be great, thanks."

He followed her into the kitchen, and on her way past the window she looked into the driveway where he'd parked his car under the magnolia — a taupey-colored convertible, the top down. It was exactly the car she'd expect a man who looked like he did to drive.

"What is that?" she asked, pointing out the window.

"Crossfire."

"It's lovely."

"Lovely is just one of its attributes."

"Fast?"

"Sure." He grinned. "What's the point of having a slow sports car?"

"True."

"So, tell me about your friend," he asked as she took a glass from the cupboard.

"It's a long story." She opened the freezer for ice cubes, which she popped into the glass.

"Start at the beginning. That's what I'm here for."

"Are we on the clock?" She reached into the refrigerator and took out the pitcher of tea she'd made earlier, and filled the glass. "Because I might have some reservations about this."

"The clock doesn't start ticking until I decide if I want to take the case, so you can give me the long version. And it will be strictly up to you, if you want to think about it a little more, or if you decide against hiring me. There's no obligation. We haven't signed any contracts. Right now, we're just talking. So go on. Tell me from the beginning."

She did.

"So that's it, that's all they have on this woman? A body with skull fractures front and back, and old signs of child abuse? And a kid who said he dropped Jason off at home and he was never seen again?"

She nodded. "That pretty much sums it up."

"Doesn't sound like a very solid arrest to me." He rubbed his chin thoughtfully. "You might not have much of a decision to make after all. I think they're going to end up dismissing the charges."

"Why would you say that?"

"They really don't have anything of substance. Can you think of any reason why the chief of police would jump on an arrest this fast?"

"You mean some personal issue?"

"Right."

"Not off the top of my head, but I haven't lived around here in a long time. All I know is what I remember from before, and what the police are telling me now. I do know that the boy Jason was with that last night said he dropped him off around three and saw him go into the house. No one — except his mother — admits to having seen him after that."

"Maybe the other boy didn't drop him off at home. Maybe he took him someplace else. Maybe he killed him."

Lorna stared at him. Had anyone considered that?

"The point is, there's only the boy's word that he'd taken Jason home, just as there's only Mrs. Eagan's word that she didn't kill him." He sipped his tea. "Why would the boy's word be more credible than the mother's?"

"One, because the mother was an alcoholic and an admitted child abuser. Two, because her daughter had disappeared a few weeks before Jason and she had been one of the first to be suspected, and I think they might have still harbored some suspicion there. Chief Walker was a patrolman at the time, and was involved in that investigation. Maybe he has some issues with having let her go back then, I don't know. And three, because the boy who dropped Jason off was the son of a woman who, at the time, worked for the county."

"So they might have taken his story as gospel?"

She shrugged. "I have no way of knowing if they had corroboration for that or not. I was only nine at the time, and my best friend was missing. I had no real understanding of what was going on, as far as the investigation was concerned, and I didn't care. I just wanted my friend to come home. I knew the police suspected Mrs. Eagan — and, to be honest, I sort of did myself. I knew she'd been rough with Melinda, and I knew that Mellie was afraid of her. To my nine-year-old's mind, that was enough to make her a bad person."

"What changed your mind?"

"What do you mean?"

"You're willing to put up bail, willing to take on the expense of a private investigator to prove her innocent. Why?"

"I guess because there's no one else to help her. I think everyone is going to assume the worst about her. She was an alcoholic. She did hurt her kids. Easy enough to believe she killed at least one of them."

"But you don't?"

Lorna hesitated.

"No, I don't. And I believe that if my mother were still alive, she'd take Billie's side. If for no other reason than to make sure the truth came out. My mother's no longer with us." She could have said more, but her throat tightened right about then, so she let it go. How important was it that he understand that she felt honor-bound to her mother, as well as to Mellie, to help find the truth?

"Your mother and Mrs. Eagan were close friends?"

"She says they were."

"Who says they were? Mrs. Eagan?"

Lorna nodded.

"You mean, you only have her word that she and your mother were friends?"

Lorna nodded again, slowly. "Does that

make me appear as stupid as I'm starting to feel?"

"Not stupid, no."

"You're searching for another word — perhaps, oh, *gullible?*"

"*Gullible* could work." He smiled. "Can you think of any reason Billie Eagan would lie about being your mother's friend?"

"Not offhand. The truth is, I don't have any more reason to believe her than to not believe her. I just don't know."

"But you jumped in with an offer to help, all the same."

"An emotional reaction, I'm afraid. One I'm not certain I'm not beginning to regret."

"Hey, so far, this has cost you nothing but a little bit of your time. Like I said before, there's no fee for talking to me about it. You can take all the time you need to think it over. And if you decide to go forward with an investigation, you can call it off whenever you want. Two hours or two days, it's up to you. I work for you."

She did like the sound of that.

"I would like to think it over before I sign anything with you."

"I won't hold it against you, either way."

"You're awfully accommodating. How do you stay in business with that take-it-

or-leave-it attitude?"

He laughed. "Well, actually, we just sold the business, my partner and I. He got married and moved to Ocean City, Maryland, and it got to be too much for him to be driving back and forth to Baltimore. There's too much work for one person, and after these past three years working only with my partner — who's also my cousin — I'm not inclined to hire another PI. There was someone interested in buying us out, so we sold the business, the building, the whole works. So, basically, I'm more or less unemployed right now."

"Oh." Lorna frowned. "Maybe it isn't a good time for you to take this on."

"I still have my license, and I'm coming off a month at the beach. I'm ready to get back to work. And I have all the time in the world."

"Are you sure?"

"I would have referred Mitch to someone else if I weren't. This doesn't sound like a very complicated case. If you're still undecided, I can always get copies of the police reports and look them over with you, see if there's anything there that's worth pursuing."

"I don't know what I want." She stopped rocking. "I think I'd just really like to know what happened to Melinda and Jason. I want to know the truth."

"And if the truth leads back to Billie Eagan and proves she killed one or both of her kids?"

"Then I hope she's convicted and rots in prison."

He nodded. "Fair enough."

"So, where do we go from here?"

"You tell me."

"Where would you start if I hired you?"

"Like I said, I'm going to want copies of the old police reports. Then I'd track down the kids Jason was with that last night, talk to them. Talk to Billie. And I'd like to take a look at the place where his body was found."

"That's easy enough. It's across the back field."

"Maybe we could take a look while I'm here."

"Sure. I'll get my keys and drive us over," she said, rising from the rocker.

He stood as well, asking, "How far is it?"

"Not far. But it's already so hot and humid, I figured you'd be more comfortable driving."

"Won't bother me if it won't bother you."

"Then we'll walk." She smiled in spite of

the fact that the very thought of walking in the hot sun across acres of dry, dusty field made her want to whine unpleasantly in protest. "Ready?"

"Sure."

They started toward the porch steps, then Lorna paused and said, "Be right back," before grabbing the near-empty glasses of iced tea and disappearing into the house. She returned in less than a minute, carrying two bottles of water, one of which she handed to T.J. "Just in case."

"Good idea."

He moved closer to the steps, then stopped while she locked the house behind her.

"We didn't used to have to do that," she explained, "but since I'm here by myself, I try to remember to keep the door locked. It annoys me that I have to do it, but you never know."

"I noticed you have an alarm system, though."

"After my younger brother and sister left home, Mom lived here with my grandmother until Gran died, about six years ago. Mom had the alarm installed then."

"You don't use it?"

"I know the code to disarm it, but not the one to set it."

"Isn't it the same code?"

"Oh. Maybe." She frowned. "I guess I could call the alarm company. I just figured with the locks on the doors, I should be all right."

"Still, if you're paying for the service, you should look into it."

"I don't know if it will be worth it, frankly, since I'm not sure how long I'll be here."

They walked past the barn, and a few of the feral cats poked out tentatively to watch. Lorna noted the water bowl she'd left for them was empty, as was the bowl of dry food.

"I wonder if they're eating that," she muttered.

"What?"

"The barn cats. I was just wondering if they were eating the dry cat food I left for them, or if it was being eaten by raccoons or field mice or whatever."

"I doubt the mice would stand a chance. I counted four cats in the doorway. How many more are there?"

"I don't know. They've been out there in the barn for as long as I can remember. A few years ago my mother rounded up the kittens and took them to the vet down the street to neuter them so they'd stop multiplying, but who knows if there aren't others? Gran liked them because they kept the mice population down, and she never had to resort to traps or chemicals to get rid of them." Lorna smiled. "Gran called the cats 'nature's mousetraps.' "

At the edge of the field, T.J. stopped and took in the vista.

"How much is yours?" he asked.

"All of it, except for the back section, where the body was found. We sold off thirty acres a year and a half ago to pay for my mother's radiation and chemo."

"I'm sorry."

"Thank you." Lorna pointed off to the right. "There's a pond behind that wooded section, and a small orchard. There's also a small family burial ground." She turned toward the left and said, "Down there is an old vineyard my great-uncle started back in the 1940s. It was pretty much ignored after he died."

"I thought I smelled grapes."

"That wouldn't have been from Uncle Will's vineyard, I doubt there's much going on down there after all these years. The grapes you smelled were from the arbor in the backyard. My gran's jam grapes. An altogether different kind of fruit."

"Can't you make wine from jam grapes,

and jam from wine grapes?"

She laughed. "All I know is that the grapes on Gran's arbor are big and dark purple. I only saw the other ones — the wine grapes — when I was little, before the weeds and the trees started taking over the vineyard and it got too spooky to play in."

"Spooky?" He cracked a smile. "Did your young imagination convince you that it was haunted?"

"Oh, sure. I went through a stage where I saw ghosts and haunts everywhere. I think it started after I found out that there really were bodies buried in the family cemetery. Then when Uncle Will started acting up, it made a believer out of me."

"Uncle Will acts up?"

"He died in the late forties, and he's never really left." When T.J. chuckled, she shrugged and said, "Hey, you can believe it or not, but I've heard him and seen him. Once you've met a ghost head-on in your upstairs hall, it isn't much of a stretch to believe that those weird sounds coming from the vineyard are caused by demons. The older kids in the neighborhood used to tell me that, and I believed them."

"I noticed that up along the main road there were a bunch of houses that had really large properties in the rear. Makes it more of a real neighborhood, I suppose, than a typical farm community."

"Right." Lorna pushed a long strand of hair from her face. She wished she'd grabbed one of the straw hats hanging near the back door. Sweat was beginning to bead on her face and some more ran down the front of her shirt, making her skin itch. "Most of those houses have ten acres or more out back. Callen was founded by six brothers — they each built one of those red brick houses along Callen Road, where you came in. Three on one side, three on the other. They wanted their houses fairly close together, but also wanted to farm. The three brothers on one side shared the acreage behind their homes, the brothers on the opposite side of the street did the same. It's only been in the last fifty years or so that the farms have been broken up and the properties sold individually. When I was growing up, there were kids in every one of those houses, and we all went to school together and played together. Summers, everyone swam in our pond and we played in everyone's yards." She twisted the cap off her water bottle. "We really had the best of everything. Farm life, and town life, too. It was a great way to grow up."

She paused to take a long drink from the

bottle, then asked, "How about you? City boy? Small town?"

"Small New Jersey town near the bay."

"Beach town?"

"Actually, it's an old seaport town." He stopped at the top of the ridge and looked over his shoulder. She'd fallen a few steps behind, and he waited for her to catch up before asking, "I'm assuming that's where they found him? Where the yellow caution tape is on the ground?"

"I'll bet the local kids just couldn't resist coming up here to look at that hole in the ground," she grumbled as she passed him and kept walking straight ahead.

"Any of those houses occupied?" He caught up with her easily.

"I don't think so. I did hear that one of them was sold, the white one there on the corner. Not sure about the others. The brick one is the sample house for the development."

They stepped around the lot markers on their way to the makeshift grave that had recently held the remains of Jason Eagan.

"I guess the police department has closed down construction for a few days."

"I would expect that they did. I saw a few police cars out here this morning. I was wondering if they were looking for

Melinda. For her grave, I mean." Lorna stood with her hands on her hips, about ten feet away from the excavation where Jason had been found.

T.J. walked to the edge of the excavation, then knelt on one knee. He studied the hole in the ground for a long moment, leaning forward to get a better look. Finally, he asked, "Did the police dig down beneath the remains, do you know?"

"No, I don't. Why?"

"Because if the killer dug the hole to this depth, I'm guessing he — or she — was pretty strong physically. There appears to be considerable rock once you get past the top layer of soil." He looked over his shoulder to where she stood, and asked, "Is Mrs. Eagan a large woman?"

"Mrs. Eagan? She's shorter than I am and probably weighs about half what I weigh. She's always been thin and on the frail side. She's a recovering alcoholic, apparently at one time a heavy smoker. Even twenty-five years ago, she was pretty thin. Pale." She walked to the excavation and looked down. "I see where you're going. If the killer dug this hole, chances are, the killer was not Billie Eagan."

"So that's one thing in her favor." He

stood up. "When do you suppose she'll be getting out?"

"I think she'll be out today or tomorrow. Do you want to speak with her?"

"I do. I think we need to hear her side of the story and make certain she's agreeable to working with us. Do you know where she lives? So you can get in touch with her?"

"She lives right over there, behind the vineyard." Lorna pointed off to the left.

"Think we could walk over and take a look?"

"I don't see why not." She glanced back at the hole in the ground where they'd found Jason Eagan. As she had when she heard his bones had been discovered, Lorna reflected that she'd never liked Jason. That he was mean to Mellie and to her, and had a foul mouth. She couldn't remember he'd ever had a nice word for his little sister. Still, she wouldn't have wished this on him. "You ready?"

"Yeah, I'm finished here." He fell into step with her.

"Those are Uncle Will's vineyards," she told him as they headed toward the overgrown maze.

"Was he a winemaker?"

"No, but he wanted to be. If he'd lived,

he would have been." She told him the story as they walked the distance to Billie's cottage.

She had just finished the story — "Unfortunately, the trellises were taken over by weeds and the vines all choked out" — when they came to the back of the small cottage. T.J. pointed to the last few rows of vines, which were obviously alive and doing just fine.

"Not quite all choked out."

"I can't believe it." She stared at the vines that twisted gently over the T-shaped structures. "How could they have survived all these years?"

"Someone's been taking care of them."

"It must have been Billie." Lorna shook her head. "I wonder what she's been doing with the grapes."

The irony of a recovering alcoholic tending grapes that would be made into wine was not lost on Lorna.

T.J. picked a small bunch of grapes and popped a couple into his mouth.

"These are great," he said, nodding. "Nice flavor."

"Those have to be some of the vines Uncle Will brought back from France."

"I'll bet they made some delicious wine."

"Well, they probably did in France. He never got to make any here." She pointed to the house. "What were you planning on doing here? Peeking through the windows?"

"For starters." He walked through the backyard, around to the front, and up the one step to the tiny porch, eating the rest of the grapes along the way. When Lorna came around the corner, he was standing on the scruffy front lawn, looking from the road to the porch.

"No neighbors close by, no streetlights. When Jason's friend dropped him off, he would have gotten out of the car out there, on the side of the road."

"Oh, the Eagans weren't living here then. They lived down the road a bit." She pointed off to the left. "We used to go through the back field as a shortcut. That would only take about ten minutes."

Lorna held a hand up to her forehead to block the sun's glare. "That's the way she went home from my house, that night. Through the field."

"Anyone else use it as a shortcut?"

"Just about every kid in town. We stopped planting to the end of the property line because whatever crop went in got trampled. If it wasn't the kids, it was the deer. After awhile we stopped planting about five to eight feet from the edge."

"Could we walk back that way?"

"Sure. Are you done here?" She nodded in the direction of the cottage.

"For now. I'll want to come back and speak with Billie once she's released. At the moment, though, I'd rather see the house they used to live in."

She stumbled slightly on some rocks and rolled her eyes at her clumsiness. *Way to impress the hot guy,* she told herself. *Story of my life.*

"It's cooler over along the tree line," she told him as she headed for the shade. Her shirt was sticking to the area between her shoulder blades and perspiration was pooling at the waistband of her shorts. T.J., on the other hand, was barely breaking a sweat. By the time they reached the back of the house where the Eagans used to live, her hair was wet and stringy. *This is not a good look for anyone,* she told herself as she polished off her bottle of water.

"Do you know who's living here now?" T.J. asked.

"No. No clue."

"Let's walk around to the front."

He was already on his way, so she followed him along the fence. They reached the road that ran past the house, and he crossed it to take a look at the property from that angle.

"Is this the way the house looked twenty-five years ago?"

"It's been painted a few times since then, but if you're asking me if the front door was over there," she pointed to the front of the house, which actually faced sideways on the lot, "then yes, it looks the same. The front of the house and the porch were always facing the side of the property."

"And that rise was always there, on this side of the house?"

"Yes, there used to be shrubs growing along it."

"So cars would have stopped out here, along the road?"

"Yes. There's no real driveway, as you can see. There never has been one. Mrs. Eagan didn't have a car, but times when my mother would bring Melinda home from something, or pick me up if I'd been playing here, she pulled along the other side of the house, where the rise slopes to almost nothing." Lorna pointed to the opposite side from where they'd been looking. "She'd park there, between the house and the fence."

"Well, as I see it, unless Jason's friend

got out of the car and walked him to the door, there's no way he could have seen over the rise, or past the house if he parked where your mom did. The front door is on a side of the house that faces away from the road, from any space to park. How could he have seen where Jason went once he got out of the car?" T.J. stood with his hands on his hips.

"Good question. But what difference does it make? Remember, Billie admitted she and Jason argued after he got home, admitted that the argument got violent. What difference does it make whether or not Dustin Lafferty — that was the boy who was driving that night — could see whether Jason went into the house?"

"It's a minor point, I agree. But it just makes you wonder, if he lied about that, what else did he lie about?"

Seven

Lorna was still asking herself that same question — if Dustin Lafferty lied about having seen Jason go into the house that night, what else had he lied about, and why — later that afternoon as she turned into Veronica Hammond's driveway and parked her car. T.J. had left shortly after they'd walked back to the farmhouse, after he'd given Lorna his card with several phone numbers and the suggestion that she give him a call the next day after she'd had time to think things over.

She still wasn't sure what to do. It seemed that with every hour that passed, she had more and more questions, and fewer answers. She was hoping that Mrs. Hammond, as an old friend of the family, might be able to shed some light on the situation.

"Lorna, for heaven's sake, walk a little faster and get out of this heat." Veronica Hammond stood in the open doorway, looking as tall and formidable as she did when Lorna was a child. Neither her hair, which was now snow white, nor her cane diminished her presence. "Can't remember the last time we had so many hot days in a row like this, can you?"

"It is pretty hot." Lorna greeted the older woman with a hug, then stepped inside. Mrs. Hammond quickly closed the door behind her. "Hey, when did you get central air?"

"Summer before last." Mrs. Hammond led her into the living room. "I couldn't take it anymore. I'd held out all those years, thinking I didn't want to shell out the money, then remembered how old I was and that I wasn't going to be able to take any of it with me, so I said, 'What the hell,' and called Sears. They did a nice job."

"It feels so good in here. The farmhouse is stifling."

The room was just as Lorna remembered it, all the same furniture placed in exactly the same spot where it had stood thirty years ago. Iron plant stands, dripping with enormous Christmas cactus and African violets in heavy bloom, stood in front of every window, and the end tables held stacks of books. Even Mrs. Hammond's old sewing basket sat in the same place next to her favorite chair.

"Well, if it gets too bad, you can always

come down here and spend the night. I have extra rooms." Mrs. Hammond plopped herself into her favorite chair and pointed to the sofa, where Lorna assumed she was supposed to sit. "Johnny's here for a while, not sure how long this time."

"Your grandson?"

Mrs. Hammond nodded. "My son Charlie's boy. I swear, I don't know what's wrong with Johnny. Can't stay married to save his soul. He's on his third wife, and she just tossed him out." She shook her head in disgust. "Not sure what the problem is — not sure, frankly, that I want to know — but every time a wife kicks him out, he ends up here."

Lorna, for her part, didn't quite know what to say. Offer sympathy? Make some banal remark? She decided to let it pass altogether.

"So, you're back in Callen. It's wonderful to see you, Lorna." Mrs. Hammond leaned over to pat her hand. "I do miss your mother. She was such a darling girl, all her life. It seems like only yesterday Alice was dressing her up and showing her off . . ."

She sighed deeply.

"I can't tell you how sorry I am that she's gone, Lorna."

"Thank you, Mrs. Hammond. And thank you for the lovely card you sent. My sister and brother and I all appreciated your kind words."

Well, that wasn't entirely true. Rob hadn't bothered to read any of the cards, but why get into that?

Mrs. Hammond nodded again, acknowledging Lorna's thanks. "How long will you be staying? And what are you planning to do with the old place? And please tell me what you were thinking when you offered to post bail for Billie Eagan."

Lorna almost laughed out loud. Mrs. Hammond definitely had her priorities.

"I'm not sure how long I'll be here. We have pretty much agreed to sell off the property, as much as we all hate the idea. None of us can afford to buy out the others right now, and we've all established ourselves elsewhere. So selling makes the most sense. I don't know what else to do with it. It hasn't been an easy decision, I assure you. That farm has been Palmer land since the eighteen hundreds, as I'm sure you know. We just don't have many options."

"Have you contacted a Realtor yet?"

"No. I was putting that off. I've only been here since Sunday, and I think I'd like a little time to unwind. Between my mother's illness and getting my business off the ground, it's been a tough few years for me. I want to take my time, and make sure that whatever decisions I make now are the right ones."

"That's smart of you." Mrs. Hammond was nodding that head of white hair, and once again patting Lorna's hand. "Don't rush into anything you'll regret. Once the farm is sold, it will be gone forever. You're wise to take your time."

"Well, I don't have all that much time. I do want to get back to Woodboro. My business is there, my friends . . ." Lorna was getting tired of the same old explanation. "In any event, I'll need to go through the house, see who wants what, that sort of thing."

"It'll take you forever," Mrs. Hammond said bluntly. "Your grandmother was a collector. You're going to have to get people in who know what they're looking at, or you'll get robbed."

"I promise, I'll check out the reputation of every dealer who passes through the front door."

"Your grandmother would appreciate that, I'm sure. She did have some lovely things."

Lorna was about to respond, when Mrs. Hammond leaned forward and tapped her on the left arm. "Now, about Billie Eagan's bail. Not that it's any of my business, of course . . ."

"I did offer to put up her bail, and I spoke with the attorney who was appointed to defend her. He didn't seem to be too interested, frankly, so I —"

"Overworked, they all are. Too many cases, too little time to prepare. I watch all those law shows on TV, I know what's going on."

"I'm sure overwork has something to do with it. But it seems to me that everyone has basically decided that Billie's guilty."

"Pretty much everyone has," Mrs. Hammond agreed, as if Billie's guilt was a given. Lorna decided to let it slide. She wasn't about to go toe-to-toe with an eighty-something-year-old woman.

"Mrs. Hammond, did you see my mother very often before she got sick and came to live with me?"

"Oh, yes. At least once a week. She stopped by on her way to the supermarket, to see if I needed anything, bless her heart. And she always checked to see if I had my heart medication, or if I needed a ride someplace. She was very thoughtful that way, you know. She looked out for everyone, it seems."

"Do you know if she had much of a relationship with Billie Eagan?"

"Well, I can tell you that after Billie was evicted from that house she'd been living in, and rambled about for a while, Mary Beth moved her into the cottage out there on the farm. So I guess she was her landlord. Not that Billie paid much in rent, but that was between her and Mary Beth." She shook her head and said, "You know, once your mother got something into her head, that was that. And she never asked me for my opinion, but if she had, I would have told her —"

"Do you know if they were friends?" Lorna interrupted, trying to steer the conversation back on track. She had a feeling she knew what Mrs. Hammond would have told Mary Beth.

"Friends?" Mrs. Hammond appeared to consider it. "I don't know that you couldn't call them friends, as unlikely as it was, Mary Beth being as sweet as she was, and Billie being the ornery little piece of work that she was. I do know that Mary Beth shopped for Billie's groceries and took Billie to her doctors when she had no other transportation. She did a lot for

Billie, but Billie wasn't the only one she helped."

"She wasn't?"

"Well, like I said, she picked up things at the store for me, mailed packages if I needed it. Even went to the library to get books for me. She did the same for two others I know of." Mrs. Hammond tapped her fingers on the arm of the chair. "But friends? I don't know if I want to call it friendship. I can't imagine why your mother would even want to be her friend. Though I do know Mary Beth was defensive where Billie was concerned."

"In what way?"

"Always reminding people how hard Billie had had things, how her husband up and left her for that young girl who worked in the flower shop. How Billie had two small kids to raise by the time she was twenty." Mrs. Hammond's head bobbed up and down. "I even asked her, 'Why would you want to be friends with a woman who treated her kids so bad, Mary Beth? How can you overlook all she did to those children?' "

"What did she say?"

"She said Billie'd spent the last twenty-odd years paying for what she'd done, that losing her kids should be punishment enough, and that she wasn't about to judge someone else's past." Mrs. Hammond paused, then added, "And she said that she felt somewhat responsible for what those kids went through. Said she had wondered about bruises she'd seen on Melinda, and had been tempted to ask, but never had. She said maybe if she'd done something back when it might have mattered, things could have turned out differently for all of the Eagans."

"Mom said that?"

"Billie did have her hands full, that's for sure. That Jason was one nasty boy, even when he was a small child. You wouldn't believe the things I heard come out of that mouth of his."

Oh, yes I would. Lorna thought back to the many times Jason had hurled curses at her and Melinda. She knew firsthand how vile he could be.

"And your mother always told me how Billie was remorseful, how much she regretted that she'd been so rough with her kids. Well, sorry's easy to say, when both kids are gone God knows where and you don't have to deal with them anymore, isn't it? Of course, now we know where Jason had gone. Most people think he only got what was coming to him. There are a lot of folks who still think he killed his sister."

"There are people who think Billie killed her."

"I don't know about the girl, but I do think there's a good chance Billie killed the boy."

"Why?" Lorna asked.

"Everyone knows that Billie and Jason had a screaming match that night when he came home so late."

"How does everyone know that?" Lorna asked.

"Well, that's what Nancy Lafferty says, anyway."

"Dustin's mother?"

"Yes. He was a friend of Jason's. He knew what was going on down there."

There was a rumble from outside the windows, and Mrs. Hammond started out of her chair.

"You sit, I'll see what that was." Lorna stood and went to the window. "Must have been thunder. There are a lot of low, dark clouds up toward Route One."

Someone dashed out the back of the house next door and ran to the black pickup in the driveway. He opened the driver's-side door and turned on the ignition, then rolled up the windows before jumping out of the pickup and running back toward the house.

"Is that Fritz Keeler?" Lorna asked.

"Yes, he still lives in his parents' house. You'd think a good-looking young man like Fritz would have found himself a nice girl to marry by now. I swear, I don't know what he's waiting for." Mrs. Hammond shook her head. "Now, Michael — you remember Michael, his younger brother?"

"Sure. My first crush." Lorna turned away from the window.

"He's married to Sarah Watts, you remember her?"

"Two years ahead of me in school, sure."

"Yes. Well, they live out on Cannon Road in a nice little ranch house. Two kids. Michael and Fritz bought that gas station and convenience store, the one that sits right before the intersection, after their mother died. Pooled their inheritance, I suppose, and bought the business."

"Quik Stop?" Lorna frowned, trying to recall if she'd heard that news before. "I don't think I knew that. I'm surprised I haven't seen Fritz or Mike there. I buy my coffee at Quik Stop every morning."

"I heard lots of folks do, they say the coffee's good. The boys are doing real well, from what I hear. But Fritz," another solemn shake of the head, "he's an odd duck."

"In what way?"

"Well, he's got no life. Spends most of his time in that house or working. Takes a week off here and there and takes himself on trips. Don't know where he goes, but he leaves every other week or so."

Sounds like me. Without the trips. Hope he goes someplace good. "I'm sure he gets bored, staying in that house alone all the time. And if he works that much, he's probably tired and just needs to relax."

"Yes, well, then there are the roses."

"What roses?"

"I swear, every time I look out the window, Fritz is planting another rosebush. Says his mother loved roses, so he plants them for her."

"Did he plant them for her when she was still alive?"

"Oh, yes. Just look at their backyard. It's one huge rose garden."

"I'd think you'd like that. It must be very fragrant early in the summer. And it's got to look beautiful from your house."

"Well, it does that. Strange, though. He's still odd, in my book."

"Fritz always was a little shy, Mrs. Hammond. Maybe he still is."

"Could be. His father never had much to say either, though God knows his mother made up for that. She could talk the ears off a —"

Another rumble of thunder, louder, closer.

"I think I should go before the rain hits," Lorna said.

"I won't argue with you, dear. They're predicting quite a storm." Mrs. Hammond reached for her cane, then eased herself out of her chair. "But you'll have to come back to see me again soon."

"I'd love to," Lorna said.

"Well, I'll look forward to that." The old woman leaned upon her cane. "Now, I don't know what you're planning on doing, far as Billie is concerned, and I don't know that anything I say could sway you, one way or another, and that's fine. We're all entitled. I suspect you're inclined much as your mother was, and if I told her once, I told her a hundred times, I said, 'Mary Beth, that is not a good woman. She beat her children, she drank half of every dime she ever made,' and like I told you, she'd say, 'Miss Veronica, that was a long time ago. Billie's stopped drinking, she's worked hard to clean up her life, she'll never for- give herself for the way she treated her kids,' " Mrs. Hammond sighed. "Sounded like too little too late to me, but you know how your mother was, Lorna. If any woman ever had a softer heart, I swear I never met her. I suppose if Billie Eagan said the right words and shed enough tears, Mary Beth would have bought into it. I never did. I'm thinking you have, though."

"You really think she's guilty?"

"Yes, I do. I think sure as I'm standing here, Billie Eagan smacked that boy in the head and broke his skull. And I can't help but wonder if she hadn't done the same to that little girl of hers." Mrs. Hammond leaned heavily on her cane. "And don't you have to wonder what your mother would be saying if she were alive today."

"I think she'd say, 'Innocent until proven guilty.' "

Eight

The cardboard coffee container all but singeing the skin of the palm of her hand, Lorna sat it on the kitchen counter and grabbed at the ringing phone just in time to hear the click on the other end.

"Nuts."

She took a mug down from the cupboard and poured the hot liquid into it, at the same time questioning her choice of a hot drink over a cold one when the temperature was climbing and the humidity was closing in around the house like a damp cloak after a night of pounding rain. Old habits die hard, she told herself, and went into the dining room to turn on her computer.

She watched out the window as a red-winged blackbird chased a hawk, the larger bird soaring ever higher, the smaller one flapping wildly to keep up. The blackbird swooped and pecked, harassing the hawk, who calmly continued to soar upward. The goal was to lure the hawk as far from the blackbird's nest as possible, but in the process, the constant flapping of the smaller bird's wings would wear it down, while the hawk rode the thermals and expended little energy. Once the blackbird had exhausted itself, the hawk could raid the nest to feed its young.

Lorna had to turn away from the window. She loved the hawks, loved watching them circle overhead, but hated that they preyed on the smaller, weaker birds. She understood all too well the ways of nature, but hated to watch when she knew what was inevitably in store for the blackbirds.

She read email from her closest friend back in Woodboro, who wanted to know how long she'd be staying in the sticks. Lorna smiled. Bonnie was from Los Angeles, and considered even Pittsburgh, where she was currently living, somewhat bucolic. She had no real conception of life in a small rural community like Callen, and so fell back on every farm and small-town stereotype she'd ever heard to tease Lorna. Today's email contained a list of all the worst farmer's daughters jokes she could find. Lorna laughed and shot back a quick response, then turned off her email and prepared to go to work.

The phone rang just as she opened her first files of the day. Roger the bail bondsman from West Chester had forms for her to fill out. He'd be there until ten. If she wanted Billie out that day, she had to get into his office before then. Since it was Saturday, he was taking the afternoon off to go to the track. Oh, and bring cash. Seven thousand dollars in cash.

Lorna showered and changed, then at nine a.m. drove to the savings and loan where her mother had kept her savings account. Mary Beth had added Lorna's name to the account two years ago, so withdrawing the funds wasn't a problem. What would be a problem would be explaining to her sister and brother where the funds went if Billie should bolt.

Lorna made it to the bail office in just under thirty-five minutes. Not bad, considering all the roadwork they were doing on Route 896. Roger had all of the paperwork laid out for her on the worn and pocked counter in the front room of his two-room office, and after a quick ten minutes, the deed was done.

"Your friend should be out by late this afternoon," he told her.

"How will she get home?"

He looked at her as if she were speaking a foreign tongue.

"That's her problem."

"How will I know when they release her?"

"You can call the prison in a few hours and someone there should be able to tell you."

"Well, how does this work?"

"I go to the courthouse — which, lucky for you, is open till noon — and tell them that bail has been posted. The clerk will give me what they call a Release of Prisoner form. I take that to the prison, they let her out. I don't provide transportation home, though. That's on her. Oh, and you just make sure she shows up at the preliminary hearing, or it's bye-bye." He held up the envelope containing the cash she'd handed over.

"She'll be there."

"She'd better be. Else I'll have to go out and find her. I hate it when I have to do that."

"Thanks."

"Don't mention it," he muttered as she walked out.

Unsure as to when and where to pick up Billie, Lorna stopped at the Callen police station on her way home. Chief Walker would know what to do.

She could not have been prepared for her reception.

134

"You have your nerve, coming in here this morning." Brad stood in front of the reception desk with his arms folded across his chest.

"What?" Lorna looked behind her. Was he talking to her?

"Who the hell do you think you are, calling in the fucking FBI?"

"What are you talking about? I haven't spoken to anyone from the FBI. Why would I have called the FBI?"

"You're telling me that guy who came here yesterday, you didn't call him in? He wasn't here on your account?"

"I spoke with a private investigator, yes, I did that. I still haven't decided whether to hire him, but I spoke with him. What makes you think he's with the FBI?"

He reached onto the desk and grabbed a fax and waved it in front of her.

She snatched it out of his hand to take a look.

"You telling me that's a fraud and it's not from the FBI?"

"It sure looks official, but I don't know why . . ." She skimmed the typed request for copies of all the reports relative to the disappearance of Melinda Eagan and that of her brother, Jason Eagan, all reports relative to the discovery of the body of Jason

135

Eagan, and the subsequent arrest of Billie Kay Eagan. She frowned, confused, until she came to the signature at the bottom. *Mitchell Peyton, SA, FBI.*

Regan's friend.

"I don't understand." She shook her head. "Mr. Dawson, the PI, did say yesterday he was going to stop in here to pick up copies of the reports, so why Agent Peyton — whom I do not know and did not call, by the way — why he's requesting the same reports, I don't know."

She handed the fax back to Brad. "You gave Mr. Dawson the copies of the reports, didn't you?"

"No, we did not."

"Why? At the very least, the reports on Melinda's disappearance should be public record. Anyone can get a copy of a police report. Reporters do it all the time. Why didn't you give him what he asked for?"

"Because it was late in the day when he came in, and Mrs. Rusk was working by herself, and didn't know if she should give them to him."

"She doesn't know that the police reports are public record? No one's told her that in the . . . how many years she's been working here? Don't you train your employees?"

"Don't get smart, Lorna. She just didn't know if she should give them out, that's all." He paused, then said, "Or maybe she didn't know where the files were."

"She couldn't have asked someone? Maybe called your father or you at home and asked where the files were?"

"She was just concerned, what with all the papers calling and everyone talking about how you were bailing Billie out and that sort of thing. She didn't know what to do, okay? He'd have gotten his reports if he'd come back this morning. He didn't have to call in the fucking FBI."

"Look, I'm sorry if you feel this puts you in an awkward position, but . . ." She held her hands out in front of her but he jumped in.

"Awkward position?" He snorted. "I'd say it's awkward. It's not enough that you're hiring someone to check to see if we dotted our *i*'s and crossed our *t*'s, but now we're going to have the fucking FBI looking over our shoulder."

They stood and glared at each other for a long moment. Dotting *i*'s and crossing *t*'s was the least of it, but Brad wasn't going to want to hear that.

Finally, she said, "So, did you fax over the reports?"

"Yes, we faxed over the reports," he singsonged back at her.

"Okay, then. Asked and answered." She turned and left the office, closing the door quietly behind her.

She dialed T. J. Dawson's number on her cell phone as soon as she got into her car and found his business card in her wallet.

He answered on the third ring.

"What were you thinking, getting the FBI involved in this? What was the point of that?" she said without identifying herself.

"Well, hello, Lorna. Nice to hear from you."

"Why did you feel it necessary to call in the FBI?"

"First of all, I did not 'call in the FBI.' I called a friend to request some documents because the local police department was not cooperating, and I had every right to see those reports. The receptionist wouldn't even show them to me, and when she called the chief of police on the phone, he told her to put me off, not to show me anything. It pissed me off."

"Couldn't you have waited one more day to get copies of those police reports? Did you have to call out the troops immediately?"

"I thought if I was going to be working

this case, I'd be better off establishing right up front that the local cops were not going to push me around."

"But we hadn't decided if you'd be handling this case, remember?" She blew out a long breath, then said, "Officer Walker didn't mention that Mrs. Rusk had called his father."

"Gee, that comes as a big surprise."

"I understand that you felt you were being stonewalled, but I wish you'd called me instead of your friend at the FBI. You've put me in a very awkward position here."

He was silent for a moment, then said, "I apologize if I've made things awkward or uncomfortable for you. I thought I was expediting things. It never occurred to me that it would have repercussions. I wanted to get the facts as soon as possible, so that you could decide what you wanted to do sooner rather than later. Again, I am sorry."

She was still trying to decide how to respond when he said, "Mitch faxed over the reports an hour ago. I found them quite interesting. How 'bout I drop them off to you, point out the things I think you might want to take a closer look at, and I'll just be on my way."

"That would be fine, thank you."

"Mrs. Eagan still in prison?"

"She's supposed to get out this afternoon. I took care of the bail this morning. At least, I think she's supposed to get out this afternoon." She sighed heavily. "That's what I was stopping at the police department to find out. How do I know when she's going to be released? I don't suppose they'll provide transportation for her, so I thought I'd pick her up. But I don't know where or when."

"Call the warden at the prison and ask."

"They'll tell me? And I can just pick her up?"

"Unless she's made other arrangements."

"I don't know if she has any other friends or relatives around here. I think her family is still in West Virginia. I'm not sure I remember where Melinda said her grandparents lived, exactly."

"What would be a good time for me to stop by?"

"Depends on what time I'll be picking up Billie."

"How 'bout I plan on coming up around seven tonight?"

"I should be able to pick her up and take her home by then. That would be fine. Thank you."

"You're welcome. And again, I'm really sorry to have caused problems for you there. I've never had a situation like that before. I guess I could have handled it better."

"You've never had anyone refuse to give you the information you asked for?"

"No."

"How have you managed that?"

"Must have been the old Dawson charm."

"Too bad Mrs. Rusk didn't fall for it."

"Lorna?" The voice on the phone was thin and soft.

"Yes. Billie, is that you?" Lorna looked at the clock on her laptop. She'd called the prison twice to ask about Billie's release, but hadn't gotten a callback.

"Yes. I just got home, I wanted to call and thank you. For getting me out of there. I didn't expect to be out for a long time. I don't know how to thank you."

"Don't skip."

"What?"

"Don't leave town, or I forfeit the bond."

"I got no place to go, so you don't have to worry about that."

"I'm not worried, Billie. But how did you get home? I left messages at the prison

141

earlier for someone to call me when you were getting out so I could come pick you up."

"They're all screwed up out there. They told me I was getting out, then made me sit and wait for a couple of hours while they played around with the paperwork. I was lucky, though, 'cause Eileen Sherman was at the prison visiting her sister when I finally got the word I could go, and she offered to drop me off. Stopped at the supermarket for me, too, on the way home. Nice of her."

"It was." There was a bit of an awkward pause, then Lorna asked, "Did you talk to your lawyer? The one the court gave you?"

"Only that one time."

"I think you should call him and let him know where you are."

"It's Saturday. And besides, wouldn't they tell him I've been released?"

"I have no idea, but even if someone did, it doesn't matter. He's your lawyer — Saturday and every other day of the week. You need to communicate with him yourself, as soon as possible."

"I don't have his number."

"I wrote it down, let me get it for you. Hold on . . ." Lorna searched the pile of paper scraps next to her computer until she found the one on which she'd written Joel Morgan's phone number. She read it off to Billie, adding, "Call him now. Leave a message if he isn't there. And if you haven't heard from him by noon on Monday, call him again. Make sure you get to talk to him."

"I hate to bother him like that."

"Bother him. He's your lawyer. He works for you in this, remember, not the other way around."

"All right. I'll call him."

"Billie, do you know what the charges are against you?"

"Seems there were three things." Billie was breathing heavily into the receiver. "Third-degree murder, that was one. Then some manslaughter. And something else . . . I forget what it was. My lawyer should know that, though."

So should you. Lorna shook her head at Billie's nonchalance.

"Billie, one more thing. I was thinking about hiring a private detective to look into this. I don't know how much real investigation the police are doing. I'm afraid they just assume you're guilty and they believe that having found Jason so near to your house is enough. If we're ever going to find out the truth about what happened back then, we'll have to do it on our own." She paused to let it sink in. "How do you feel about that?"

"About finding out what happened to my kids?" Billie said softly. "I still wonder, every night. But that's going to cost way more money than I'll ever see. I appreciate the thought, Lorna, I really do, but I can't see how I can pay for such a thing."

"Let me figure that out." She was thinking about using an IOU for some of her share of the proceeds from the sale of the farm. She wasn't sure what the property was worth, but she knew it would be a substantial amount. She hoped T. J. Dawson would accept that, and figured anything she spent would be more than covered. "I'm sure it's what my mother would do, if she were here."

"I don't know how I'll ever thank you, I swear I don't. And it's too much for you to do."

"Maybe we won't be able to find out what happened back then, but I do believe it's worth a try. I don't know how much I can put into this, but once the investigator looks over all the reports and statements from back then, maybe he'll have some ideas. If he thinks he can find something, we'll give him a chance to do that. If he thinks otherwise, well, then, we'll deal with that. I only ask that you cooperate with him."

"I'll do whatever he wants." Billie started to sob quietly. "I don't know why you'd do all this for me."

"Melinda was my friend. It's time we found out what happened to her."

"You sure are your momma's daughter, Lorna Stiles." Billie blew her nose. "You surely are."

"Thank you. That's one of the nicest things anyone has ever said to me. Now, don't forget to call Joel Morgan," Lorna reminded her. "It's very important that you speak with him."

Lorna hung up, wondering how hard Billie would try to track down her lawyer. It wouldn't surprise her in the least if she had to call him herself before next week was out. The woman didn't seem to have a lot of motivation, even considering what was at stake.

It occurred to Lorna that maybe Billie had expected to be arrested, sooner or later, that maybe she'd lived with that expectation for the past twenty-five years. *Does she believe her conviction is a given? Are her expectations from life so low that she assumes she'll be found guilty? Or does she expect to be found guilty because she is guilty?*

Maybe Billie felt guilty not because of what she did, it occurred to Lorna, but because of what she'd failed to do. Failed to cherish her children, failed to protect them, failed to care for them when she had them. Billie Eagan had been a crappy mother, and maybe, after all these years, she expected to be punished for it.

Either way, it's time to find out, Lorna told herself. *No more second-guessing — should I commit to this, should I not. Just move it along, find the truth, then get on with my life.*

The grandfather clock in the front hall chimed five. She saved her work and turned off the computer and went into the kitchen to scramble some eggs for dinner. She tossed in a handful of cheddar cheese and some hot peppers she'd picked up at the Amish farmers' market stand two miles down the road. One of the best things about living out in the sticks, as Bonnie called it, was being able to buy directly from the farms, if you didn't garden yourself. Her grandmother had had a wonderful garden, right out there past the magnolia. Her mother had kept it up until she'd fallen ill. Then all her energies had been diverted to beating back the tumors that seemed to come from nowhere to invade her body. Lorna finished eating and walked out the back door.

The bones of the garden remained, and she stepped through the gate and inside the white fence that surrounded it. She leaned over to pick up the pickets that had loosened and fallen to the ground over the past two years, and she stood them up in their places. The stakes her grandfather had cut to tie up the tomatoes were still lined across the back of the garden, though the plants were long gone. The weeds had grown out of control, and without thinking, she stooped and started to pull the tallest ones. Where her mother had planted green beans that last year, wild thistles now stood. They were thorny and deep-rooted, and her bare hands were no match for them. She went into the small potting shed and searched for a pair of garden gloves and a weed digger, then set out to annihilate the invaders. A large pile of the offenders lay on the pebbled path when she heard a car pull into the drive. She looked up to see T.J. unfold from the small sports car sitting so low to the ground. She wondered how he got out when the top was up.

"Hi," she called to him while she hastily wiped her hands on her cutoff jeans. "I'm sorry. I lost track of time."

"What have you got growing back here?" he asked as he walked toward her, a leather folder under his arm and a white cardboard box in his hand.

"A bunch of weeds."

"Well, they certainly look robust. What are you feeding them?"

She laughed. "They're apparently quite capable of feeding themselves. I'm afraid the plot's gone unattended for two summers now. These things have taken over. My mother would be appalled if she could see it."

She pulled off her gloves and tucked them between two pickets.

"There's still mint." He pointed to the far corner of the garden. "At least, it looks like mint from here."

She went to the corner to check it out. "What do you know, it is." She smiled up at him. "And I've been drinking my iced tea plain all week."

She broke off a few stems and sniffed at them. "Nice. How'd you know what it was, from over there?"

"Hey, I grew up in New Jersey. They don't call it the Garden State for nothing."

148

She went through the gate and closed it behind her, making a mental note to come out tomorrow with a hammer and a few nails to mend the broken section of fence.

"Oh, here." He handed her the white box.

"What's this?"

"Peace offering."

She raised an eyebrow.

"The best napoleons in Baltimore. Hands down."

Lorna lifted the lid and peered inside. Four plump, sky-high pastries marched single file across the bottom of the box.

"How could you have known that this is my all-time favorite thing?"

"You look like a woman who understands good pastries." He smiled. "My grandmother worked in a bakery back in Tuckerton, years ago. She used to bring these bad boys home for special treats. Good report cards. Winning touchdowns. Honor roll. Even college vacations, she'd drop off some before I left to go back to school."

She held the box to her chest. "Well, I hope you bought a couple for yourself. I'm not sure I want to share."

"Mine are in the trunk."

"I was kidding. I'd share. Thank you.

This wasn't necessary, you know. You already apologized."

"Some women like to drag that out awhile."

"I'm not one of them."

"So I won't need to grovel?"

"Groveling is demeaning to the groveler as well as to the grovelee."

"I'll remember that. And thank you. I swear I didn't mean to put you between a rock and a hard place."

"We're past that. Let's just deal with what is, see what can be done."

"Have you determined if Billie has used her get-out-of-jail card yet?" he asked.

"She's home. I spoke with her earlier. She hitched a ride with someone who was visiting a relative out at the women's prison earlier today."

"Did you remind her not to leave town?"

"Yes, but she's not going anywhere. Even she admitted she had nowhere to go but home."

"I have the copies of the police reports, if you want to take a few minutes to look them over."

"I would. Thanks. Come on in." She waved him on and he followed her into the house. "I'm sorry it's so hot in here. I'm pretty much dying without air-conditioning, but there's only one old unit and it doesn't work very well, especially since the humidity's been so brutal."

They walked into the dining room. She turned on the lamp on the sideboard, and hoped they'd finish up before it got dark enough that they'd need to turn on the overhead light. It was hot enough without it.

"Let me tuck this box into the refrigerator. Can I get you something to drink while I'm there?"

"A glass of water would be fine."

She brought back two bottles of spring water, handed him one, and twisted the lid off the other and took a long drink.

"Thanks," he said, setting the bottle on the table. "Where would you like to start?"

"You tell me." She pulled out the chair at the head of the table and started to sit, gesturing for him to take a seat as well. He took the one to her left.

"I guess we'll go in order." He started pulling files from the leather folder.

"In order of what?"

"The crimes. Let's start with the disappearance of your friend."

"I remember that night very well."

"Tell me again, everything, just as you remember it."

She did.

"Was anyone with Jason when he arrived to pick up Melinda?"

"Not that I recall." She chewed absently on a cuticle. "No, I'm pretty sure he was alone. I remember standing on the back porch and watching them walk out past the barn."

"You lived here at the time?"

She nodded. "We've always lived here, as long as I can remember. My grandfather died when I was three, and my parents moved here so my grandmother wouldn't be alone. We all grew up here."

"Any chance anyone would have been waiting for Jason out near the barn?"

"I guess anything is possible. But I didn't see anyone, and I was out there for a while."

"Doing what?"

"Looking for a star to wish on." She hesitated, then told him, "I was worried about Mellie's mother finding out about the dress. We put it in a bag, and I was afraid she'd have trouble sneaking it into the house. That her mother would see it and punish her. I was looking for a star so I could wish that her mother wouldn't hurt her."

"You knew that Billie was rough with her kids?"

152

"I pretty much knew. I told myself that maybe I was wrong, but deep inside, I pretty much knew. If it turns out that it went too far that night, and that Billie really did kill her, I don't think I could ever forgive myself for every time I suspected something wasn't right but kept my mouth shut."

"Is that what this is really about? You trying to decide if you have to carry that guilt around for the rest of your life?" he asked softly. "Because if it is . . ."

She brushed him off. "So what else do you have?"

"I have the police reports from the night Melinda disappeared. Everyone they spoke with. Billie Eagan. Your mother. Your father. You. Jason. Someone named Evie Kemp."

"She lived next door to the Eagans. Died a few years ago." Lorna held out a hand. "May I see what she had to say?"

He handed her the file. Lorna quickly scanned the Kemp report.

"She says she didn't see Melinda at all that night. She saw Jason in the yard with his mother . . . heard Billie yelling at him. Never saw Melinda, though." Lorna looked up at him and smiled. "And Mrs. Kemp would have known. She knew everything that everyone was doing, all the time."

"Nothing like a nosy neighbor."

"I guess sometimes that's true, right? Sometimes the neighbors see things that can help out in an investigation."

"Sometimes."

She glanced over the other reports in the file, the early investigations following Jason's questioning right through to finding the body in the back field. The clock in the hall chimed ten. No wonder she was tired. And T.J. still had to drive back to his home.

"I didn't realize it was so late. May I keep this tonight?" she asked. "Then maybe we can talk tomorrow."

"Sure."

"I need to decide how much money and how much more time I want to put into this."

"I don't blame you. You take your time." He stood up. "Actually, I'm busy tomorrow. Call Monday, anytime. I'll be around."

"I thought you said you sold the business. Will I be dealing with someone else?"

"No. If you go forward with this, you'll work with me."

She walked him to the front door.

"Thanks again for the napoleons. Unnecessary, but very much appreciated."

"You're welcome. Thanks for being so understanding."

"You have any thoughts at all on this?" She went out the door with him and across the porch.

"One thing I was wondering. Was the dress ever found?"

"Her birthday dress, the one in the bag?"

"Yeah. I didn't see any mention of it having been found that night, and it wasn't on the evidence inventory. Actually, you're the only person to have mentioned it."

"I don't know that anyone else would have been aware she'd had it with her. Her mother didn't know she had it, and Mellie sure wouldn't have told Jason. My mom and I knew, but I don't recall that anyone asked me about it." She shook her head. "I don't really know if my mother said anything to the police about Mellie having a bag with a dress in it. But they wouldn't have been looking for something they didn't know was missing."

He walked down the steps with his hands in his pockets.

"What are you thinking?" she asked from the top step.

"Melinda had to have disappeared somewhere between here and her house. According to Jason's statement, he stopped off at a friend's house, and his sister continued on through the field. So whatever happened to her, obviously it happened in that field. Or started in the field. Someone else had to have been there, someone had to have taken her from there. If we're assuming someone grabbed her, chances are the bag with the dress in it would have been dropped someplace. I'd expect her to fight, wouldn't you? And in fighting, she probably would have dropped the bag."

"She would have fought. Melinda was tough, chippy." Lorna nodded solemnly. "She would have fought like a demon if a stranger had tried to grab her."

"Then where is that bag?" He opened his car door and stood next to it. The driver's seat looked barely large enough to accommodate a man of his height and broad shoulders. "Where's Melinda's birthday dress?"

"I never thought about it. It never occurred to me that it might be missing." She gazed off into the field. "Maybe it's buried out there someplace, turned over into the field by the tractor when the field was plowed."

"Or maybe," he said as he got behind the wheel and started the car, "it wasn't a stranger she ran into that night."

Nine

Mosquitoes. The bane of summer.

Lorna swatted at the air around her head and pulled the covers up a little higher. *Why do they always seem to know when you're having the best dream?*

She hunched under the covers, but the buzzing persisted. It was another long minute before she realized there was no mosquito in her room. Someone was buzzing the doorbell.

She got out of bed and went to the side window. Looking toward the front of the house, she saw a black-and-white police car, engine on and the lights silently whirling. She threw up the sash and called out, "I'll be down in a minute."

She pulled on her clothes and slipped her feet into rubber flip-flops and went downstairs, grumbling to herself. It was eight a.m., and she hadn't had coffee. She hadn't slept well, what with Uncle Will prowling around, though thankfully he'd settled into his old room at the end of the hall by two this morning and hadn't been heard from since. And then there was the matter of T. J. Dawson and what to do about him. She'd spent all day Sunday and well into the night wrestling with herself over the issue.

Hire him? Not hire him?

Hire him? Not hire him?

Part of her wanted to hire him, just to have him around, just to be able to spend a little more time with him. Not a good enough reason to spend a considerable amount of money. She couldn't remember the last man she'd met who'd interested her as much as he did, though.

Actually, she could, but he'd turned out to be a dud, she reminded herself.

She unlocked the front door and opened it to find Chief Walker, looking annoyed.

"I'm sorry, Chief, but I didn't sleep well last night so I overslept and —"

"Sorry to wake you." It was obvious to Lorna he wasn't the least bit sorry. "But we have a problem."

"Chief, I told Brad I didn't call the FBI, I only —"

"Not that problem," he cut her off again. "The construction crew seems to have hit gold again."

"What are you talking about?"

"They found another one."

"Another . . ." It took a minute for it to

sink in. "Another body?"

"Well, bones. Definitely human bones."

"Please tell me it's not a small child," she whispered.

"It's not a small child. A bone from one leg is missing, but I'd say the person was five-seven, five-eight, in that range." He paused. "It wasn't Melinda Eagan, that much I'm sure of. I just wanted to give you a heads-up, is all, let you know what's happening. You're going to be seeing a lot more activity out there this time, once the press gets ahold of this."

"I appreciate it, Chief."

"The ME is on his way, same routine as before." He stared at her for a minute, then said, "Any idea what the hell went on back there, Lorna?"

She shook her head. "I'm as mystified as you are. More so, because that was Palmer land, we owned it at the time Jason and this other person were buried there."

"I guess it would be too much to hope that at some point over the years, you noticed something funny going on out in your fields."

"Never. I'm sorry. Finding Jason's body was one thing, finding another one so soon after . . ." She shook her head. How could this be happening on her family farm?

"Might give your brother and sister a call, see if they remember anything. If you think of something, even a little thing — like maybe some homeless person you used to see hanging around a lot, anything like that — you give me a call."

"Will do," she said, thinking he'd like nothing better than to be able to pin this on some nameless stranger. "Chief, how will this affect the case against Billie Eagan?"

He visibly prickled. "You sound like a reporter. Won't affect it at all. Why should it?"

"It's one thing to think that she killed her son in a fit of anger, which appears to be your theory. It's another altogether to think she killed some stranger."

"Now, we don't know that it's a stranger we found, do we? Let's not put the horse before the cart." He turned and walked to his car. "We'll get back to you if we need you."

Lorna watched from the doorway while the police car made a circle in the drive. The chief looked straight ahead, not bothering to wave on his way past, though surely he knew she was still standing there. *Guess he's still pretty pissed off.*

She closed the door and went back upstairs to look for her keys, debating whether to change her clothes before running out to the mini-mart for her morning coffee. Deciding against changing, she grabbed her handbag from the floor next to the bed, where she'd dropped it the night before. Troubled by the latest finding, she set out, distracted, on her morning errand.

Lorna had just walked into the Quik Stop when she heard someone calling her name. She looked around but didn't see anyone she recognized. She was pouring her coffee when she felt someone a step or two too close to her.

Then someone whispered in her ear, "That cup's on the house."

"Fritz!" She laughed, looking over her shoulder.

"Lorna, put that cup down so I can give you a real welcome-home hug."

She set the cup on the counter and put her arms around him.

"It's so good to see you," she told him. "I stopped to see Mrs. Hammond just the other day, and she told me you and Mike bought this place. I come here every morning and this is the first time I've seen either of you."

"Mrs. Hammond said you were stopping

in for coffee every day, so I thought I'd start watching for you. I'm in the office for the first few hours of each day, and Mike comes in around four."

"I'm late this morning. I'm usually here by seven."

Another customer reached past her for a cup, and Lorna picked up her coffee and stepped aside.

"I heard you were right in the middle of this thing with Mrs. Eagan," Fritz said, guiding her out of the way of a woman searching for the right color sweetener packet. "I can't believe they found Jason after all these years. And right out there, on your farm."

"That section isn't ours anymore, but yeah, it's crazy. And this morning, it got even crazier." She told Fritz about Chief Walker's early-morning visit.

"Holy shit, another body?"

Two customers at the pastry counter turned around to stare.

"That was exactly my reaction when he told me." She lowered her voice. "I can't believe someone brought bodies onto our farm to bury them, but that's apparently what happened."

"Any idea who this latest person was, how he or she died?"

"Nothing so far. The ME hadn't even arrived yet. I guess it will be awhile before they know anything. And they're not likely to tell me. I'm persona non grata around the police station right now."

"I heard about that, too."

"You did?" She frowned. "What exactly did you hear?"

"I heard that you bailed out Mrs. Eagan — which I can understand you doing. She was a friend of your mother's, and you and Melinda were friends, right?"

Lorna nodded. "What else did you hear?"

"I heard you pulled some strings and had the FBI brought into the case."

She shook her head. "Not true. First of all, I have no strings to pull. Second, I did not call the FBI. What I did was talk to a PI about the possibility of him looking into the case. It's important to me to know the truth. If Mrs. Eagan killed one or both of her children, I want to know. If she suckered my mother into believing she was innocent so that she could use her and their friendship, I want to know that as well."

"No offense, Lorna, but don't you think Chief Walker wants to know the truth, too?" Fritz said softly.

"Of course I do. It just seemed to me

there was a total rush to judgment to arrest Billie Eagan with only the scantest bit of evidence."

"I agree it's circumstantial — from what I've heard, anyway — but it does make sense. I can see how it happened the way he thinks it did."

Before she could respond, he said, "Just think it through logically. Mrs. Eagan's daughter disappears, and suspicion falls immediately on her, which right there gets a lot of people talking. Then suspicion shifts to the son. Just before the son is going to be arrested, he disappears. Now, suppose for a minute that Jason did kill Melinda. He comes home after drinking with his buddies, and maybe he says something about it. Maybe he even admits it. Mom picks up something heavy and smacks him in the head with it. Maybe on his way down, she smacks him again. Then she realizes what she's done, and she has to get rid of him. She takes him out into the field and buries the body. Maybe she's shocked it's not discovered."

"It wouldn't have been." She shook her head. "Fritz, you didn't see how deeply those remains were buried. There's no way she could have dug that deep on her own. And there's no way she could have gotten his body clear across the field, in the dark. She isn't strong enough."

"She was strong enough to beat him good whenever she could."

"You knew about that?"

He nodded, a look of distaste on his face. "I knew. I was in one of Jason's classes, I saw the bruises. I never knew why he didn't fight back."

"She was his mother." Lorna shrugged. "I think that's very common among abused children. They don't fight their abuser. Whether they think they deserve to be treated that way, I don't know. And I think it's too deep a subject for us to resolve in this conversation."

"But you have to agree, it could have happened that way."

"Yes, it could have happened that way. If it did, let's find out."

"So you hired a PI? That may be a good thing. I think everyone wants to know what really happened." He got a cappuccino from the machine. "Have you tried this? It's pretty good."

She shook her head. "I like my coffee straight."

"Well, I'll be interested in hearing what your guy finds out. If you're willing to share, that is."

"He's not my guy yet. I haven't officially hired him. I was still thinking it over, but now, with this latest find, I'll go ahead with it. And as far as sharing information is concerned, it's all going to come out, sooner or later. Either now or at Mrs. Eagan's trial."

"Well, if you need anything, anything at all, you give me a buzz, hear?"

"I will. And say, your backyard looks gorgeous. I can't believe you still have so many roses blooming, this late in the summer."

"Yeah, how 'bout it?" He beamed proudly. "I've spent a lot of time out there, watering, battling the Japanese beetles, black spot, mildew, aphids, you name it. But Mom always managed to keep the roses going right into the fall, so I feel obligated to do the same."

"Well, you're doing a great job."

"Thanks. I'll bring you some one of these days."

She started up to the cash register and he waved her away.

"I told you, it's on the house."

"Just for today."

"We'll see." He squeezed her arm. "Great to see you, Lorna."

"Good to see you, too, Fritz."

He held the door open for her and she walked out just in time to see the county ME's car go by.

She drove back to the farm, hoping that the remains would be identified soon. If the bones were bare, no tissue left on them, it could be some time before they knew the identity of the second person buried in the Palmers' field.

Or Palmers Woods, as the sign pronounced.

The person could even be a few hundred years old, she rationalized. There had been skirmishes here during the American Revolution. Or perhaps it was a Native American. There were settlements all along the river, and every child who grew up in Callen knew that the road that wound past the farm and through town had once led to the old Baltimore Pike. Or the body they'd found in the field that morning could have been a traveler who took ill and died along the wayside. Whoever had found him could have buried him right then and there, depending on the circumstances. Sure, it could have happened that way, she told herself as she dug into her nutritious breakfast of coffee and a napoleon, which she was happy to discover lived up to its hype.

It could be coincidental that the remains just happened to have been buried in the same field as Jason Eagan, maybe hundreds of years apart. A lot of things must have been buried in these fields over the centuries. Best not to jump to conclusions.

She tried to hold that thought as she climbed the ladder to the old hayloft and watched out the barn window. A small crowd of police officers, rescue-squad members, and county personnel hovered around the site. It didn't take her long to figure out that sitting there wasn't going to get her anything except hot and irritated. The temperature in the loft was at least ten degrees higher than it was in the house. There was absolutely nothing to be gained by staying there. She wasn't going to see a thing. Better to use the time constructively.

She glanced at her watch. It was almost nine. Time to go to work, anyway. She climbed down the ladder, startling the cats who'd ventured out to peer at her. She closed the barn door behind her and went back to the house.

Her cell phone was ringing but she couldn't remember where she'd left it. By the time she recalled it was in her handbag, the ringing had stopped. She checked the screen, but the number was private.

She grabbed a bottle of water from the refrigerator and turned on her computer. She'd started the billings for the Cut 'n Curl yesterday, and had promised the owner of the hair salon she'd have them to him by noon today. Like most salons, Cut 'n Curl was closed on Mondays, but the owner went in to catch up on paperwork and restock inventory.

At eleven-forty she called her client to let him know the file was on its way. The machine answered and Lorna left a message. She hung up and forwarded the work via email. He emailed back his thanks, with a reminder that she was overdue for a cut.

She stretched and decided a break was in order, and that the best use of the break would be to call Andrea and Rob and let them know what was going on. Besides, the chief had asked her to. If either of them had any recollections that could help his investigation, maybe he'd forgive her PI — and therefore her — for that fax from the FBI.

That reminded her that she still had to call T.J. and talk to him about his fee and about how much investigation she would have him do.

Andrea first.

She ended up leaving a message for her sister to call her. She didn't think voice mail was the way to deliver the news.

Rob's phone rang and rang. Finally, he answered just when she was expecting to hear a recording.

" 'Lo?" he rasped.

"Robbie, it's Lorna." When he didn't respond, she added, "Your sister."

"I know who you are, thanks," he said flatly. "Do you have any idea what time it is?"

Oops.

"It's eight forty-five out there, by my calculations."

"Middle of the night," he muttered.

"Rob, I'm sorry for waking you, but I just called Andi and she wasn't home, so I thought I'd try you. I'm sorry. Want me to call back?"

"Why? So you can wake me again?"

"I said I was sorry." She bit her tongue. Same old Rob. "Don't you have to get up for work, anyway?"

"I'm sorta between jobs right now. So what do you want?" he grumbled.

"Rob, last week, they found Jason Eagan's remains. In our back field." She explained how the backhoe had uncovered the grave.

"Jason Eagan, eh? There's a name out of the past." Rob yawned. "They say how he died?"

"Blunt trauma to the head, front and back."

"Cracked his skull, huh?" He was starting to wake up. "Well, no sympathy here. Jason was a mean bastard. He used to scare all the little kids."

"This morning they found the remains of someone else."

"Who?"

"We don't know yet. The medical examiner has the body now. I'm sure there will be a full-scale investigation."

"All this on our farm, eh?"

"All this on what used to be our farm. Both skeletons were found in the section Mom sold off."

Rob changed the subject abruptly. "Speaking of which, what's happening with the sale of the rest of it? I could use my share of the proceeds."

"Rob, I told you it wasn't going to happen overnight. For one thing, before we can sell the property, we have to have it appraised. Then we have to talk to a couple of Realtors and find out what's the best way to sell it. Do we sell as one parcel, or do we try to have it subdivided?"

"We sell for the most money, as soon as we can. I told you, I'm between jobs right now."

"Well, then, since you're not working, why don't you hop on a plane and get yourself out here and give me a hand? There's a whole houseful of stuff here to be sorted through, furniture, things that have been in the family for generations. The house has to be cleaned out —"

"Just sell it all," he interrupted her. "Get someone in there to buy it all, and be done with it."

"Gran had a lot of fine collections, Rob. She had all that cranberry glass, she had carnival glass, she had —"

He cut her off. "I don't care about that stuff, not any of it. Just get rid of it all."

"It's not that easy. For one thing, we need to have an appraisal for the estate, and we haven't done that yet."

"What are you waiting for?"

"Excuse me, but I work every day. I have a business to run."

"Hey, don't complain. You volunteered to go there and take care of everything." He was fully awake now.

"I *volunteered* because you couldn't get back to L.A. fast enough, and Andrea has a family to take care of. There wasn't anyone else, Rob."

"Look, I don't see what the big deal is. If you're worried about getting ripped off, just call a couple of dealers in to look things over. Then once you know what everything is worth, sell it. And it's done."

"Andi wanted some things, some of the furniture."

"Fine. She can take whatever she wants, we'll deduct the price from her share after everything is sold."

"Is there anything you want, Rob?"

"From there?" He snorted. "I can't think of one thing I want from Callen."

She was stung by his words, startled by the angry undertone.

"Was there something else, Lori?" His voice had softened slightly.

"Actually, there is. Chief Walker wanted me to ask both you and Andi if you remember ever seeing anyone around the farm who didn't belong here. Maybe some drifter or stranger, out in the area of the fields, or back behind the barn. Or if you ever saw anything that didn't seem right, out there by the woods."

Rob fell silent.

"Robbie?"

"I heard you. I'm thinking." He paused briefly. "Nope, sorry. Can't think of a thing. Anything else?"

"Look, since you're not working and have some time on your hands, why don't I send you a plane ticket and you can come out here and give me a hand. I could really use the help, Rob."

"Sorry, Lorna." She could hear the resignation in his voice. "I left Callen for the last time years ago. I can't think of a good enough reason for me to go back there, now or ever. But thanks for the offer of a plane ticket. Keep in touch, okay?"

The line went dead in Lorna's hand. It was another moment before she hung up the receiver, several more before she got up and poured herself a cold drink, then went out on the back porch, trying to come up with a reasonable explanation as to why her brother was so adamant about never coming home again.

Ten

"You're kidding. Remains of a second body? Same era as the first? Same sex, same cause of death?" T.J.'s questions shot at Lorna through her cell phone with a speed that defied response.

"Whoa. Slow down," she protested. "I have no information other than there was another finding. I detected a definite coolness from Chief Walker, though, so I suspect I'm still on his shit list, which means it's not likely he'll be willing to share any news with me."

Lorna slumped in her chair at the dining room table. There'd been a steady stream of police and emergency vehicles appearing over near the new development all day, but she had no idea what was going on. She'd walked across the field around two o'clock, but the EMT who'd been posted guard on her side of the property wasn't about to let anyone near the site of the grave. From where she'd stood, she could see the ME's car and those marked *County CID*, but other than being able to note the high level of activity, she couldn't tell what was going on.

"I think we need to know right off the bat if there's any chance this could be connected to Jason's death, and if so, are they going to be eyeing Billie as a suspect. I wonder if the chief would talk to me."

"Ah, apparently I need to remind you why I'm on his shit list in the first place."

"Good point." He fell silent for a moment, then said, "But there are other law enforcement personnel there, right? Didn't you say there were county cars on-site?"

"Yes."

"Well, maybe I could get some information from one of them. You know, lawman to lawman."

"Do PIs qualify as lawmen?"

"Hey, I'm ex-FBI. We could get lucky. And remember, the only person who saw me at the police station was the receptionist, so neither the chief nor any of his officers knows what I look like."

"What information are you searching for?"

"Whatever we can learn about the victim. For starters, cause of death. How long the remains have been there."

"They wouldn't necessarily know that right away, would they?"

"They'd have a damned good idea of

what killed the victim if the skull was bashed in, and clothes can give you an indication of the era."

"But they couldn't determine the age of the victim just by looking at the bones, could they?"

"It's possible, if your ME is very good. That will require some lab work, though. I don't know how well equipped your county facilities are, and I don't know how good the lab techs are. A lot of smaller labs don't have the funds for the more sophisticated equipment."

"So assuming that we don't have what it takes here, the bones would be sent elsewhere for testing, right?"

"Right. Most likely to the FBI lab."

"Oh, that would go over big." She grimaced. "I suppose they'll blame that on me, too."

T.J. laughed. "I promise to take the blame for everything. I don't have to live in that town."

Motion at the far side of the field caught her eye.

"T.J., hold on, there's something else happening out there." Lorna walked outside and to the end of the front porch.

"What's going on?"

"It looks like another ambulance just arrived. Why would they need another ambulance?" She frowned. "Unless they found another body . . ."

"I'm on my way."

She disconnected the call and walked up the drive to the barn, then along the edge of the field and to the family burial ground.

"Do you believe this, Mom?" she asked as she went through the gate.

Lorna watched from the closest possible vantage point, but realized that she wasn't likely to see a thing from anyplace other than the barn, so she started walking back. She'd spent a half hour in the hot sun, and all she'd learned was that a couple of TV stations had sent their news vans, which were parked along the road. Which meant that someone had been alerted to what was happening in Callen and found the story newsworthy. The thought made her uneasy. The last thing she wanted was publicity.

She was almost to the corner of the barn when she heard voices in the drive. Not expecting anyone except T.J., she peered around the corner, and saw two news vans parked next to her BMW.

"Shit."

She went into the barn through its back

door, and climbed to the loft. Besides giving her a better view across the field, it allowed her to avoid the reporters she'd seen lurking around the vans.

Damn. She was supposed to be selling the farm. This kind of attention would not be to her advantage. Who would want to buy a property where dead bodies kept turning up?

She kept one eye on the field, and another on the drive. The reporters didn't appear to be in any hurry to leave, and the fact that she hadn't answered the door buzzer didn't stop them from occasionally going back to the front door and ringing it again. She was thinking perhaps it would be better to face them once and hopefully get rid of them, when another car pulled into the driveway. She watched the small, sleek sports car zip up to the porch and stop.

She crouched at the front loft window and watched as the reporters rushed T.J. After he'd said whatever it was he'd had to say, the reporters and cameramen climbed back into their respective vans and drove off. She waited until they disappeared out onto the road, then made her way down the ladder.

Walking toward the front of the house,

she saw T.J. sitting on the front steps.

"How'd you get rid of them?" she called to him.

"Told 'em it was obvious that you weren't here, but you'd call as soon as you had a statement to make."

"I'm not going to have any statements."

"That's pretty much what I figured." He grinned as she drew closer. "Got rid of them, though."

"And I thank you for that. The last thing I want is to have pictures of this farm plastered all over the news. We're going to be putting the property on the market. I'd rather prospective buyers not get their first look at it on the evening news." She sat down next to him. "I'm thinking if we keep a low profile here, the fallout won't be so bad."

"Well, I did learn a little something from them." He moved over a little to make more room for her on the step. "They definitely found more remains over there. At least one more, but they're apparently still digging."

"Oh, my God." She put a hand over her mouth. "I can't believe this. What the hell?" She looked up at him, wide-eyed. "Someone must have been sneaking onto our property and burying bodies." She covered her face. "At some point, while we were living here, someone was coming onto our property and burying bodies and we never knew."

"It is pretty creepy, I'll give you that."

"Okay, where do we go from here? How do we find out what's really happening? Not rumors, but facts."

"Well, seems to me the shortest distance is still a straight line."

She shook her head. "Chief Walker won't tell me a thing."

"Then we go to plan B." He got up and dusted off the back of his shorts. "I'll walk over and see what I can find out."

"Am I going to have to bail you out before the day is over?"

"I'll do my best to avoid confrontation with the Callen PD," he told her, "but if I'm not back in an hour, call Mitch."

"I don't have his number."

"I was kidding." He walked toward the field.

"Oh," she said, though he'd already turned the corner of the house.

Lorna retreated to one of the rocking chairs, and sat down with her feet crossed at the ankles and resting on the porch railing. Her eyes flickered to the road every time she heard a car, then back to the field.

T.J. was back in less than twenty minutes.

"So. How'd you make out, lawman to lawman?"

"Let's just say those county boys don't know the meaning of professional courtesy, and we'll leave it at that." He took the steps two at a time and sat in the other rocker.

"That bad, eh? Walker see you coming?"

"No. But I didn't see him coming, either."

"He kicked you off the site?"

"Yeah, but it could have been worse. At least he didn't arrest me, like he did one of the reporters who got too close and started snapping pictures."

"So I guess we need to talk about plan C."

"This is new territory for me. I've never had to go beyond B." He rocked for a moment. "I could give Mitch a call. I'm sure the Bureau is going to be getting the remains at the lab."

"Calling Mitch is what got us into this spot. If we contact him before the chief calls them in, we're just in that much deeper."

"Good point." He rocked a little more. "You know, I think we're getting side-tracked. Our original plan was to speak with some of the witnesses who gave statements back when Melinda disappeared, and a few weeks after that, when Jason disappeared. Let's get back to that, see if we can develop any new information."

"Okay. Where do we start? Who should we talk to first?"

He raised an eyebrow. "I thought you were hiring me to do the talking."

"I am. But that doesn't mean I can't come along, does it? I know almost everyone on that list. I can tell you things about them you wouldn't otherwise know."

"I'd expect you to tell me, anyway."

"Well, I would. But I think it makes more sense if I come along."

T.J. went to his car and opened the trunk. He returned to the porch with the leather portfolio he'd had with him the other night. He opened it and took out a piece of paper and handed it to Lorna.

"What's this?" she asked.

"It's the list of people I want to talk to." He sat back down in the rocker. "Start at the top, let's go through the first five. What can you tell me about them?"

"Billie Eagan, you already know about." She looked up at him. "I need to take you over to meet her."

He nodded, and she continued.

"Chris Taylor — his sister Corrie was a friend of mine all through school, she's married and living in Syracuse now. He was in Jason's class." Her eyes scanned the list. "A lot of these people were Jason's classmates. Fritz Keeler — I just saw him this morning, he and his brother, Mike, own the gas station–convenience store down past the intersection. Dustin Lafferty, he's the boy who drove Jason home the night he disappeared. Eddie Franklin, he and Dustin and Chris all hung out together, they were all five or six years ahead of me. I mostly knew them because they had sisters I was friendly with." She read to the bottom of the page, then looked at him. "What would you like to know?"

"Who should I start with?"

"I don't think it matters, after all this time." She shrugged. "Start at the beginning."

"Can you check off the ones you know are still in the area?"

"Sure."

He took a pen from the folder and handed it to her. She checked off fewer than a dozen names.

"Actually, I'd start with Fritz. He'd already heard about me hiring you, he asked about it this morning, so he's a good person to start with. I think he'll cooperate with you, answer whatever questions you ask."

"Then we move Fritz to the head of the line." He paused, tilted his head slightly, and asked, "Is that your phone?"

"It's my cell. I'll be right back." She ran into the house and grabbed the phone.

"Lorna? It's Regan."

"Hey, Regan. How are you?"

"Oh, I'm fine. I was just wondering how you're doing."

"What do you mean?"

"I turned on the news in time to see the story, and I was wondering how you're holding up."

"The story?" Lorna's stomach twisted. "Of course. The story. Shit. What are they saying?"

"After their big lead-in to The Body Farm?"

"Are you serious? Which channel?"

"Actually, all of the networks."

"Damn it." Lorna stalked outside, the phone still up to her ear. "What are they saying?"

"That the remains of four bodies . . ."

"Four? Oh, my God, they found another

186

one? What the hell is going on? I'm assuming this one was also found on the section we sold off to a developer."

"They did mention that work has stopped until the entire area has been searched."

"Oh, swell," Lorna grumbled. "I'll never find a buyer for this place now."

She put her hand over the phone and told T.J., "It's Regan Landry. She's watching the news. The press has dubbed this place 'The Body Farm.' "

"Ask her if Mitch can find out if the FBI has been brought in yet."

"T.J. wants you to ask Mitch if the FBI is on this yet." She listened, then said, "Okay, that's great. I'll be here."

She disconnected and slid the phone into her pocket.

"She's going to call Mitch, then she'll get back to me." Lorna paced the porch to the far end. "Body Farm. That just stinks." She made a face. "I should probably let this settle down before I put the house on the market, shouldn't I?"

She paced a little more. "Or should I sell it quickly, before they find more bodies?"

"Have you spoken with a Realtor yet?"

"I haven't had time. I've only been home a week."

"You really want to sell this place?" His gaze started at the roadside fence and went right on back to the field. "It's such a beautiful property. If I were looking for a place with some ground, I'd jump on it. It has charm, Lorna. It has history."

"Unfortunately, most of which is buried."

He laughed. "When was the house built?"

"My great-great-grandfather built it in 1853."

"And it's been in your family ever since?"

She nodded.

"Doesn't it bother you to sell?"

"More and more, every day." She looked past him to the barn. "My siblings and I agreed, after Mom died, to sell. I came here to get things in order, get the house cleaned out, get it on the market."

"And then?"

"And then I go back to Woodboro, where I live. My business is there. My friends." The words sounded tired now. She'd sung that song too many times the past week.

"What kind of business?"

"I'm a CPA. I do accounting for a number of small businesses."

"You own your own business?" He smiled. "Very impressive. But who's running it, while you're here?"

"Well, I am. I had a computer network set up, I hook in with my clients and take it from there."

"And your business isn't suffering while you're here?"

"Hasn't skipped a beat." She could see where the conversation was leading. "My life is there. I really don't have one here anymore. My sister and her husband live in Oklahoma. They have very young children. She doesn't want to sell. I think she has visions of bringing the kids back for summer vacations on the farm. Playing in the fields, swimming in the pond."

"You have a pond?"

She nodded. "On the other side of the family burial plot."

"Family burial plot, too?"

"Yes."

"Any chance these last three bodies —"

She cut him off. "No. No chance. I was over there earlier, no sign of disturbance."

"Are your parents buried there?"

"My dad is — though he's not a Palmer, he lived here for most of his married life — and my mother is . . . partially. Sort of."

"I have no idea what that means, 'partially sort of buried.' "

"She was cremated. She wanted some of her ashes spread around in the family cemetery." She could tell by the look on his face that he wanted to ask where the rest of the ashes were going, but he was too polite. "She wanted to be in three places: the cemetery, with her parents and my dad; her garden; and around the pond. Her favorite places."

"Is that why you were weeding the other night?"

She shook her head. "Oh, no. Not that garden. Mom wanted her ashes in her flower garden. But that's so overgrown, I couldn't do it. I don't think she realized how the weeds would take over, with her having been gone the past two summers. I'll get to it before I leave. At least, I hope I will. It meant a lot to her."

"You said 'siblings.' I understand why your sister isn't here to give you a hand, who else is there?"

"My brother, Rob." She settled back in the chair and rocked for a long moment. "I had a really odd conversation with him just this morning. I asked him to come back and give me a hand — he's between jobs right now — but he said the strangest thing. He said he'd left Callen for the last time when he was eighteen, and he couldn't think of a good enough reason to come back now. Or words to that effect."

"Did he have a hard childhood?"

"Robbie?" She laughed. "Please. He was the youngest, he was the only boy, and he was spoiled rotten. He was doted on by my grandmother like you wouldn't believe."

"Then maybe *spoiled* is the right word."

"He was never bratty, at least, not that I remember. He's seven years younger than I, though, so he was eleven when I left for college. I don't know why he feels the way he does, but he was pretty insistent about not coming home. He wants me to sell everything, send him his share, and we'll all go on with our own lives."

She was waiting for him to comment, and when he didn't, she said, "Selling would probably be best for everyone. Andrea and I together couldn't buy out Robbie, so that's that. And I don't know how I'd support this place."

"How did your mother do it?"

"She rented out the fields to another farmer."

"Really?" His interest was instantaneous. "Is he still around?"

"Gil Compton, yes, he is." She turned to look at him. "I see where you're going.

Maybe he saw something over the years, something or someone."

"Maybe we should put him on the list of people to talk to."

"It would. Good call. I wouldn't have thought of him."

"That's why you're paying me the big bucks."

"Oh, right. We need to talk about that." The phone in her pocket rang and she answered it right away. "Regan. Were you able to speak with Mitch?"

"I was. Unfortunately, the Bureau doesn't have the case yet. As a matter of fact, no request has been made. His boss is going to call the county DA in the morning and offer assistance, but until that happens, he's reluctant to get involved. There was a little fallout from the fax thing. Your police chief called the Bureau. Mitch got his hand slapped."

"Ouch. I'm so sorry that happened. Please apologize to him for me."

"He doesn't blame you. He blames the cops for having put T.J. in that position in the first place. They know the law. They're supposed to follow it."

"Still . . ."

"Still nothing. The reports should have been handed over. They can charge for them, but not withhold them."

A van pulled into the driveway. T.J. got up and walked down to meet it.

"There's another damned reporter here," Lorna said.

"That's only going to get worse. I think you should call your police department and tell them that you need a car there to keep trespassers off the property."

"Fat chance. No one there is speaking to me unless they have to."

"Well, they have to. They can't pick and choose who they're going to protect. Hang up and call them." Regan paused, then said, "Are you alone there?"

"Well, T.J. is here now, but he'll be leaving."

"Why don't I drive up there and spend a few days, just till this blows over and something else takes its place on the news."

"Drive up? Aren't you in Princeton? Wouldn't that be 'drive down'?"

"My dad's place is in Princeton. My house is on the Eastern Shore. Right around St. Michaels. I'm probably not an hour from you. Not a bad drive."

"I thought you had a book due."

"They moved it on the schedule, changed the publication date. I can take a little time off. What do you say? Want a roommate for a few days?"

"Actually, I'd love it. If you're certain it's not an imposition."

"Hey, I offered. I want to. Give me directions from around Rising Sun."

Lorna did.

"Piece of cake to find you," Regan said. "I'm going to hang up and throw some clothes into an overnight bag, and then I'll leave. In the meantime, call the police department. Make 'em earn your tax dollars."

They each hung up, and Lorna stood to look down the drive. T.J. was still talking to whoever was in the van. Lorna was about to walk down to see what was going on when the van made a U-turn and took a left on Callen Road.

"What was that all about?" she asked T.J. as he approached the house.

"Network news, Wilmington affiliate. I told them the farmhouse was off-limits. Not that that will do any good."

"Regan's coming up to spend the night," she told him. "She suggested I call the police and have them send a car to keep an eye on things."

"I was going to suggest the very same thing. I'm not comfortable with you being here alone. Some of these people will go to ridiculous lengths to get their story. It's better if the police are around and you have someone in the house with you. Call them now."

"I don't think my request will be well received."

His jaw tightened. "Too bad. That's their job. Go on, give them a call while I'm still here."

She went into the house to look up the number and realized that it was well past the dinner hour. She should offer to feed T.J. She dialed the number for the station and peered into the refrigerator while the line rang. Lots of vegetables . . . eggs . . . seltzer. Somehow, T.J. didn't look like the type of man you'd invite for quiche and sparkling water.

"Callen Police."

She knew the voice.

"Brad?"

"Yes?"

"Lorna Stiles."

"Yes?"

"Brad, I'm having a problem here, with reporters coming to the house."

"And what would you like me to do about it?"

"I would like you, acting on behalf of my local police department, to send a car over

195

to patrol the property during the night, more than just the quick drive-by you've been doing."

"Need protection from a few reporters, do you?" He laughed. "Maybe you should call your friends at the FBI."

"And what do you suppose the feds would say if I told them my local police department refused me protection when I felt threatened?"

A long, unpleasant silence followed.

"I'll send Bobby Markham over." He paused, then asked, "Will there be anything else?"

"No, thank you very much. I appreciate it, Officer Walker. Be sure to thank Chief Walker for me."

She hung up, and grinning, walked back outside.

"They're sending a car," she told T.J. "I'm ordering pizza. What's your preference?"

Eleven

"Lori?"

"Andrea?" Lorna glanced at the kitchen clock. "You're up awfully early. What time is it out there, five-thirty?"

"I couldn't sleep. The baby kept me awake all night so I got up" — Andrea's words shot through the phone, gathering speed — "and came downstairs and turned on the TV . . ."

Uh-oh.

". . . and what do I see but our house . . ." she took a breath, ". . . at least, it looks like our house, Lori. But back when I lived there, it was referred to as the 'old Palmer farm.' The house on the TV was being called 'The Body Farm.' "

Andrea paused, then said, "Please tell me they're talking about somebody else's farm."

"I wish I could."

"Well, what the hell is going on out there?" Andrea sounded close to tears. "Where are all these bodies coming from?"

"I don't know. And I haven't seen the

news today, so I don't know what's being said."

"They're saying four bodies have been found out in the fields."

"It's actually the old woods. The developer cut the trees down. I guess to the reporters it looks like part of the field. And I guess, technically, it is now."

"Well, so much for finding a buyer. Who's going to want to buy the property now that bodies are popping up all over the place?"

"Trust me, any one of the builders down here would love to get their hands on this much land. They won't care. At least, they won't after this blows over."

"Well, won't the police keep the property off-limits for a while?"

"For a while, maybe, while they search around to see if there's anything else here, but that won't last. Are you worried we won't be able to find a buyer?"

"I'm more worried that we will." Andrea sighed. "I don't know if it's the baby that's making me nostalgic, or if it's just a slightly delayed reaction to Mom's death, but I find myself more and more wishing we didn't have to sell. Even if we could just save the farmhouse and the barn, maybe that stretch along the road, down to the pond. That way we'd still own the family plot."

Andrea was sniffling.

"Why can't we do that, Lori? Why can't we keep that much?" The sniffles turned to sobs. "Why do we have to sell it all?"

"We'd still have taxes, and maintenance on the house. We can't leave it vacant indefinitely," Lorna said as gently as she could.

"But we could come for a few weeks every summer, and the kids could see what life on the farm is like."

"Does it make sense to hold on to it just for those two weeks when you bring your family on vacation?"

"Well, you could vacation there, too, and Robbie . . ."

"Andrea . . ."

"And Christmas. What about Christmas? We could all come back at Christmas. Mom would have liked that."

"Yes, she would. But there'd be no 'all,' sweetie. Rob told me he'll never come back."

"I don't know what's up with that, Lorna." Andrea was back to sniffling. She blew her nose away from the phone, then said, "He told me pretty much the same thing, last time I spoke with him. I asked him how he could feel that way about our home, and he said that my memories were apparently better than his, then he changed the subject."

"He said he only wants his share of the proceeds of the sale. He's out of work right now, and I guess he needs the money."

"Why can't we buy him out, you and me? Why can't we just sell the fields and give him that?"

"Andi, honey, it doesn't make sense. Someone has to live here. Someone has to take care of the place."

"But Mr. Compton —"

"Mr. Compton did it for Mom. Mom's gone now, and we can't expect him to watch over this place forever."

"But you could —"

"No, Andi, I can't. I'm sorry, but I can't. This isn't my home anymore. I love it, every bit as much as you do, but like you, I've made a home elsewhere. Sooner or later, I'm going to have to get back to it."

"Maybe I can talk to Robbie. Maybe I can bring him around."

"Good luck."

"I'll let you know what he says."

"You do that, sweetie."

Lorna hung up the phone and blew out a long breath. Andrea was always sentimental when she was pregnant. Maybe her attachment to the farm would pass when the baby was born.

Maybe not.

Well, Lorna couldn't dwell on that right now. Her houseguest was on her way down the steps, looking for coffee, no doubt. Lorna opened a cupboard and took down the sealed bag of ground coffee she'd bought at the supermarket earlier in the week, then found the coffee pot. She hadn't bothered to make her own since she'd returned to Callen; buying it already made had seemed easier. Today would be a good day to start.

Lorna was filling the pot with water when Regan came into the room.

"Oh, yay. I was hoping there'd be coffee." Regan smiled.

"Well, there will be, once I figure out how much coffee goes into this thing." Lorna set the pot on the counter and searched through one of the nearby drawers for a pair of scissors to cut the top off the packet of coffee.

"My dad had one of those old percolating pots. He used a heaping tablespoon of coffee per every cup of water."

"Works for me." Lorna hunted for a measuring spoon and cup, then dumped the water out of the pot. "We'll start over, though, because I have no idea how much water I put in there."

"It looks like it's going to be a gorgeous day." Regan stood at the screen door.

"It is, much less humid than it's been. Which is a relief. It's been wicked hot here."

"Can we take a tour of the farm?"

"Sure. Before or after breakfast?"

"Before. We can take our coffee. It's a nice morning for a stroll."

They waited while the coffee perked, then left through the back door, mugs in hand.

"Barn on the right, gardens on the left," Lorna pointed out. "Straight ahead is the field, at the opposite side of which is the section of field where the bodies were found."

"You have any thoughts at all on that?" Regan asked.

Lorna shook her head. "Not a clue. My first thought was that maybe they'd come from the family burial plot somehow, but there's no sign of the graves having been disturbed."

"Could that have happened at some other time? Maybe a few years ago?"

"Someone would have noticed. My

family has lived here continuously since the mid–eighteen hundreds. If the graves had been dug up, someone would have known."

"Where's the family plot?"

"Right down here." Lorna led the way. They walked several hundred yards, then stopped by the fence. "Grandparents, great-grandparents, great-greats, and several generations of aunts, uncles, cousins, and of course my dad and some of my mom's ashes are here now."

"It's lovely, isn't it?" Regan leaned on the fence. "All those pretty vines and the wildflowers. It's just the way I'd picture a small country graveyard."

"I thought it needed some tending — the grass was getting long — but it looks as if our neighbor, Mr. Compton, came down and mowed. I'm going to have to give him a call and thank him."

Lorna walked around the back of the small cemetery, Regan following.

"Down here's the pond and, beyond that, a small orchard."

"I can smell the apples."

"Rotting on the ground, no doubt. No one's been down to pick them for years. I don't imagine there's much good fruit anymore." Lorna stopped at the edge of the pond.

The cattails were tall and straggly, their pods having already burst to release the seeds. A small dark bird took cover on the opposite side of the pond, and from deep within the reeds bullfrogs grumbled.

"I haven't heard one of those in the longest time." Regan laughed. "Don't you love that sound?"

"I do. We used to try to catch them when I was younger, but they're so fast. And some of them are just huge."

Lorna stood with her hands on her hips. Someday soon she'd have to come back with that second urn of her mother's ashes. She'd been deliberately avoiding it, but she knew she couldn't put it off forever.

"And the area where the remains were found?" Regan asked.

"Straight ahead. Want to see how close we can get?"

"Sure."

They walked around the pond and through the orchard. At the far end, Lorna grabbed Regan's arm.

"I forgot. The police have cordoned off the field with yellow tape," she said. "They want to make sure no one gets close to where they're working."

"Probably a smart thing to do, to keep as many people away as possible. Otherwise, this field would be teeming with reporters and cameramen, more than it already is. The police don't need that when they're trying to investigate something as serious as this."

"I wish I had binoculars."

"Me, too." Regan raised her hand to her forehead to block the sun. "I can't see a damned thing."

"The only good vantage point is the old hayloft in the barn."

"Well, it could come to that before the day's over, if our curiosity gets the best of us."

"Seen enough?" Lorna asked.

"I haven't seen anything, and I'm not likely to, so I'd put breakfast next on the agenda."

They started back across the field. They'd gotten halfway, when Regan pointed off to her right and asked, "What's that wild area we passed?"

"It used to be a vineyard." Lorna told her the story of her great-uncle Will's dream of bringing a winery to Callen.

"That is so cool." Regan grinned. "Can we walk over there? I'd love to see it."

"I'm afraid there's not much to see, but sure." She led the way.

As they drew closer, Lorna said, "I think

most of the vines are most likely dead. They haven't been tended in years." She paused, then added, "Except for those few rows up there near the cottage. Billie Eagan's been living there, at my mother's invitation, and she dug all the weeds out and somehow got the vines to grow up on the trellises again."

"You said your great-uncle brought the vines from France?"

"Some of them. I don't know if he planted American varieties as well. No one seems to know much about the venture, except he did cultivate the grapes for a few years and was planning to make wine."

"He had the equipment here?"

"No, I don't think he'd bought equipment yet. If he did, it was disposed of before I was born. But he did have a wine cellar dug, and he brought a lot of barrels back from France, so I guess he planned on making a lot of wine."

"Where's the wine cellar?"

"It runs under the barn and out below the field a ways. I'm not sure how far. When I was little, it seemed like it went down into the center of the earth, but I haven't been to the cellar in years."

"Is there wine down there?"

"Like I said, Uncle Will never actually

got to make any before he died." Lorna grinned. "Which is not to say he hasn't contemplated it since."

"What do you mean?"

"He's still around the house sometimes. If you believe in that sort of thing."

"I do," Regan admitted somewhat sheepishly. "I always have. Growing up in England, I had relatives with very old houses. Some of them had unexplained goings-on, so I've had some exposure to the real thing."

"Uncle Will is definitely the real thing."

They walked toward the house and were almost to the end of the field when Regan stopped and looked back over her shoulder.

"It's really beautiful, don't you think? The vineyard?"

"It used to be. Now, overgrown like that, and with all the vines barren and twisted around the trellises, it's sort of sad-looking." Lorna paused. "When I look at it, I can't help but think about how Uncle Will must have felt, after his wife and son died. Back then, the vineyard would have been beautiful, well tended and the vines healthy, but they lost their beauty for him after he lost his family."

"Have you thought about restoring

them? Raising grapes? You have the basic infrastructure already in place."

"I know nothing about growing grapes, nothing about making wine. It's probably more complicated than you think. And I have one business to run. I don't have time to learn another."

"Too bad." Regan resumed walking. "It would probably be fun."

"Sure it would, if your idea of fun is worrying about crop failure and the weather." Lorna took one last fond look behind her before falling in step with Regan. "But it might be worth mentioning to the Realtor. There are several really fine vineyards and wineries here in the southeastern part of the state. Someone thinking about starting up their own small winery might be interested."

"So you're definitely selling?"

"As soon as I can get around to lining up a Realtor and having everything appraised."

"Where will Billie go, after you sell the property?"

"I haven't really given it any thought. Actually, I haven't given selling as much thought as I should have."

"My dad's been gone for a year, and I still haven't had a serious discussion with an agent about selling his place. I've had a few out to look, but I've never gotten beyond that. I keep meaning to, but for some reason I've found myself putting it off."

"It's hard to give it up. Especially if it's your childhood home."

"Well, I didn't grow up on Dad's farm, but I have spent a lot of time there. I feel the same way, though. I don't know, maybe it's just an attempt on my part to hold on to my dad."

"You were really close, I guess."

Regan nodded. "Especially those last few years when we worked together. I came to see him in a whole new light, as someone other than simply my father. He was a brilliant writer, and was totally devoted to finding the truth and seeing the bad guys pay. He received citations from police departments all over the country. Cops loved him. He treated them with great respect in his books, never blamed them for not being able to solve a crime, even when their investigations had proven to be sloppy or lazy. He had a huge following in the law enforcement community. When he had book signings, the stores would be filled with cops."

"We could sure use him now," Lorna

said, thinking of her situation with the Callen PD.

"Well, you've got me. Granted, compared to my dad, I'm just a rookie, but if there's anything you think I could do to help you out . . ."

Lorna stopped for a second, her thumbs hooked into the pockets of her jeans, a slow smile working at the corners of her mouth.

"You know, Regan, there just might be."

"Chief Walker, I can't thank you enough for agreeing to see me on such short notice. I know this must be a busy time for you and your men." Regan smiled into the chief's eyes.

"Busiest we've ever been, with the body count rising every day." He guided her by the elbow to his office. "But when you called, how could I say no? I've been a big fan of your father's — and you, too, of course — for many years now. He was a great friend to law enforcement, Ms. Landry, and well respected."

"Thank you, Chief. And it's Regan." She sat in the chair he pointed to. "Please call me Regan."

"Well, Regan, we're honored to have you here. Now, what's this about a book in the works?"

"As I told you, it's really just a gleam in my eye right now, but I thought if I were to give it any real consideration, I should go right to the source, and what better time than now, while events are still unfolding?"

"I'll help you where I can, but there's still a lot we don't know, you understand."

"Oh, I'm sure. And I hesitated to call, but you know, the more I heard about your case through the media, the more I thought it sounded familiar. Like something I read in one of my dad's files. And I thought, hey, if it turns out that these cases are related, and there was something I could share with you — well, I just had to call. It's a long shot, of course . . ."

"Long shots have been known to pull through sometimes."

"True enough." She nodded as she took a notebook from her shoulder bag. "I thought we could compare notes."

"You know the basics. What more did you want to know?"

"First of all, have you determined if there's a connection between the little girl who disappeared all those years ago —"

"Melinda Eagan."

"Right. Melinda Eagan." She paused, then asked, as if the thought had just occurred to her, "Was any trace of her ever found?"

"Nope. Nothing."

"Not a shoe, not a —"

He cut her off. "Nothing."

"Do you think her disappearance is somehow connected to the victims you've found this week?"

"Don't know. The ME says the remains we've uncovered are all males. Adolescent males. 'Course, so far, we haven't been able to identify anyone but Jason Eagan, her brother. We're still working on that."

"Similar cause of death?"

"Yes, ma'am, fractured skulls, every one of them."

She pretended to make notes in her file while she asked, "Have there been reports of boys of that age going missing over the past years?"

"Only Jason."

"So these boys would have come from someplace else."

"Most likely. Unless those remains are better'n fifty years old or so, I'd say they'd have to have been brought in from elsewhere. I've lived here all my sixty-five years, and I'd have heard if anyone else had disappeared."

"The FBI files might be able to help you

there," she said. Then, noticing the way his eyes narrowed, she added, "But of course I'm sure you have contacts with other local police departments. Those boys could have lived in some of the nearby towns."

"Most of the towns out here are little bigger than this one. And some of them have no police force. Much of the area falls to the state police. Here in Callen, we've always had our own department. Some of the other towns never have."

"Well, that's quite remarkable, don't you think, that your career has spanned all those years successfully, here in your hometown?"

He nodded. "Only job I ever had, after I left the army. I've been grateful for the opportunity to serve my community."

"I was wondering, will you be reopening Melinda's missing-persons case? It seems like it all started with her."

"In a sense, maybe it did." He tapped his fingers on the desktop.

"Is her mother still under arrest for Jason's murder?"

His eyes narrowed again.

"I was just wondering," she shrugged nonchalantly, "since the mother has been arrested for killing her son, and he died of a fractured skull . . . if all these other boys were killed in the same manner, is it likely that she killed them all?"

"I still believe she's guilty of the death of her son, yes. I haven't seen anything that would rule that out."

And not much to rule it in, either, Regan thought.

"Far as these other boys are concerned, how does that match up to the case you were looking into?" he asked. "That case of your father's that you mentioned."

"Actually, it doesn't match up at all, now that I have the facts straight from you." She folded her notebook. "The cases I was interested in were all gunshot victims. Had I mentioned that?"

"No, you did not."

"I thought I had." She tucked the notebook back into her bag and stood up. "I can't tell you how much I appreciate your time, Chief."

"That's all you wanted? You sure?" He stood, but remained behind his desk.

"I'm sure." Regan turned on the charm. "I'm disappointed to learn that our cases aren't as similar as I first thought they might be. I would've enjoyed working with you."

"Well, perhaps some other time. And who knows, maybe the next victim we dig up might have some bullet holes in him."

"You think there are more victims out there?" she asked as he escorted her to the door.

"Yeah, there are more. We're working to keep it quiet, because we want to keep the press out, keep the publicity down. The county boys are excavating as cautiously as they can, but it's tedious work. They're trying not to lose any evidence. We're not sure just how carefully those first couple boys were dug up, between you and me."

He opened the door and held it for her.

"Thanks again for your time."

"Been a pleasure."

Chief Walker stood in the doorway of his station and watched Regan drive off. She gave a little wave when she passed him, and he waved back.

Now, what was that about? he wondered as he watched her drive away. He shook his head and went back inside, walking right past Mrs. Rusk as if he didn't see her and straight on to his office. He closed the door and sat in his old brown leather chair. He lit a cigarette — opening the window to let the smoke out, since Callen's municipal building was supposed to be smoke-free — and leaned back in the chair. The interview had left him unsettled.

He had been a great fan of Josh Landry's, that was certainly true enough. His gaze searched the nearby bookcase for some of Landry's titles. He'd meant to point them out to the daughter, but they hadn't gotten far into the conversation before something seemed off-kilter. Of course, he'd never been interviewed by a writer of her stature before, so maybe he simply wasn't aware of how it was done. He'd expected more questions about the remains they'd just found, and fewer about the Eagan kids. And he hadn't expected any questions about Billie.

Thinking about the Eagan kids always made him uneasy.

He'd always believed Billie had killed her son. There'd been no doubt in his mind about that. He could see how it happened, how she'd killed him in anger, smacked him in the head with something hard, something they'd never found. But the girl . . . he'd never had a feel for what had happened to the little girl.

He blew out a long breath, and recalled the night when the call had come in from Billie Eagan that her daughter was missing. His first year on the job, and he'd been so eager to make a good impression on the chief. He was one of the first ones on the scene, and helped lead the search party through the fields, calling for her.

He was on his way back across the field when he found the brown paper bag. He'd looked inside and seen the yellow-and-white fabric. He'd tucked it under his arm, and was almost back to the Eagan house when one of the others called him for assistance. Billie Eagan had just about collapsed at the edge of the field. He set the bag down to help carry her into the house.

When he went back for the bag a few minutes later, it had disappeared.

He had walked into the field again, and looked all around the back of the house, but the bag was gone.

Some of Jason's friends had gathered in the yard — they'd all taken part in the search for Melinda — but the bag wasn't there. He'd thought maybe one of them had picked it up, but when he asked if anyone had found anything that might have belonged to Melinda, they all said no.

He'd hoped against hope that the bag hadn't contained anything important. All he'd seen was some yellow-and-white fabric.

But as soon as he'd spoken with the Stiles girl, he'd known what was in the bag.

Melinda Eagan's birthday dress.

He should have told someone at the time, but he hadn't. He was new to the force. If the old chief had known that evidence had disappeared because the rookie had left it unattended in the field, well, they probably wouldn't be calling him Chief Walker today. It was a lesson Walker had never forgotten.

He'd turned his back for just a few minutes, and the damned bag had disappeared into thin air.

Billie hadn't taken it. She was with him and his partner. Jason was being questioned at the time.

So, who had taken it? And why?

And why did it seem to matter more now than it had then?

Twelve

"Hey, Regan, how'd it go?" Lorna called from the front porch, where she sat in one of the rocking chairs.

"Pretty much par," Regan replied as she walked toward the porch. She smiled at the man sitting in the rocker next to Lorna. "You must be T.J. We have a mutual friend in Mitch Peyton."

"So I understand." T.J. stood and offered both his hand and the chair. "He mentioned you when he called me on Thursday."

"No, keep the rocker, I'll sit right here on the steps." Regan lowered herself to the top step. "So what did he say?"

"What did who say?" Lorna asked.

"Mitch," Regan responded, looking intently at T.J.

T.J. shrugged. "Oh, just that you had a friend who needed a little help with something he thought I might be able to assist with."

"That's all?" She frowned.

"Well, he did say that you and he were friends, that you worked together on some case up in New Jersey a couple months ago, and you've stayed in touch."

"Oh." Regan appeared disappointed to hear that Mitch hadn't had more to say about her.

"What did you learn from Chief Walker?" Lorna asked.

"Not a whole lot," Regan admitted. "There's been no trace of Melinda found, not an article of clothing, nothing. I asked. So to answer your earlier question, the dress wasn't recovered. He still thinks the mother killed the brother, by the way. This in spite of the fact that all the remains recovered show that every victim was an adolescent male with a fractured skull. What are the chances the mother killed all the other vics? Is she a big woman? Could she have taken these guys?"

"She's a tiny thing, thin, frail. And back then, she was a heavy drinker. I don't think she'd be hauling strangers across the field to kill them. She wouldn't have had the strength."

"What makes you think the bodies were all strangers?"

"There haven't been that many young males reported missing in Callen since the beginning of time. They had to have come from someplace else."

"Is someone doing a search on missing persons in the area?" T.J. asked.

"Not yet. I asked about that, and Chief Walker said they don't have the manpower right now." Regan leaned back against the porch rail. "Apparently everyone is out in the field, digging."

"I'm sure they have computers," T.J. said.

"Maybe they don't have anyone on staff trained to do the searches," Regan offered. "I've run into a lot of smaller police forces that don't know how to access or input information into the national databases. Some others, I've found, simply don't want to be bothered."

"Maybe we could help them out. Do a little research for them." T.J. smiled.

"How would we do that?" Lorna asked.

"We'd call Mitch and see if he can do a search for missing boys between the ages of, say, twelve and eighteen, over the past, what, twenty-five years?" T.J. thought for a moment, then said, "They should probably be bringing in the Bureau, anyway. They're going to be in over their heads, if they aren't already."

"You'll never get Chief Walker to admit that."

"It's a capital case, there's every indication that there could be a serial killer involved here. It has FBI written all over it," T.J. told them. "Regan, why don't you give Mitch a call, see what he thinks."

"I'll do that. And we'll ask him to go back thirty years, just in case." Regan reached for her handbag and took out her phone and began to dial.

"When's Billie's preliminary hearing?" T.J. asked Lorna.

"One day next week, I haven't heard a date yet."

"I'm betting the charges are dropped between now and then. You know I haven't thought they had enough evidence against Billie, but with these other victims being found," he shrugged, "I don't see them proceeding at this point. Unless they can finger her for all the killings, I think they're going to have to go back to square one. I guess I'll have a better feel for it after I've met Billie."

"We can do that now, if you like," Lorna suggested.

"The sooner the better." T.J. stood. "You're coming with me, though, right? I think she'd be much more comfortable if you were there."

"Sure. I'd planned on being there. Let me give her a call and let her know we're stopping over." Lorna got out of the chair and went into the house.

"Where is everyone going?" Regan asked as she put her cell phone back in her handbag.

"Lorna and I are going over to talk to Billie Eagan."

"I'll wait here. For one thing, I think the poor woman would probably feel over-whelmed if the three of us showed up. Besides, I'm waiting for Mitch to call back. I had to leave voice mail."

"Are you sure you don't mind?" Lorna asked as she came out through the front door.

"Not at all." Regan got up and walked over to the rocking chair Lorna had been sitting in. "It's a beautiful day, the humidity has dropped, it's nice and shady here on the porch, and I have a book in here somewhere . . ."

Regan began rooting through her handbag.

"Here we go. The newest thriller from my favorite author." She moved the chair, then sat and rested her feet on the porch railing. Since she was shorter than Lorna by several inches, the rail would have been out of reach if she hadn't moved the rocker. "I'll be right here when you get back."

"Okay, if you're sure." Lorna swung her bag over her shoulder and followed T.J. down the steps.

Regan waved them on.

Lorna paused next to T.J.'s car.

"Maybe we should drive over."

"Isn't Billie's house right across the field?"

"Yes, but it *is* several acres away." She was still staring at the car.

"You're incredibly subtle." He took his keys out of his pocket and opened the driver's-side door.

"Great. I've been dying for a ride in this machine all week." Lorna grinned, opened the passenger door, and got in.

"You should have said something. I'd have been happy to show 'er off." T.J. slid behind the wheel and started the engine. "You want the top up?"

"You're kidding, right?"

"Just asking. Some women don't like to have their hair blown around."

"I'm not one of them."

He turned the car around and stopped at the end of the drive.

"Which way?"

"Turn right," Lorna told him. "Then right again in about a quarter of a mile."

He accelerated slowly, then proceeded to

the intersection, where he made a right at the stop sign. Lorna leaned her head back and closed her eyes, letting the breeze blow around her. She was smiling, and he found himself smiling, too.

"That was nice," she told him when he pulled up in front of Billie's house and cut the engine.

"Not much of a ride. We'll take the long way home."

"Yay." She got out of the car and waited for T.J., then walked up the two steps leading to the front door. She was about to ring the bell when the door opened.

"Billie, this is T. J. Dawson, the private investigator I told you about," Lorna said.

"Pleased to meet you." Billie did not offer her hand, but appeared to be studying him. After a long moment, apparently approving of what she saw, she stepped aside and gestured for her visitors to come inside. "I don't know what there is to investigate, but we can talk."

She led them into the living room, which was furnished with an old blue sofa — the cushions of which were sagging slightly — one end table, a floor lamp that Lorna recognized as having come from her family's attic, a chair with a makeshift slipcover, and a television set on top of a bookcase.

Billie must have caught Lorna's glance at the lamp, because she said, "That lamp, your momma gave it to me. If you need it, or you want it, you can have it back."

"No, no, I don't need it," Lorna assured her.

"Well, you ever feel you do, you just tell me." Billie sat in the corner chair.

Lorna and T.J. sat side by side on the sofa.

"Billie, have you been hearing about all the bodies found in the back field?" Lorna asked.

"You tell me what that all means," Billie visibly shivered, " 'cause I never heard tell of such a thing. Bodies all through the woods, they're saying on the news." She looked from Lorna to T.J. and back again. "You don't think they believe I had anything to do with all that, do you?"

"Billie, I honestly don't know what anyone is thinking at this point," Lorna told her. "But if they gave it serious thought, they'd figure out that you're not a likely suspect. You're not physically big enough, or strong enough, to have pulled it off. So I think that shouldn't be a worry right now."

"Well, it ain't like I got nothing else on my mind." She turned to T.J. "Lorna said you wanted to ask me some questions. You go right ahead. What do you want to talk about first?"

"Let's talk about the night Jason disappeared," T.J. said.

"Go 'head."

"Do you remember where you had been that night before Jason came home?"

"I was right there at home. I'd worked until nine-thirty at the diner, then had to wait for almost forty minutes for Stella's husband to come pick us up." Billie turned to Lorna and said, "Stella Rusznick worked the same shift as me, and her husband picked her up every night. Nights when I didn't have a ride, they'd drop me off. Most nights he was there by ten, but that night he was a little late. He'd stopped at Kelly's Tavern on the way and had himself a few."

Billie laughed hoarsely.

"I never knew how scared you could get when a drunk was behind the wheel. All the times I drove drunk, or rode with someone who was, I never was scared. Once I stopped drinking, though, whoa! Scared the bejesus outta me to be in that car with Stella's husband. Never knew what sober people felt, driving with me, until I sobered up myself."

"So you got home around ten after ten that night," Lorna said.

" 'Round there. I went into the kitchen and made myself a cup of tea. Never drank it until I stopped — Well, anyway, I made tea and took it outside and I sat on the back steps. Looked out across that field, looked up into the sky. Wondered where my girl was." Billie stopped and swallowed hard. "With Mellie gone, I had a lot of time to think, mostly about how bad a mother I'd been. Mother from hell, I'd say, and that would be the truth. I prayed every night that wherever she was, she might know how sorry I was for every time I hurt her. Every time I raised my voice when I didn't have to. Every time I ignored her or made her feel like she didn't matter. I sat there each night after she disappeared, wondering if she was still alive . . . wondering if she'd just gotten so tired of me being the way I was that maybe she simply up and ran off."

The small house was still and silent as a tomb. Billie's pain and guilt were palpable, her words so soft, both Lorna and T.J. had to lean forward to hear her.

"Hasn't a night passed since that I haven't wondered." Billie's gaze shifted and she stared out the window to her right. "Even now . . ."

"Where were you when Jason got home that night?" T.J. tried to steer the conversation back on topic.

"I was still there, out on the back steps. I heard the car pull up and I heard the door slam and I waited to see if he was going to come out, but he didn't, so I went on into the kitchen."

"Talk to me about that," T.J. said. "About what happened when you went into the kitchen."

"Well, it's like I told Walker. I went inside and there he was, stumbling drunk. Pissed me off so bad, I could hardly see. I hadn't had a drop since my girl disappeared, and there was my boy, drunk as a skunk at three in the morning. He's there, looking for something to eat, and we have words. He's fourteen years old and he's shit-faced in my kitchen."

"What did you say?" T.J. asked.

"What do you think I said?" Billie raised an eyebrow. "So he starts yelling at me, about the pot callin' the kettle black. We stood around doing a lot of shouting, I remember that. He's yelling at me, about me teaching him how to be a drunk, and I'm yelling at him to look at my life and learn from it. That I wanted better for him, that

I may not have given him much in the past, but I was trying to give him something right then and there. Drinking like that ain't no kind of life. I ruined myself and I ruined my children, but it could end with me, if he did better than what I had done. And then it just stopped."

Her voice was thin, almost wistful, like a girl's.

"The yelling just stopped. And I told him how sorry I was for the way things had been, for all I'd done to him and to Mellie." Her eyes filled. "And he said, 'That's easy to say, now that she's gone.' "

Billie wiped her eyes with the back of her hand. "Well, that was like a slap in the face, but one I deserved — I did — and I told him that. I deserved to have him hate me and I wouldn't have blamed him one damned bit if he did."

"And then what?" Lorna asked.

"And then my big, strapping, drunk fourteen-year-old man-child put his head on my shoulder and he started to cry." She nodded her head. "Just like that. Jason started to cry. Hadn't cried since he was maybe three, four years old. And I put my arms around him and I rocked him, just like I did when he was a baby. At least, I rocked him best I could, him being so much taller than me and all. But it was okay, he was okay after that. And I thought, 'Maybe it's not too late, for me to be more of a mother, him to be more of a son.' "

"Why did he leave, Billie?"

"Sir, I have asked myself that question a hundred times, I surely have." She turned to T.J. "One second, he was all peaceful and resting his head right here," she patted her left shoulder, "and the next thing I knew, he was cursing and running out the back door."

"What did he say?" a puzzled Lorna asked.

"He said, 'You son of a bitch,' and went right on out the back door like he was being chased. I looked out the window, but I couldn't see nobody, not even him. I don't know why he started cursing at me after he'd been so calm, or why he ran out like that."

"Where was the window in relation to where he was standing?" Lorna asked.

Billie thought for a moment, then said, "It was to my left."

"Could you see out the window, Billie?" T.J. resumed the questioning.

"I couldn't, no, I wasn't facing it." She thought for a moment, then said, "But he probably could have. His head was on my left shoulder, looking away from me." She focused on them and said, "He probably could have seen out the window, but if he did, he wasn't saying what he saw."

"Did you hear anything? Voices, conversation, anything at all?"

She shook her head.

"When Jason didn't come back in, I went out onto the back steps and called him, but there was no answer. And I didn't hear nothing out there, nothing but the wind blowing through that field." She bit her bottom lip. "I figured he'd started to remember how bad I'd been and it pissed him off all over again, and maybe he'd run away."

"Had you seen anyone around that night? Heard any cars?"

"Just the one that dropped off Jason."

"Billie, did anyone have it in for Jason?"

Billie's eyebrows raised. "Mister, just about everyone who knew Jason had it in for him. He had a way, brought out the worst in everyone he met. That boy had a chip on his shoulder, big as the moon."

"Did he mention anyone in particular?" T.J. continued. "Ever talk to you about anyone he was having problems with?"

"No. He wasn't the type to tell you

much of anything. Kept it all to hisself, mostly." Her voice dropped slightly. "Guess when you know no one's listening, you just stop talking."

"The police report also indicates that the police spoke with your ex-husband, who stated he'd had no contact with you or the children in many years. Is that correct?"

Billie nodded. "Buddy didn't have nothing to do with us at that point. He had hisself a new wife and a new family."

"Did you ever seek child support from him?" Lorna asked.

"Not much point in that," Billie told her. "He didn't have nothing for me to get. I didn't see much reason to bother with him. Once a man washes his hands of you, that's pretty much it."

"But they were still his kids," Lorna protested. "He should have helped support them."

"He wasn't working for a long time. Never seen anyone get blood from a stone."

"Any idea where he is now? How we can get in touch with him?"

"What d'you want with him?" Billie's eyes narrowed.

"Well, the police interviewed him then, I'd like to speak with him now."

"He didn't have nothing to say on the subject back then. Chances are, he'd have less to say all these years later."

"They were his kids," T.J. reminded her. "A lot of times, when a child disappears, it turns out that the noncustodial parent has taken them."

"I can guarantee you, right now, that Buddy Eagan did not take Melinda." Billie's jaw set. "And we all know where Jason has been, all these years."

"Still, I'd like to speak with your ex."

"Well, good luck finding him, then. I don't know where he is."

T.J. opened the file he'd brought with him and had tucked on the floor next to his feet.

"Billie, this is a copy of the police report from the night your son disappeared. It says that you told the officer who interviewed you that you and Jason were arguing and that he stormed out of the house."

"We weren't arguing no more by the time he left."

"But the report indicates that you were."

"That's not the way I would have told it. That's not the way it happened." Billie shook her head for emphasis. "We weren't yellin' no more then. I wouldn't have said that we were."

"But you initialed the pages that you'd read it and it was right," T.J. pointed out to her.

"I didn't read real good back then. I wouldn't have known what he had written on that page." Her cheeks colored slightly at the admission. "He told me he'd written down just what I said, and he just needed me to write my initials, which he told me meant that I had said those words."

Billie frowned. "Never occurred to me that he woulda wrote down something else."

"It's an important detail, Billie. The way it's written, it sounds as if Jason left the house because you two were arguing. From there, it's not much of a stretch to think maybe you followed him."

"All these years, I did think he'd left the house that night because of me."

"But it sounds to me as if you and he had, well, come to an understanding," Lorna said.

"I thought we had, but then he left sudden like that."

"Maybe he saw something or someone outside," T.J. pointed out. "You said his head was facing the window."

"You mean, maybe he'd seen someone

out there, through the window?"

T.J. nodded. "If he wasn't cursing at you, he was cursing at someone else."

"Huh. Wouldn't that beat all, if it had been someone else he'd been cursing at. Wouldn't that be something." She shook her head slowly. "All these years, I thought he'd been cursing at me . . ."

"You think she was telling the truth?" Regan asked after T.J. and Lorna had filled her in on their interview with Billie. "You think she seemed sincere?"

"Either that, or she is one fine actress." T.J. settled himself on the top porch step.

"I think she was telling the truth. I think Melinda's disappearance was a real wake-up call for her. I think she did stop drinking, and I think she would have tried to reconcile with Jason at that point. It all makes perfect sense to me." Lorna looked at Regan, then T.J. "Is anyone that good an actor?"

"You'd be amazed at how resourceful people can be when they're trying to save their skins," T.J. told her. "An accomplished liar could easily have pulled off that kind of performance."

"The question is, is Billie Eagan an accomplished liar," Regan interjected. "Do you think Jason really saw someone outside the window that night? Or do you think she's making that up now, to offer another plausible scenario? If she could convince people that there was someone else there, and Jason ran out to confront that person, it's just a short step to suggesting that this other person killed him."

Lorna nodded. "I agree, it's convenient that she hasn't told this story to anyone else."

"We don't know that she didn't," T.J. reminded her. "Billie said that this is the story she gave the cop who interviewed her after Jason disappeared. She says he wrote it down wrong, and because her reading skills were so poor, she didn't realize that he hadn't gotten it right."

"That happens more often than you'd believe," Regan said. "I've found that in my own research, for my books, that sometimes the cop taking down the information uses words that intimate something other than what was intended. Or sometimes the cop doesn't take real good notes, he'll think he'll remember something, but forgets it and writes down his impressions rather than what the person really said. And if, like Billie, the witness or suspect doesn't read well, he or she could sign something as being correct when it's not a true account of what happened."

T.J. shuffled through his files, then, finding the one he was looking for, opened it and took out a sheet of paper.

"The cop who signed this report was a Duncan Parks." He looked at Lorna. "Do you know if he's still around?"

"I have no idea. Chief Walker would know, but I'd prefer to keep my face out of his for a few days. I've pissed him off enough for one week." She tapped her fingers on the side of her chair. "Fritz might know, though."

"Fritz, who is on the list of witnesses we wanted to talk to?" T.J. asked.

Lorna nodded.

"This gives us a real good excuse to pay him a visit," he told her. "Know where we can find him?"

"I know where to start."

"Let's do it."

"I'll stay here and wait for Mitch," Regan said. "He told me he'd be here around dinnertime." She smiled. "Typical Mitch."

"We should think about dinner," Lorna said as she stood.

"Pizza would be good," Regan suggested. "Got beer?"

"Got a state store about three miles down the road," Lorna told her.

"Excellent. I'll just sit here with my book while you two fetch food and drink."

"Any preferences?" T.J. asked.

"Nope. As long as the pizza's hot and the beer's cold, I'm a happy woman." She leaned back in the rocker and opened her book. "I'm starting to feel a little like I'm on vacation here, and I like it. At least, till Mitch arrives and shakes things up, as he usually does. So you two just go on and see what you can pry out of Fritz, and I'll stay right here and enjoy what's left of the afternoon."

Thirteen

"Fritz, I really appreciate you making time to see us on such short notice," Lorna said as Fritz led them into his living room.

"Hey, I'm just glad you were able to catch me before I left town," he told his visitors. "Is it okay if we talk in here, or would you rather go out to the sunporch?"

"I'd love the sunporch," Lorna replied. "I'll bet there's a beautiful view of the garden from there."

"The best." He winked and gestured them to follow him through the house to the back. "Some areas are starting to fade out now, sadly. The daylilies, for example, peaked a few weeks ago. July was spectacular, and we did have fabulous roses this year, if I do say so myself."

"You mentioned leaving town," T.J. said. "Vacation?"

"Just a mini. I don't have time to take a full week off right now — the store is always so busy in the summer, you know, with all those people using Callen Road as their shortcut out to I-95. From there it's just a short hop to the Delaware beaches."

Fritz led Lorna and T.J. through a white louvered door onto a screened-in porch that overlooked the backyard. "Sit," he instructed. "Make yourselves comfortable."

Lorna and T.J. took the chairs on either side of the door, leaving Fritz to sit on the sofa.

"You really outdid yourself this year," Lorna noted, looking out the back screen to the lush gardens beyond. "The colors are just wonderful."

"Everything came up as planned. That doesn't always happen. And of course, my mother always took great pride in her roses. I try to keep them going in her memory." He looked from Lorna to T.J., then said, "But you didn't come to talk about gardening."

"You're right. We came to talk to you about Jason Eagan," T.J. told him.

"Right. You'd be Lorna's private eye, then." He nodded knowingly. "What is it you want to know?"

"Just your recollections of the night Melinda disappeared. Your name is on the list of people interviewed, though the notes on that interview and several others appear to be missing."

"Probably because I didn't tell them much of anything. I had nothing important

241

to say." Fritz shrugged. "We were over at Matt Conrad's, just hanging out in the backyard."

"Matt's house was that big white clapboard one on Callen Road, the first house past our fence," Lorna explained to T.J. "It's the only house between our farm and the house the Eagans lived in at the time."

"Right. We used to all hang out there a lot because Matt's parents both worked and we usually had the house to ourselves till seven o'clock or so, when they got home from work, then we'd all leave."

"Tell us about the night Melinda Eagan disappeared," T.J. prompted.

"Matt and I were in his backyard, then Jason stopped by. He said he was on his way to get his sister but he'd stop by after. He was back in maybe five, seven minutes. It hadn't taken him very long."

"Did you see his sister?" T.J. asked.

"No, I didn't. Matt and I were sitting on the stump of a tree that had been cut down, smoking cigarettes Matt had swiped from his mother's purse before she left for work that morning. Our backs were to the field. As I said, Jason joined us a few minutes later. He had a bag with some of his sister's birthday cake, and we polished that off. Then, maybe after he'd been there for ten or fifteen minutes, we heard Jason's mother calling him from their house. He handed me the cigarette he'd just lit and took off like a bat out of hell." Fritz glanced at Lorna and added, "Mrs. Eagan had quite a temper. When she told Jason to jump, he jumped."

"So he went home, and you stayed there for how much longer?"

"Maybe another fifteen, twenty minutes after that. Then my brother, Mike, came by to get me home for dinner, and Dustin stopped over. But before we could leave, Jason came back and asked if any of us had seen Melinda. We hadn't, but we all started looking for her."

"How did you go about doing that?"

"We just all went through the field, calling her. I went down to the pond, thinking maybe she was there, then back through the orchard. Everyone pretty much fanned out."

"Were you able to keep track of where everyone else was?" T.J. asked.

"Nah," Fritz replied. "Most of the corn had been cut by then, but in spots it was still maybe knee high or a little better. And of course the field is hilly, so you didn't have a good straight-on view of where anyone else was. And by then it was getting dark. You couldn't see much of anything."

"So if someone had been hiding there, you could have missed him," Lorna said.

"It's possible, but we covered that field pretty well. And then after awhile, the police came, and they covered it, too. If anyone had been hiding back there, I think they would have been seen by someone." He stopped for a minute, then added, "I seem to recall your mother and father were there, helping us search."

"That's right," she said, nodding.

"There wasn't a sign of that kid. Later, after we'd been through the field for what seemed like about the tenth time, the police went in to talk to Mrs. Eagan. We gave our statements — pretty much what I just told you — then we went home. It was all anyone talked about for the next couple of months, though. Melinda Eagan disappearing like that, then Jason . . ." Fritz glanced at Lorna. "You might have been too young to remember, but I'll never forget the sense of panic that went through the school back then. That anything like that could happen around here was inconceivable."

"Did Jason ever talk about his sister?" T.J. asked.

"Not really. Oh, he liked to give her and

her friends a hard time. Creep them out, harass them a little, nothing that would really hurt them. I had the feeling he really did like his sister, but he never would have shown it. It wouldn't have been cool, you know?"

"Creep them out, how?"

"Just do things to scare them a little. One time, I remember, he caught a couple of little garter snakes and put them in her room to scare her and that other girl she was friends with, the one from Arnold?" Fritz looked at Lorna.

"Danielle Porter," she supplied.

"Right. Danielle." He nodded.

"How about the night Jason disappeared?" T.J. looked at his notes. "Which most likely was the night he was murdered."

"Again, we were all together. We met up at Matt's, then we went to Dustin's, and he drove us to White Marsh Park. He was sixteen that year, had his license."

"How old were you?" T.J. asked.

"I was sixteen," Fritz told him. "Jason was fourteen, but he looked older."

"So did Mike," Lorna recalled.

"True. He'd turned fourteen at the end of the summer, but he was always a big kid. He shot past me when he was twelve.

He got the genes from our dad's side of the family, I guess," Fritz said. "Anyway, Matt, Jason, and I walked out to Dustin's. His parents were out for the night, and he'd managed to score a couple of six-packs, I guess one of the older guys picked it up for us. I honestly don't remember who we got it from. We took it out to White Marsh Park and drank it. Talked about stuff. Girls, of course. Matt had just been kicked off the soccer team for arguing with his homeroom teacher, so we had to talk about the injustice of that for a while. Later, Dustin drove me home, then Matt, and he was going to drop Jason off last, on his way back to his house. And that's what he said he did."

"Your brother wasn't with you that night?"

"No, I don't remember what he was doing that night." Fritz glanced at Lorna, then asked, "What's that little grin all about?"

"I was just wondering how you managed to sneak in half-drunk in the wee hours of the morning."

"Oh." He laughed. "My mother visited her sister in Rehoboth once a month. That was her weekend at Aunt Kitty's."

"How did you find out about Jason disappearing?" T.J. asked.

"When he didn't show up in school for a couple of days, we stopped out there at his house, and his mother told us she didn't know where he was, that the police were looking for him, and if any of us heard from him, we should let her know." Fritz raised his eyebrows, as if revisiting the surprise of that moment. "We were just stunned, you know? He was just gone."

"And you had no thoughts about that? What did you think might have happened?" T.J. probed.

"Truthfully, we figured he'd run away. That after his sister disappeared, maybe he figured, what the hell, there was no point in hanging around." Fritz looked at T.J. "And right about then, the story was going around that the police wanted to question him about Melinda's disappearance. Some people thought maybe he'd done something to her."

"Did you?"

"No, Mr. Dawson. I knew he hadn't done anything to her. For all he liked to tease and torment her, I always thought she was the only person he really cared about. I figured it was more likely that he thought that, with her gone, he didn't have much reason to hang around."

"He ever talk about running away?"

"Back then we all talked about running away. Kids do that. No one took him seriously. But then when he was gone like that, we — Matt and me — thought maybe he'd done it after all. Dustin believed Jason's mother might have had something to do with it, but I never did. She just didn't have the strength to take down someone who was bigger and stronger."

"Do you know if he ever saw his father?"

"No. He never saw him, far as I know. Mr. Eagan had nothing to do with either Jason or Melinda. And frankly, Jason wanted nothing to do with his dad. There was no love lost there, on either side, I think."

"I know you've been asked this before, and it has to be something you've thought about yourself, so I have to ask." T.J. leaned forward a bit. "Can you think of anyone who might have wanted to harm either Melinda or Jason?"

"Jason could be a bully sometimes, so I know there were a lot of people who didn't like him, maybe some who wished he'd disappear. But not liking someone, and killing them, that's two different things. And as far as his sister was concerned, I'm sorry. I didn't really know her well enough to have a feel for what could have happened to her. All we knew back then was that she disappeared one night, then a few weeks later, Jason disappeared the same way."

He paused, then added, "Only now, we know what happened to him. Maybe she'll turn up soon, too."

"Is Matt Conrad still around?" T.J. asked.

"No, but Dustin lives out near Elk Run. Last I heard, they'd been in touch. I can get his phone number for you." Fritz rose and started out of the room.

"And your brother?"

Fritz seemed to pause momentarily in the doorway. "He's still around. You can probably catch him down at the store till seven."

"How about this cop who made out the reports, Duncan Parks?" T.J. asked. "He still around?"

"Last I heard, he retired to Florida about ten years ago, had a heart attack, and died a month later."

T.J. stood and went to the back of the sunporch and stared out at the rose garden. When Fritz returned a minute later, he handed the paper with the phone number on it to Lorna.

"Matt is married now and lives out near

Reading, I think. Dustin's still pretty friendly with him, so he should know how to get in touch with him."

"You didn't stay in contact?" T.J. asked.

"Not really." Fritz shrugged. "We don't have a whole lot in common anymore."

"That happens, doesn't it? Anyway, we appreciate the number, Fritz. Thanks." Lorna tucked the slip of paper into her jeans pocket. "And thanks for taking some time from your travel schedule for us."

"No big deal. Besides, I want to help if I can. That was such a sad thing, those two just disappearing like that." He shoved his hands into his jeans pockets. "Sure would be a shame if Melinda had met the same fate her brother did, wouldn't it?"

"How well do you know Fritz?" T.J. asked when they were back in the car.

"I used to know him pretty well. He was a bit older than me, but we were neighbors. The Keelers live right up around the bend on Callen Road. He taught me how to drive a stick shift after my dad died. I had just turned sixteen a couple of months before and Dad was teaching me how to drive his old pickup when he had his heart attack. Fritz later showed me how to work the clutch so I could drive the truck around the farm, like I'd wanted to do. He's always been a nice guy. Quiet, for the most part, and devoted to his mother, who died a few years ago. She'd been ill, and he stayed home to care for her."

"And his brother?" T.J. started the car and backed out of Fritz's driveway.

"Mike had a different agenda."

"What does that mean?"

"He was much more popular, especially with the girls. Everyone wanted to go out with him — me included — but he was really selective. Didn't date a whole lot. His wife was a quiet girl all through school. I think a lot of people were surprised when he married her."

"Why?"

"Well, like I said, he could have had his pick." Lorna thought for a minute, then added, "She's not as flashy as he is, if you know what I mean."

"Maybe he figured one peacock in the family was enough."

"I think you might be right." She stared out the window, then said, "Slow down. The pizza place is up here on the left. I know we just had pizza last night, but I have the feeling we'll have a lot of 'splaining to do if we go back to the house without it for Regan, and this pizza place is better. The state liquor store is right across the road there, so we can grab a few sixpacks of beer while we're here."

T.J. parked in front of the restaurant and turned off the engine. They went inside and read the menu, debated topping options, then agreed on one large pepperoni, one large with everything. T.J. went for the beer, and when he returned he joined Lorna at a small table while they waited for the pizzas.

"I got two six-packs of Sam Adams and two of Bud Light, that okay?" he asked.

"Sure. Thanks." She pushed a can of Diet Pepsi across the table. "Soda will have to do for now."

"No problem." He leaned back in his seat, then thought better of it when the plastic back groaned slightly. He sat forward and asked, "Who's this other girl Fritz mentioned?"

"Danielle? She went to our school, and was about two grades ahead of us, if I recall correctly. I think Melinda had just started to get to know her the spring before she disappeared. I don't know how well they knew each other, or how Mellie got to know her. She didn't say much about her, but that last summer and fall, she spent a lot of time at Danielle's house. Weekends, mostly."

"The police did interview her, I saw her name on the list." He popped the tab on the soda can. "She didn't have much to add, though."

"I don't know why she would. She wasn't around that night."

"They would have talked to anyone who might have been in contact with Melinda during that time," T.J. told her. "They'd want to know if Melinda had mentioned any stranger who might have approached her, or if she'd felt someone had been watching her, that sort of thing."

"I always thought there was something odd about Melinda's relationship with Danielle." Lorna got up and went to the counter and returned with two straws, one of which she silently offered to T.J.

"No, thanks," he declined. "What did you think was odd?"

"I could never figure out how Melinda knew her. Or when she got to know her."

"She never talked about her?"

"She talked about her, but she never really *said* anything about her." Lorna appeared pensive. "I can't explain it."

"Did she go to Danielle's house, or did Danielle go to hers?"

"She almost always went to Danielle's. I

can only think of one time when Danielle was at Melinda's. But Mellie never talked about what they did at Danielle's. I just remember that she was always excited about going. As a kid, I was probably a little jealous — you know, my best friend had a new friend. I guess I was afraid Melinda would dump me for her and then I wouldn't have a best friend anymore."

"Did you know Danielle?"

"I knew who she was. As I said, she went to our school, but she was a couple of years older. The school we attended was a regional elementary, it went up to grade eight. It was odd that a sixth grader would want to be friends with a fourth grader. Especially since they didn't seem to have much in common."

"Why would you say that, if you didn't know Danielle?"

"The girls she hung around with were a little more advanced than Melinda and I were, socially. So it just never struck me as a good fit, that's all. The one time I remember Danielle stayed at Melinda's for an overnight, she seemed bored to death."

"Well, now I'm intrigued," T.J. said. "I think we're going to have to find this Danielle person and see what was going on. In the meantime," he said as he pushed his chair back from the table, "it looks as if our dinner is ready. Let's continue this conversation back at the house. Maybe we can get Mitch to use his FBI skills to track down Danielle."

As it turned out, Mitch had already begun to apply his skills to the case.

"First thing in the morning, I'll be making the acquaintance of your local police force," Mitch told Lorna.

"Good luck there." She laughed. "Are you planning on just walking in and introducing yourself?"

"Actually, that's exactly what I'll be doing." He grinned. "As the special agent assigned to the case, I'll be —"

"Whoa, back up." T.J. twisted the cap off a beer and handed the bottle to Mitch. "The FBI is in on this now?"

Mitch nodded. "As of about three this afternoon."

"How the hell did that happen?" T.J. joined him at the table.

"I started discussing the case with my boss, and told him about Regan getting involved through Lorna." He took a swallow of beer. "He'd seen the coverage on the news, of course, and thought by now we'd have had a request from someone to send an agent in to assist. Since this is apparently a serial killer's work, and they have a small police force here with no experience in this area."

"So what did . . ." T.J. paused. "You still working for John?"

Mitch nodded.

"How did he manage to get you in?"

"He called the district attorney and asked if he thought the Bureau could be of service. And the DA was happy to get the call, from what I understand. He's up for reelection next year and the last thing he wants is something like this hanging over his head for the next twelve months."

"So John graciously offered to send a man down to assist." T.J. nodded. He knew John Mancini's MO all too well.

"Who's John?" Lorna distributed four plates from the stack she'd set on the table.

"John Mancini. He's the head of the unit I work for," Mitch told her. He turned to T.J. and said, "He told me to tell you he'd pull the reprimand from my file if you came back in to talk to him."

"What reprimand?" T.J. asked.

"The one he gave me after I sent that fax to the Callen Police Department asking for the reports on the Eagan case."

"Who's he kidding?" T.J. shook his head.

"He didn't put any such thing in your file. Not his style. Not for something like that. And you're on the case, so you know he's not even pissed off at you."

"I told him you'd see through that, but he wanted me to give it a try." Mitch shrugged. "He would like you to come in for a sit-down, told me to tell you he has a few select openings he needs to fill."

"I'm not looking to go back to the Bureau, Mitch, but tell John I appreciate the offer." T.J. got up and grabbed a beer from the six-pack he'd left on the kitchen counter.

"You worked for this John Mancini?" Lorna asked.

"With Mitch," T.J. told her. "We went through training together, actually."

Lorna stepped aside to permit Regan to place both pizza boxes on the table.

"You've been out now for what, six years?" Regan asked.

T.J. nodded. "Something like that."

Lorna handed out napkins, then took the seat across from T.J. She opened the lids of both boxes and told her guests, "Pepperoni on the left, the works on the right. Please help yourselves."

"So, you left the FBI to start your private investigation business?" Lorna asked T.J.

"My cousin and I started one, yes." The slice of pizza he'd just slid onto his plate appeared to have garnered an inordinate amount of his attention.

Lorna didn't have to be hit over the head. His leaving the Bureau was off-limits. Okay by her.

She turned to Mitch. "So, what's your plan to aid and assist the Callen Police Department?"

"The first thing I want to do is see if we can start putting together a list of young men who went missing over the past twenty-five to thirty years from the Pennsylvania, Delaware, Maryland, and New Jersey area." He drew an imaginary circle on the table, encompassing the points where those states came together. "Then we'll see what evidence we have that will enable us to start matching up the remains with the missing. At least, that's the goal. Once we're able to start identifying victims, we'll try to find some commonality among them."

"Meaning?" Lorna asked.

"There has to be a reason why each of these victims was chosen. Once we figure out what that reason was, we'll be closer to figuring out who we're looking for," Mitch explained.

"After all these years, isn't it likely that the killer is gone from here? All of these victims were killed a long time ago," Lorna pointed out. "What are the chances the killer stayed in Callen?"

"That's a good question," Mitch told her. "Right now, we have no way of knowing if he moved on, or if he simply found another means of relieving whatever it was that compelled him to kill in the first place."

"So he could still be here," Regan said, "but he might not be feeling any pressure to kill."

"Swell." Lorna put her pizza on her plate. "What happens if he starts feeling the pressure again?"

Mitch looked at T.J.

"This is really your area of expertise, Dawson. I defer to you."

T.J. shook his head. "Not anymore, pal. I hung up that hat a long time ago."

"Hey, you know what they say around the Bureau." Mitch took a sip of beer, then set the bottle back down quietly on the table. "Once a profiler, always a profiler."

"You were a profiler?" Lorna tried to keep her jaw from dropping.

"Long ago and far away," T.J. said, as if to dismiss it as having no importance.

There were other questions she could have asked, questions she wanted to ask, but he'd clearly closed that door. She glanced beside her and met Regan's eyes.

Later, Regan told her silently.

"So, Regan," Mitch turned his attention to her. "What's the latest on your search for Eddie Kroll?"

"Who's Eddie Kroll?" Lorna asked.

"I don't know who he is. I know a little about him, but I don't know who he is," Regan told her. "I found his name in a file in a box of things that belonged to my father."

"What kind of things?" T.J. appeared relieved to have the topic of conversation shift from his former occupation.

"Old report cards, mostly. All from a Catholic grade school in Illinois from back in the forties. I did try to contact the school, but it closed about fifteen years ago." She smiled. "I tried tracking the name through the diocese schools, but the trail seems to end in ninth grade. There was no record of him after early March of his freshman year at St. Ambrose High."

"You're not giving up, are you?" Mitch asked.

260

"Are you kidding? I'm hot on this guy's trail." She grinned. "I'll be in Chicago at the end of the week, Saturday, to do a TV show. If Eddie Kroll is out there, I'm going to find him."

"He probably changed schools — maybe his family moved out of the city — and is happily retired in Florida by now," Lorna said. "And what's the big deal with him, if you don't mind my asking?"

"My dad kept all kinds of things, newspaper clippings, letters, postcards, you name it, that related to specific incidents. But in this case, he kept this guy's report cards. Why?" She put down her glass. "Why have them? Why keep them? What significance could they have had to my father, who wrote true crime books?"

"Then what you really want to know is, who is Eddie Kroll, and what was he to Josh Landry," Lorna summed it up.

"Exactly." Regan nodded. "And one way or another, I'm going to find out. However long it takes, I'm going to find Eddie Kroll."

"Well, you've got your mystery man, I've got my serial killer," Mitch said. "Sounds like we're both going to have our hands full for a while."

He looked at T.J., who was working on

another slice of pizza.

"Would you at least be willing to take a look at whatever information I get, once we start compiling data on the victims? Sort of a thank you for me getting those reports for you this weekend?"

T.J. looked distracted, as if chewing on Mitch's question along with the pepperoni.

Finally, he nodded slowly. "Your paybacks are a bitch, Peyton, you know that? But, okay, I'll take a look. As a thank you. Then we're even."

"Sure." Mitch looked pleased with himself. "Then we're even."

Fourteen

The early-morning air was steamy and dense. Summer was reasserting itself, and it wasn't pretty. Lorna rolled out of bed and into the shower. Thirty minutes later, she felt as if she could use a second one. She'd dried her hair with the blow dryer, but by the time she reached the first floor, the strands around her face were already coils of light brown frizz. She turned on the air conditioner and her computer in the dining room, then followed the smell of brewing coffee into the kitchen.

"I was just debating with myself, whether it was too hot to make coffee," Lorna said, taking two cups from the cupboard and setting them on the counter. "But you beat me to it, and it smells too good to pass up."

"I hope you don't mind," Regan said from her seat near the window. "I'm such an early riser and it never seems too hot for me to drink coffee. It's my addiction."

"I don't mind at all. I appreciate it. Nice to have it waiting for me." She got out the half-and-half and a bowl of sweeteners, real and artificial, and placed it all on the table in front of Regan. "I feel like making breakfast this morning."

She opened the refrigerator and peered inside. "Are you up for eggs? I bought some the other day at the Amish farm about a mile down the road."

"I could always eat," Regan replied.

"Scrambled all right?"

"Perfect."

Lorna set about preparing the eggs while Regan poured two cups of coffee.

"So," Lorna said as she added butter to the frying pan, "what's the story with T.J.? Why'd he quit the FBI, do you know?"

"It has something to do with a case he worked on in Georgia, that's all I know. All Mitch would tell me was that T.J. and his cousin, who was also an agent, both quit at the same time and started up their own business. He said they were really successful, apparently got a lot of work out of the DC area. Politicos and socialites. I guess they had a lot of contacts from being in the FBI. Anyway, the cousin got married last year and moved to some small beach town in Maryland with his wife. They sold off the business and now T.J.'s trying to decide what to do with the rest of his life. The only other thing I know is that the Bureau wants him back — bad. He was apparently very good at what he did."

"Well, that's more than I expected you to know." Lorna smiled as she whipped the eggs in the bowl, then slid them into the pan on the stove.

"I ask a lot of questions."

"Do you want toast?" Lorna walked to the bread box, passing the dining room door as she did so. She glanced at the computer on the table, and noticed the large reminder message on the screen. She went closer to take a look, then grimaced. "Damn. *Damn.*"

"What's wrong?" Regan appeared in the doorway.

"I forgot I had a meeting today. *Damn it.*" She closed the reminder screen and quickly opened a file, then turned on the printer. "I can't believe I forgot about this meeting. It's with one of my oldest clients."

"Where's the meeting?"

"At my client's office, back in Woodboro." Lorna bent over the computer, selected several pages, and hit *Print.*

"Can you make it?"

"Yeah, if I leave within the next ten minutes." She grabbed the coffee off the counter. "I'll have to stop at my town house and change, all my business clothes are there. God, I completely forgot what day it was."

"Well, you've had plenty to think about, these past few days," Regan reminded her. "You go on and get yourself ready to leave. I'll finish up the eggs and you can grab a few bites on your way out the door."

"I'll have plenty to think about on that long ride back to Woodboro," Lorna told her as she raced up the steps. "Like how to tell my client he's operating at a loss."

She grabbed her handbag, stuffed in the little travel case containing her makeup, and found her shoes. She raced back downstairs, apologizing to Regan as she flew through the kitchen. Regan held a plate out to her and she grabbed it on the fly.

"Stand still for twenty seconds and chew," Regan said, laughing.

Lorna took a bite. "Thank you. I wish I had time to sit and eat with you. I'm so sorry."

Regan waved away the apology as unnecessary. "Do you need your laptop?"

"I do." Lorna rolled her eyes. "Haste does indeed make waste."

She started toward the dining room and Regan stopped her. "Finish your eggs. I'll get your computer."

"I am so sorry to bail on you like this," Lorna said as Regan came back into the room with the white laptop in one hand and its carrying case in the other. "I should be back tonight. I'm so sorry . . ."

"Stop apologizing, and just go." Regan slid the computer into the case and handed it to Lorna, who had just finished rinsing her plate in the sink. "I can lock up the house when I leave."

"You don't have to leave," Lorna told her from the front door. "I know you're really getting into this case, and I'd expect Mitch to be by later. There's no reason for you to go, unless you have something else to do. You know where everything is in the house, so please feel free to stay. Besides, I'm just as happy to have someone here, frankly, what with all that's going on. You don't know what will turn up next. It might be better if someone is in the house."

"Then I'm more than willing to stay." Regan walked out onto the porch with Lorna. "You go take care of your business. The house will be fine, I'll be here when you get back. Go do what you have to do."

Lorna tossed her briefcase holding the files she'd hastily printed out onto the passenger seat along with the laptop. She'd never forgotten a meeting before, never let down a client, and she wasn't going to start now. She hit the highway, determined to make it to Woodboro in record time. She listened to a book on tape for a while, then turned it off to make phone calls. One to another client who liked a touch-base call every few weeks, another to her friend Bonnie, to see if she was available for a quick bite after work. Since the meeting was at three, it made sense for her to grab dinner before she left to drive back to Callen. Bonnie, a criminal lawyer, was in court, so she left voice mail suggesting they meet at a favorite restaurant at five-thirty, if Bonnie was free.

She made it to her town house in just under five hours, which was a record. Plenty of time to change and to prepare for the meeting.

She parked in her garage and went through the door that led to the kitchen. She'd never been quite so aware of how still an unoccupied house could feel. It was as if all the energy had left with her last Sunday. She walked from room to room, each one marred by the memory of her mother's pain. She opened the guest room closet and looked at the clothes. Her mother's shoes were still on the floor next to the chair she'd last sat in; the last book she'd started reading was still on the bedside table. Lorna sat on the side of the bed and held her face in her hands.

"I miss you, Mom. I hate it that you're not here anymore." She spoke the words out loud, as if her mother could hear. "I hate that you had to die."

She stared at the closet's contents. Mary Beth had wanted her clothes to go to Goodwill or the Salvation Army. "Whichever is most convenient for you, sweetie. Either would be fine."

"It's not fine. It's never going to be fine," Lorna had replied.

"Well, I just hate the thought of clothes hanging here, when someone else could be wearing them," Mary Beth had said softly. "Would it make it easier for you if I were to write things out, things I'd like you to do after, rather than discuss it with you?"

"Whatever is best for you, Mom," Lorna had said, regretting the show of anger.

"No, honey. I've already accepted what is. You're still fighting it. I need to do whatever is best for you now. Whatever will make it easiest for you when I'm gone."

"I'll never accept it. Nothing could make it easier. I don't want you to die."

"Well, nobody wants to die. But when you know how short the time is, you can't cheat yourself out of what little you have left by pretending that things are other than what they are." Mary Beth had struggled to sit. "I hate it, too, sweetie, but that's what is. I don't want to leave my children. I don't want to leave my friends or the places I love. But the choice isn't mine." She had reached for Lorna's hand and held it. "If I use my energy fighting against it, I lose what strength I have to enjoy what I still have. Understand?"

Lorna had nodded, unable to speak. Her mother had been so much braver than she had been.

She got up and left the room, closing the door behind her. It hurt to be here, more than she'd expected. If anything, she'd have expected to have felt the loss more at the farmhouse, where her mother had lived for most of her life, rather than here, in these small rooms where Mary Beth had lived for less than two years.

The message light was blinking on the answering machine, and Lorna paused to listen. The only one of the seven messages she listened to more than once was the message from Jack Corey. She'd dated Jack for six months before she brought her mother out to stay with her, but he wasn't inclined to continue the relationship once she had Mary Beth's illness to contend with. She'd barely seen him over the past year and a half.

"Hey, Lorna. Jack here. Say, just heard about your mother. So sorry, I know how close you were." After what she thought he'd have imagined to be a respectful pause, he continued, "So, I just thought I'd give you a call and see if you were free for dinner one night next week, maybe we can pick up where we —"

She hit the *Delete* button.

What a colossal ass. Whatever had she seen in him?

She went into her bedroom and took another quick shower, tried to tame her unruly hair, then pulled on a dark blue skirt and a white cotton shirt, dark heels, and a red belt. She found earrings and put on simple makeup, then left for her meeting. She closed the door of the town house behind her and headed off to meet with Larry Myers to give him the bad news.

"Ugh." Lorna shivered and took a sip of wine. "Remind me again why I dated Jack Corey in the first place."

"Tall, good-looking, successful tax attorney." Bonnie Jacobs rested her arms on the edge of the table and grinned. "And considering that the pickin's out here in the badlands of western Pennsylvania are so damned slim, it must have seemed like a good idea at the time."

"I should have saved the message to play it for you. You could hear the swagger in his voice. I'm sure he must think I've been praying he'd call."

"Does this mean you're not going to call him back?"

Lorna rolled her eyes, and her friend laughed.

"I'm sure I'll hear about it in the coffee shop someday soon," Bonnie said. "You seem to have forgotten, I work in the same building. Sooner or later, he's bound to corner me."

"Well, if he does, tell him I won't be around for a while, I have family business to take care of. Tell him I'm . . ." Lorna swirled the wine around in the glass, then grinned. "Tell him I'm starting a winery."

Bonnie laughed. "A winery? Where did that come from?"

"It just popped out," Lorna said, taking a sip of her wine. "But there are the vestiges of an old vineyard on the farm. My great-uncle started it sixty years ago but it's fallen into ruin."

"The vines are all still there and every-thing?"

"A few random plants may have sur-vived, but for the most part, I think the weeds choked them out. Most of the trel-lises are still standing, but there are trees and all sorts of things springing up among them. It probably would be really difficult to clear it all out. Not that I have any in-terest in doing that." She grinned again. "But it does make a fun story for Jack."

"Consider it told." Bonnie stabbed at her salad and asked, "So, can you tell me what the hell is going on down there in Southern Bumfuck, for Christ's sake? It seems as if every time I turn on the news, there's another body being dug up."

"There have been four at last count. And I'll be damned if I know where they came from. It's pretty horrific. Those remains have been there for years."

"Well, it's a farm, right? How come the tractors didn't plow them up before this?"

"Until that parcel of land was sold off to a developer, it was all wooded. So it was never plowed. It's only been recently, when they took out the trees to start building the houses, that the graves were discovered."

"God, that is creepy." Bonnie shook her

blond head. "How are you making out with your plans to sell it?"

"I'm not."

"You're not selling?"

"I'm not making out well right now, but yes, I'm still planning on selling. Things have been so hectic this week. Plus, there are other factors involved right now."

"Like what?"

"Like the police — and as of yesterday, the FBI — are investigating multiple murders and could probably block the sale of the property while the investigation is ongoing. I know they're still looking for other graves. And like the fact that we're not likely to get as good a price for it at the moment, since there's so much notoriety attached to the farm. I'm afraid if we put it on the market right now, we'll attract the curious and the morbid, but no serious buyers." Lorna leaned back to permit the waitress to serve her entrée.

"You really think real estate developers care about that sort of thing?" Bonnie snorted.

"We — my sister and I — were hoping to not have to sell to a developer. We'd hate to see the family home be demolished and replaced with a row of town houses."

"Maybe you should put it on the market

and see what happens. You never know who might be interested. Though I suppose there are fewer and fewer people going into farming today."

"True enough, though you'd be amazed at how many working farms there are in the area."

"A good thing." Bonnie speared a piece of yellow summer squash with her fork and held it up. "Someone has to feed us. I for one am happy someone is still in the business of raising veggies."

"You, being a vegetarian, would be in heaven in Callen. You can go right to the farms and buy whatever is in that week. There are also several dairy farms, a few that raise organic meats, and, of course, the mushroom farms. And the vineyards. There are at least half a dozen within twenty miles of our farm."

"It all sounds so . . . rural."

Lorna laughed.

"So tell me what the police and the FBI are doing to find this killer who's on the loose."

"For one thing, no one knows if the killer is still in the area. There haven't been any recent victims found — at least none that we know of. They're still trying to identify the victims found this past week.

Mitch — Mitch Peyton, he's the FBI agent assigned to the case — is working on that." Lorna paused, then asked, "Did I tell you I hired a private investigator to help determine if Billie Eagan killed her son?"

Bonnie placed her fork on the side of her plate, then looked up. "Why, no, you hadn't mentioned that. How do you know Billie Eagan? And where did you find a private investigator?"

Lorna related the entire story. When she concluded, Bonnie shook her head and said, "And here I thought you were languishing down there in Nowheresville, and instead, you're cavorting with possible murderers, FBI agents, an internationally known true crime writer, and a private eye."

Bonnie paused, then asked, "Is he cute?"

"Is who cute?"

"The PI."

"Very. Tall, blond, built. Drives a little sports car."

"You're making this up."

Lorna laughed. "No, actually, I'm not."

"Well, I suppose we might as well party tonight, because with all that going on in Bumfuck, I don't see you hurrying to move back to Woodboro anytime soon."

"I'll be back. I just need to resolve a few things."

"A few things like multiple murders and the sale of a very large property." Bonnie shook her head. "Girl, we won't be seeing you for another six months. Fortunately, you can take your business with you. All the joys of self-employment, and all the excitement of a juicy murder investigation and a hunky PI. Some girls have all the luck."

"Hey, you're welcome to come on out and join in the fun."

"Well, if the case against Billie Eagan starts moving into dangerous waters, and you need a top-notch criminal defense lawyer, you know where to find me." Bonnie tapped Lorna on the arm. "Scout around for another hunky PI and we'll talk reduced fee."

"Oh, right. I forgot how much trouble you have finding male companionship," Lorna deadpanned. Bonnie's great looks and personality, combined with her success, ensured she never had to be alone on a Saturday night unless she chose to be.

"There are lots of men around, but no one all that interesting. Most nights I'd rather be working." She resumed eating. "At least with a criminal case, you can be assured that some of the reading will be good. As a matter of fact, a few of the statements I've read lately rival some of the best fiction on the market."

"You need a vacation, Bonnie."

"I just had a vacation."

"You need another one," Lorna told her. "Why not come for a visit sometime soon. Stay Friday through Sunday."

"You're planning on staying there, aren't you?" Bonnie asked over the rim of her glass.

"For a while."

"I bet you don't come back."

"I'll be back. I just have to take care of some business there. It might take awhile, but I'll be back."

Bonnie took a twenty-dollar bill from her wallet and laid it on the table.

"Twenty says you stay in Bumfuck."

Lorna matched the bill.

"My twenty says you're wrong."

Bonnie grinned. "You know, I never bet on anything less than a sure thing, Ms. Stiles. I say a year from now, we'll be sending your mail to the farm."

"The only way I see that happening is if they're still digging up bodies. And if that's the case, you can pretty much bank that twenty, because I'll never be able to sell the place."

"Maybe not such a bad idea, if you

get to keep the PI."

"Ha. Fat chance." Lorna shook her head. "I don't think I'm his type."

"What do you think is his type?"

"The hot convertible sports car type," Lorna told her. "Like you. You're more his type. Sophisticated. Accomplished. Gorgeous."

"Oh, please. Sophistication is a state of mind, and who needs it, really? And may I remind you which of us started a successful business on her own? How much more accomplished do you need to be?" Bonnie waved off Lorna's attempt at protest. "And as far as looks are concerned, well, let's put it this way: Jack always brags he's never dated less than a 'ten.' What's that tell you?"

"It tells me that my taste in men had dropped to a disturbing all-time low two years ago." Lorna grimaced. "It also tells me I'm better off concentrating on work than on my social life, if that's the best Woodboro has to offer."

"Well, you can work wherever you are, and right now, the farm seems like the place to be. Frankly, I don't know about you, but I always wanted to be Nancy Drew. You know, solve the mystery. Catch the bad guy. Adventure. Intrigue." Bonnie sighed. "If I were you, I'd be in no hurry to come back here and leave that all behind."

"I did want to be Nancy Drew," Lorna admitted.

"Well, here's your chance, if only for a little while. Besides, you never know what other secrets are still hidden on that farm of yours."

Fifteen

"Is this powwow invitation only, or can anyone sit in?" Lorna asked from the doorway of her dining room. Mitch, Regan, and T.J. were seated around the table, obviously in the midst of a discussion.

"Hey, it's your table." Mitch waved her in.

T.J. pulled out the chair next to his, and she draped the strap of her shoulder bag over it.

"Sorry I didn't make it back last night," Lorna said to Regan. "I had dinner with a friend, and by the time we were finished . . ."

"No apology necessary. I told you when you called that I didn't mind, and I thought you should stay there. A five-hour drive after a night out would have been too much. And besides," Regan smiled, "you needed a night out to have fun. Things have been too intense around here practically since the day you arrived. I didn't mind staying here by myself. And I wasn't really alone, you know."

Lorna glanced sideways at Mitch, wondering if perhaps he'd kept Regan company while Lorna was in Woodboro. It was obvious there was something between them.

Regan caught the quick glimpse and sidestepped it. "Your Uncle Will."

"I hope he behaved himself."

"He was a perfect gentleman," Regan assured her.

"Uncle Will is the ghost?" T.J. looked from one woman to the other.

Lorna nodded. "Right."

"And you saw him?" he asked Regan.

She shook her head. "No. I only heard him."

"What did you hear? What did it sound like?" Mitch asked.

"It sounded like someone was pounding first on the wall, then the window, in the back bedroom."

"Are you sure someone *wasn't* pounding on the windows?" Mitch rose, alarmed. "Jesus, Regan, they've been digging up bodies right and left around here. And you hear someone pounding at night and you think it's a ghost? You think this is Great Adventure?"

"I know when someone is trying to break in, Mitch." Regan's eyes narrowed. "I can tell the difference."

"Let's go take a look." Mitch pushed

back his chair. "Which bedroom is it?"

"The last one at the end of the hall on the right," Lorna told him, amused.

"You coming, PI?" Mitch called over his shoulder to T.J.

"Sure. Why not?" T.J. followed him out the door and up the steps.

"I don't believe in ghosts, Regan," Mitch called down from the second floor, his footsteps echoing overhead.

"You haven't met my uncle Will," Lorna called back.

There was the sound of a window banging closed several times. A few minutes later, the two men returned.

"There's no sign of the window being jimmied, and the lock seems real secure," Mitch told them. He turned to Regan and added, "Maybe you were dreaming."

"Maybe you ought to sleep in Uncle Will's room one night," she smiled sweetly, "and we'll see who's dreaming."

He smiled in return. "Anytime."

"Okay, so we've established that Mitch is a nonbeliever and Regan and Lorna believe. Truthfully, I'm still on the fence," T.J. announced. "Let's move on, shall we?"

"Where were we?" Regan shuffled the notebook pages that lay on the table in front of her.

"We were talking about the responses we've gotten to our request for information on missing persons — specifically young men — over the past thirty years," Mitch said.

"From this area?" Lorna asked.

"Right. Southern New Jersey, the entire state of Delaware because it's small, northeastern Maryland, and southeastern Pennsylvania, from Harrisburg to Philadelphia, including the southernmost area from Lancaster straight on over to the Delaware River." Mitch held up a sheet of paper. "Guess how many responses so far?"

"I have no idea." Lorna shook her head. "Three?"

"Nine."

"Nine!" she exclaimed.

"Which tells me what the police have found is only the tip of the iceberg."

"But they wouldn't necessarily all be buried on my property, right?"

"Not necessarily, but I think there's a damned good chance there may be more out there. He'd have felt confident here, he'd met with success here. He'd never been discovered here." Mitch turned to T.J. "Which in itself should tell us something about him, right?"

"It tells me he's probably local. Probably

grew up here, may still be living here."

"Why would he still be here?" Lorna asked. "Wouldn't he be afraid that the remains would be found and he'd be caught?"

"No one's come close to catching him. For twenty-five years, no one even caught on that the crimes were committed. He's obviously in his comfort zone. He's killed here, he's buried his prey here, and he's gotten away with it for a very long time. And as Mitch just pointed out, he feels secure here. I don't see him having ever left. It probably gives him great comfort to have his kills close by."

"Well, if we assume you're right, and he's still living around here, what do you suppose he's thinking now?" Lorna asked.

"That's absolutely the question to be asking." T.J. turned to her. "And it's the one question no one else has asked."

Lorna felt her cheeks tinge pink. Nancy Drew, indeed.

"I think if he hasn't already begun to panic over the last few days, he's going to start very soon. I think he was okay when Jason's body was found. Okay, maybe a little tense, watch and wait, but in the end, the police blamed Billie for that. So I doubt he had much of a reaction other than maybe to feel the loss, that something has been taken from him. But it wouldn't really have affected him, I don't think, because he knew there were others, and he probably thought they were safe."

"But then the others were found," Regan pointed out. "Maybe not all of them, as Mitch noted, but enough to turn the national spotlight on the farm."

T.J. nodded. "Right. I think every day this week, things have gotten more and more tense for him. We don't know how many bodies were buried here, so we don't know if he's anticipating more discoveries — hoping, I'm certain, that no more are found. He's already upset, I believe, that four have been taken from him. He wants them here, nearby, needs to know they're there, under the ground, right where he left them. It has to be a torment for him to watch them exposed and removed."

"So what do you think he's going to do?" Lorna asked.

"I think he's going to be looking for replacements," T.J. told her.

The four fell silent for a moment, then Lorna asked, "So unless you find him, he'll start killing again?"

"If he's ever stopped — and we don't know for certain that he has — yes, I expect him to look for victims here. Remember that he could well have been killing elsewhere, but I think he needs to keep his victims close to him."

"That would involve a lot of travel on his part, though, wouldn't it? As large an area you've already canvassed for victims, and found nine, wouldn't he go beyond that to find future victims?" Regan asked.

"Possibly. Of course, there's always the chance that he stopped. The last victim we identified was reported missing in 1995."

"Ten years ago." Lorna looked pensive. "That means he was actively killing and burying his victims here for at least fifteen years."

"Fifteen years that we know of. As I said earlier, don't be surprised if there are still some surprises out there," Mitch told her.

"God, I hope not." Lorna shivered. "I've had enough surprises for one week."

"So, what's our game plan for today?" Regan stacked her notes neatly in front of her.

"*Our* game plan?" Mitch raised an eyebrow.

"Surely you don't expect to exclude me."

"Surely you don't expect to tag along

while I visit with the families of some of the victims."

"The Bureau permitted me access to interviews on previous cases, as a consultant," Regan reminded him.

"You had already shared information from your father's files on a similar case," he countered, "and you were permitted to accompany me to look over police files to see if you could spot similarities."

"Well, you don't know that I might not have some insights into this one as well."

"I don't know how welcome a civilian is going to be to a family whose long-missing son has just been identified."

"How 'bout we let John decide?" Regan smiled. John had been a big fan of her father's true crime series, and had authorized her involvement in cases in the past. She opened her bag and took out her cell phone. "That number again, Agent Peyton?"

Mitch recited the number and she dialed it, then got up and walked to the window.

"What's on your agenda for today?" Mitch asked T.J.

"I'm going to meet Danielle Porter at three," T.J. replied.

Lorna stood and collected the empty coffee cups.

"I was wondering if you'd come along, Lorna," he said. "I think you could be helpful, maybe get her to talk a little more than she might to a stranger."

"I'm pretty much a stranger, too, remember."

"Yes, but you're a local. And a woman. She might feel a little more comfortable talking to you."

"Where is she living now?" Lorna called from the kitchen, where she was rinsing the cups.

"She gave me the address, let me get it." T.J. went through his briefcase and located the slip of paper on which he'd written the number and address. He took it into the kitchen to show Lorna.

"Hmm, 724 Old Anderson Road." Lorna nodded. "That's off State Road, about two, three miles past Callen. There's no town there, per se, just a bunch of farms. I know the area. It should only take us about ten minutes to get there."

She looked at the kitchen clock, the face of which was set into the body of a black cat, a relic from her grandmother's day that Mary Beth had loved. It was just a little after one-thirty.

"Well, then, it looks as if we all have our work planned for us this afternoon." Mitch stood in the doorway. "Regan's been given the green light to come along with me — as a consultant," he emphasized, apparently for Regan's benefit. "And since we have appointments with three families today, I think we need to get going."

"I'm ready whenever you are," Regan told him from the dining room, where she was sliding her reading glasses into their case and hunting for her sunglasses.

"How about if we regroup later this afternoon?" T.J. suggested. "Lorna, do you mind if we use your home for our unofficial headquarters?"

"Not at all. I was going to suggest that Mitch feel free to use the dining room if he needs a place to work. If the weather cools off, we can clear some space from the table in the living room's front window to give you a bit of privacy, Mitch."

"Privacy's not much of an issue right now," he told her. "But thanks."

"All set?" Regan touched Mitch on the arm as she came into the room.

"Yes." He nodded. "We'll catch up with you later," he said to T.J. and Lorna.

"Good luck with Danielle," Regan called over her shoulder.

"Thanks." Lorna waved from the kitchen doorway.

After Mitch closed the door behind them, she turned to T.J. and said, "We have at least an hour before we have to leave. Is there anything else you need to do before we meet with Danielle?"

He shook his head. "No. Do you?"

"I have to check my computer, see if any of my clients have emailed me. Once I take care of that, though, I'm clear for the day." She had finished rinsing the cups and dried her hands on a red-and-white towel, which she folded and placed on the counter.

"You go ahead, then. If you don't mind, I'll step outside and walk around for a while."

"Just don't wander too close to the yellow crime scene tape on the other side of the field and get yourself arrested."

"I'll try to behave myself."

Lorna turned on her computer and pulled up that morning's emails. She had questions from one client on some account payables, and an email from another client who wanted to arrange a meeting before the end of the month. She responded to both and turned off the laptop, then went outside and looked around for T.J. He was nowhere in sight.

She walked past the barn and stood on

the edge of the field, one hand shielding her eyes from the bright early-afternoon sun. No T.J.

She called to him, but there was no response.

Lorna turned to go back to the house to search for her cell phone — she could always call and ask where he was — when she noticed the barn door was open. She went inside and called his name.

"Down here." The voice was faint and far away.

"Down where?" She frowned, looking around. Then she remembered. "Are you in the wine cellar?"

"Yes. Come on down."

"What are you doing down there?" she asked as she found the door to the steps ajar, and started down.

"Just looking around. Is it all right?"

"Sure. I don't mind. It's just a little creepy and dim."

"It wouldn't be if you replaced the lightbulbs once in a while," he teased, pointing to the electric lamps set into the wall on either side of the long narrow room. "A few still have a little life in them. How long has it been since anyone was down here?"

"Melinda and I used to play here," she

told him. "The small room back there" — she pointed past him — "used to be our secret place. We would go there to get away from her brother and his friends. Sometimes she hid in here from her mother. Gran said Uncle Will had planned to use that as the tasting room for his winery, but of course he never got that far."

She was following T.J. through the cavernous room, with its stone walls and low ceiling, past the empty oak barrels Uncle Will brought from France in anticipation of the first vintage. T.J.'s shadow disappeared through an arched doorway into the darkened room beyond.

"Is there a light in there?" she asked.

"I'm looking. Give me a second."

A long minute later, a faint light began to glow. In the dim light a round table with four tall chairs were visible in the center of the room.

"I found a candle and some matches," he told her. "I'd expect that the electric lines ran back here as well."

"They did. But we used to prefer the candles."

He turned to look back at her and she shrugged.

"Like I said, this used to be our secret

place, mine and Melinda's. Like a secret clubhouse. We came down here a lot. We'd talk or hide out, sometimes we'd bring snacks and spend a whole day. It was so nice and private. We always felt we could say anything down here." She folded her arms across her chest and wandered into the room. When she got to the back corner, she stopped and knelt.

"Our blankets are still here," she said. "We used to spread them out on the floor and lie on them to read or have picnics or whatever. Sometimes, in winter, it would be cold, so we'd wrap up in them to keep the chill off."

She stood with her blanket in her hands, then opened it up.

"Hard to believe I was small enough to wrap this around me and still have plenty left to make a little bed out of it." She held the blanket up for T.J. to see, then refolded it. "We would sneak matches and candles so that we didn't have to use the electric lights. For some reason, we thought no one passing through the barn would see the candlelight, but the lightbulbs would shine like beacons." She laughed. "So much for the logic of a couple of nine-year-olds."

Lorna paused, then walked around the room, her eyes on the floor.

"What are you looking for?" T.J. asked.

"Melinda's blanket. It doesn't seem to be here."

"Where should it be?"

"It should have been over there, with mine. We used to fold them up as small as we could, and hide them in the back corner, so no one would find them."

"When was the last time you were down here?"

"When I was nine. I was never too keen on being down here alone, and we — Melinda and I — had sworn to never tell anyone else about our secret place. I never did. I guess I always thought someday she'd come back, and I didn't want to have to tell her I'd shared our secret."

"So no one else knows this place is here?"

"Oh, sure, my sister knows. My brother. Probably some of his friends knew it was here, though they all seemed to spend more time over at the home of one of the other boys, who had horses. They all liked to play cowboys when they were younger. So much more authentic when you had a horse to ride."

"And your sister?"

"Wouldn't have been caught dead down here." Lorna laughed. "Spiders, other crawly things. Maybe some with fur and tails. Not Andrea's cup of tea."

"You didn't mention it to the police? Or to your parents?"

"No. I didn't," she said somewhat sheepishly. "I should have. As an adult, I know that. But as a child, I couldn't have broken that promise."

She wandered around and peered in all the corners.

"Still looking for the blanket?" T.J. asked.

"Strange that it's not here."

"Maybe she took it," he suggested.

"Took it where? It was here the day before she disappeared. We were down here, practicing lines for the school play. We had the blankets on the floor, right there." She pointed to the middle of the room.

"If she needed a place to hide, would she have come here?"

"What are you getting at?" Lorna asked. "What are you thinking?"

"The theory all along seems to be that Melinda was abducted from the field that night. Maybe she wasn't taken away by someone else. Maybe she ran away. What do you think?"

"I can't imagine where she would have gone." Lorna frowned.

"Maybe she came in here to hide, then left when the excitement died down out in the field."

"But hide from what?"

"That's a good question." T.J. stood in the doorway, his hands on his hips. "Would she have had any reason to hide from her mother that night?"

Lorna shook her head. "No. I already told you, my mother washed her dress so that no one could tell it had gotten dirty. She would have been able to smuggle it into the house, it wouldn't have been difficult. She wasn't afraid to go home."

"Maybe something happened between your house and hers that night, something that made her want to hide."

"Jason might have known. But of course, we can't ask him."

"Fritz didn't mention anything out of the ordinary that night," T.J. reminded her.

"I think we need to talk with the others who were there with him. Matt, Dustin . . . Fritz's brother, Mike. He was around later."

"Well, let's go back into the house and look up some phone numbers, make a few calls," he suggested. "I want to speak with all of them as soon as possible."

Lorna looked at her watch.

"How about we grab the phone book and I make the calls from the car? We're due at Danielle Porter's in less than a half hour."

"That will work."

She walked through the arch and into the wine cellar. T.J. blew out the candle and left it on the floor inside the door.

"Next time we bring lightbulbs."

Danielle Porter lived in a double-wide trailer on an acre lot surrounded by apple trees and a big flower garden. There was a two-car garage and a child's playhouse in the backyard, and a mailbox surrounded by weeds at the foot of the driveway. T.J. parked the Crossfire in front of the garage, and he and Lorna walked across new macadam to the worn path through the grass to the front door.

Danielle stepped out of the house to meet them before they could ring the bell.

"You're T. J. Dawson?" she asked.

He nodded and offered her a business card.

"And you are?" Danielle stared at Lorna.

"Lorna Stiles."

"Lorna Stiles," Danielle repeated thoughtfully. "You're from around here. I know your name. But I don't have a clear memory of you."

"I was a friend of Melinda Eagan's," Lorna told her.

"Who?" Danielle placed a hand on her hip and cocked her head slightly to the left.

"Melinda Eagan," Lorna repeated.

"Am I supposed to know the name?"

"You were friends with her, back in grade school." Lorna's eyes narrowed suspiciously. Was it possible Danielle had really forgotten someone she'd been friends with years ago? "She used to stay at your house quite often. Until she disappeared one night and was never seen again."

"Oh, the girl who disappeared." Danielle's expression never changed. "What about her?"

"I'm looking into her disappearance," T.J. said, stepping into the conversation.

"So why do you want to talk to me? I wasn't there that night, I don't know nothing about it."

"I was hoping you'd be able to give us some information we don't already have. You spent some time with her back then, maybe you'd remember if she ever told you that someone was giving her a hard time, or frightening her in some way."

"Only her mother." Danielle shrugged. "She used to beat up on her something bad, I remember that."

"Did she ever say anything to you about maybe wanting to run away?" T.J. asked.

"No." She shook her head and looked down. "We really weren't that close."

"She used to spend a lot of time at your house," Lorna reminded her. "What did you do? What did you talk about?"

"It was a long time ago." Danielle shrugged. "I don't remember what we did, or what we talked about. I guess she just didn't make that big an impression on me."

She looked from Lorna to T.J. "Was there something else?"

T.J. handed her his card. "If you think of anything, if you happen to remember something about Melinda, give me a call."

"Sure." Danielle stepped back into the house and closed the door.

Lorna and T.J. returned to his car.

"That was a waste of time," Lorna said.

"Not really. We learned something."

"What, that she was lying?"

"That could be important." T.J. started to back the car slowly down the drive. "Why would she lie about knowing Melinda?"

"I don't know, but apparently she can't wait to tell someone." Lorna stared at the open window as they went past. "She grabbed that phone and started dialing before we reached the car. Wouldn't you love to be a fly on the wall right now?"

"Nah. But I would like to know whose number she just dialed." He reached into his pants pocket and took out his phone, then dialed a number. "Mitch, it's T.J. How quickly can you get phone records?"

Sixteen

"Cannon Road is the next left, so you'll want to turn there," Lorna told T.J.

"It will be interesting to see how Mike Keeler's version of things stacks up against his brother's," T.J. noted.

"Mike was fourteen, remember. Two years younger than Fritz. He might have seen things differently."

"What's that supposed to mean?"

"Fourteen, you're still a kid. Sixteen, you're a little more mature. I think the older you are, the more you're likely to remember the little things."

"Two years isn't so great a difference."

"I just remember Fritz as being the more serious of the two. Mike was always clowning around. Nothing ever seemed to affect him. Fritz was more intense about things."

"Interesting observation."

"And that's all it is. Just an observation." She ran a hand through her hair to get it out of her face. She could only imagine what it looked like by now. T.J. had pulled to the side of the road to put the top down after they'd left Danielle's, and had taken Lorna on a zippy ride through the country-side. "Slow down so I can read the numbers on the mailboxes."

He eased up on the gas.

"It must be two houses up from here." Lorna pointed to the bright yellow mailbox at the top of the slight rise in the road. T.J. slowed even more so she could read the name on the side of the box. "Yes, that's it."

T.J. turned into the drive just as a young child in white shorts and a bright red T-shirt ran around the corner of the garage, which, like the ranch-style house attached to it, was pale gray siding with black shutters. She stopped next to a bright red crape myrtle and stared at the little car with the big man behind the wheel.

T.J. turned off the engine and got out.

"Hi," he called to the little girl. "What's your name?"

"I can't tell you," she replied. "You're a stranger and I can't talk to you."

T.J. nodded. "Good answer."

A man in khaki shorts emerged from the garage. "You must be Mr. Dawson. And hey, Lorna Stiles. Good to see you again."

Mike Keeler gave Lorna a quick hug and

offered his hand to T.J.

"Good to see you, too, Mike," Lorna replied.

"Kayla, I want you to go inside and tell Mommy she's going to have to take you and your sister to the soccer field. I'll be along later," Mike told his daughter, then turned back to his visitors. "So, Lorna, Fritz tells me you're putting the farm up for sale."

"I will be, yes."

"You have a Realtor yet?"

"No, but it's on my list of things to do."

"I only ask because Sarah, my wife — you remember Sarah, she was Sarah Watts in school . . ."

Lorna nodded. She remembered Sarah Watts, though she hadn't known her well.

"Anyway, her brother, Jim, is a Realtor, he owns Watts Real Estate out there on Route One. Maybe you could give him a call."

"I'll do that. Right now, the police are still all over that back section, and they're not letting anyone past about mid-field of our land."

"I guess they'll be going over the rest of the property, too," Mike said. "The vineyard, down around the pond, out around the orchard."

"Maybe, if they keep finding bodies, they'll expand the search. So far, they haven't done so. Although they're being really meticulous, taking their time."

"Probably afraid of missing something."

"It pays to be thorough."

"So tell me what I can do for you." Mike shoved his hands in his pockets.

"Well, as you know, there's been a lot of activity out at my place. The FBI is involved now, as I'm sure you've heard, and T.J. is working with them," Lorna told him, stretching the truth a bit. "We're hoping that once we find Jason's killer, maybe we'll be able to figure out what happened to Melinda."

"You working with the FBI, too?" Mike asked her.

"No." She shrugged. "But I am an interested party, since the bodies were found on my property. Or my former property, at least."

"From what I've heard, the boys they found buried were all about the same age, all died from the same type of head injury." Mike was facing into the sun and he squinted, his eyes becoming little slits. "Why would you assume the same thing happened to Melinda? She disappeared first, right? Those FBI profilers you see on

TV are saying that whoever killed those boys had a thing for *boys*. Why would a killer who only went after teenage boys kill a nine-year-old girl?"

"No one's assuming that Melinda was killed by the same person," T.J. told him. "But we are thinking there's a connection between the two. We just don't know what it is yet. And as far as what you're hearing on TV, you need to keep in mind that profiling is far from being an exact science."

T.J. paused, then added, "I'm not so sure *science* is even the correct term to use. It's off as often as it's on. I wouldn't put much stock into what you see on television."

Lorna glanced sideways at T.J., and caught the set of his jaw as he spoke. This was obviously a hot button of his, and probably related to his former stint as a profiler. She wished she knew him well enough to ask him about it. There was a story there, and she was dying to hear it. Maybe another time.

Sarah Keeler came outside the house and waved to Lorna. The two women exchanged pleasantries before Sarah rounded up her daughters and strapped them into the family van to head off to soccer.

"Bring some bottled water when you come to the field," Sarah called to Mike as she eased past them. "And try not to be too late. We have a double-header tonight, and they might need you to fill in for Kara's coach in the second game."

Mike waved to his wife and daughters, then turned his attention to Lorna and T.J.

"Let's go sit on the deck, it's cooler and more comfortable out back." Mike gestured for them to follow him to the backyard. "Sarah just made a pitcher of iced tea. I'll run in and grab some for us. It's been another hot one, eh?"

They climbed the three steps up to the deck and took seats around a glass-topped table that appeared brand new. Mike ducked inside the house and returned with three glasses of iced tea. He handed a glass to each of his visitors, then sat in the chair at the head of the table.

"So go ahead and ask away." Mike settled back in his chair and crossed his legs. "Where do you want to start?"

"Let's start with the night Melinda disappeared." T.J. rested both arms on the table. "You were around that night."

"Right. My mother sent me over to Matt Conrad's house to get my brother for dinner. She'd been calling him but no one was answering the phone. Matt's parents hadn't gotten home from work yet, and I said the guys were probably outside, so my mom told me to go get Fritz and tell him to come home."

"How far is Matt's from your house?" T.J. asked.

"Less than half a mile. I rode my bike."

"Do you remember what time it was when you got there?"

"No. But it was still light out. Matt and Fritz were out back smoking cigarettes. I sat down and smoked one or two with them — that was the big thing back then, cigarettes, about as wild as we got around here — then Jason came along, said he was going to collect his sister and walk her home, but he'd be right back. A little while later, he returned, then his mother started calling him, real loud, so he got up and ran home. A few minutes later, he was back, asking if anyone had seen his sister. No one had, so he asked us to help him look for her. Later the police came and they started looking, too, and me and Fritz went home. Next day in school we heard she was still missing and there was this big search."

"How long were you at Matt's before Jason arrived the first time?" T.J. asked.

"Oh, maybe a half hour or so."

"Then he went to get Melinda, came

back, and not long after that his mother called him . . ."

Mike nodded. "Right, and he left again for a couple of minutes. But he came right back."

" 'Right back,' meaning how long between the time he left to go home and the time he came back and said his sister was missing?"

"No more than five minutes."

"You sure about that?"

"I'm positive."

"What time did Dustin arrive?" T.J. asked.

"Dustin?"

"Dustin Lafferty, your brother's friend."

"Oh. Hey, I'd forgotten about him. Yeah, he was there, too. I think he got there right after me."

"So you joined in the search? Did you split up, or go in pairs?"

"We split up, we all went off in different directions, but there was nothing. Not a sign of her anywhere."

"Where did you look?"

"I took the orchard. I don't remember where anyone else looked."

"The orchard's down near the pond?"

"Yeah. I think Jason took the pond. I went around all the apple and peach trees but there was nothing to be found. Melinda was just gone."

"Now, the night that Jason died, you were all over at Lafferty's?" T.J. leaned back in the seat.

"Right. Me, Fritz, Jason, Matt, and Dustin."

"Drinking beer?"

"Yeah, we all had a few. We stayed till a little after two, then Dustin drove everyone home. He dropped me and Fritz off, then took the others home. The next day, we heard that Jason had disappeared, too."

"You have any ideas, back then, what might have happened to him?"

"No." Mike shrugged. "He wasn't the most popular guy in school, but he was okay, if you know what I mean. I liked him. For a while, the kids were saying that Jason and his sister had both run away, to get away from their mother. She used to be really hard on both of them, he told us that."

"Can you think of anything else we might need to know?" T.J. put both hands palm-down on the table, ready to push himself out of his seat. The interview was over. He'd gotten what he'd come for.

"Just that back then a lot of people thought Mrs. Eagan had killed both her kids. I'm still not so sure she didn't."

"You may have heard I put up her bail," Lorna said.

"Everyone in Callen's heard about that." Mike grinned. "You didn't make any friends in the local police department with that move."

Lorna got out of her chair, preparing to leave. "If she's innocent of Jason's murder, they should be looking for whoever killed him."

"Well, I think she's guilty as sin." Mike stood, too. "I think they had the right person all along. I think in the end, all this investigation is going to prove is that she killed them both."

"What about all the other boys they've found, Mike? Think she killed them, too?"

"Hey, like those FBI guys said, the killer had a thing for teenage boys. Who knows? Maybe that's how Mrs. Eagan got off, you know? Doing young boys, then killing 'em."

Mike stood at the end of the deck and looked down at T.J. and Lorna, who'd already stepped onto the grass at the bottom of the steps.

"Yeah," he continued, "if I were the investigator, that's what I'd be looking into. Mrs. Eagan's sex life."

★ ★ ★

"What do you think?" T.J. asked as he drove away.

"I think that was a seriously sick thing to say." Lorna shook her head. "That man clearly watches too much TV."

"Or reads too many thrillers." T.J. gunned the engine. "Or maybe not enough."

"What do you mean?"

"Either that was all smoke screen, or he and his brother need to get their stories straight. They don't match up. Fritz said Mike got to Matt Conrad's house after Jason was called home. That Dustin stopped by after Mike had arrived to tell Fritz it was time to go home." T.J. eased up to the stop sign at the top of the hill. "Which way?"

Lorna pointed right, and he made the turn.

"Fritz also said that Mike wasn't with them the night that Jason disappeared, that they were at White Marsh Park till three in the morning. Mike just now said he was with them at Dustin's — didn't say a word about White Marsh Park. And he said Dustin drove them home at two. One of them is lying."

"How do we find out which one?"

"We talk to Dustin Lafferty and see what he remembers."

Seventeen

"So you got two different versions of the same story?" Mitch sat on one of the oak chairs at the table in Lorna's kitchen. "Interesting. I got three similar versions of the story I was after."

"Are we going to hear them?" T.J. stood in the doorway.

"Sure. We're going to trade notes," Mitch told him. "We'll see who had the more productive day."

"Does everything still have to be a competition with you?" T.J. complained while taking a seat opposite Mitch.

"Not everything."

"Sorry." Lorna came through the back door holding several bags. "Burgers and fries from the café down the road are the best I can do."

"What's to be sorry about burgers and fries?" T.J. rose to give her a hand. "I don't think anyone here expected you to be feeding us this week."

"Well, it makes more sense than all of us going our own ways, then trying to reconvene to share information." Lorna set the bag she was carrying on the counter and T.J. did likewise. "Thanks, whoever set the table."

"That was T.J.," Regan told her.

"Thank you, T.J." Lorna turned to him and smiled.

"You're welcome. What else can I do?" he asked.

"You can get a platter out of the cupboard behind you and stack these burgers on it while I find something to put the fries in."

"I for one am happy we're having this info-swap," Regan said. "I'm going to have to leave tomorrow for a few days and I'd hate to go without hearing the latest."

"Oh, that's right. You have a meeting in Chicago on Saturday."

"TV interview, yes. But if you're not tired of my company, I can come back later in the week. I hate to miss out on anything." Regan looked from Mitch to T.J. "You don't suppose you'll have solved this whole thing before I get back, do you?"

"Wouldn't that be the luck?" Mitch took a burger from the platter T.J. set on the table and put it on his plate. Lorna handed him the bowl into which she'd dumped the fries, then placed a bottle of catsup in front of him. "I wish I could wrap this up by the end of the weekend. I have a stack of cases back in my office, I don't know when I'm going to get to those."

T.J. handed Mitch a beer.

"Thanks," Mitch said. "Of course, if we weren't so shorthanded at the Bureau right now, I wouldn't be backed up."

"Who are you trying to kid? The FBI's well staffed." T.J. took a bite of his burger.

"Domestic issues are taking a backseat to the terrorist units," Mitch told him. "A lot of the new agents are going that route. The drones like me who handle the routine same old, same old — serial killers, kidnappings, sex crimes — keep getting further and further behind in our work, because God knows there's no shortage of predators." He ran a hand through his brown hair, and his eyes darkened. "Honest to God, it's tough keeping up with them. You put one away in Florida, another one pops up in Wisconsin."

"If you're trying to make me feel guilty . . ." T.J. rubbed the back of his neck.

"Nah. Guilt didn't work before, it isn't likely to work now. It'll take something bigger than that to bring you back," Mitch said. "So, we'll move on. Let's get to the nitty-gritty here. Story time."

"How 'bout I eat while you tell us what

you found out today, then you can eat while I tell you what we did."

"How come you get to eat first?" Mitch asked T.J.

"Because my story is probably shorter than yours and I haven't eaten since breakfast."

Lorna sat between Mitch and T.J., poured beer from an ice-cold bottle into a glass, and prepared to take mental notes.

"Okay, here's what happened. We — Regan and I — started with the New Jersey victim first. Sixteen-year-old boy, Sid Calhoun, went missing . . ." He turned to Lorna. "Guess how many years ago."

"Twenty-something," she replied immediately.

"Damn, you are smart. You ever think about working for the FBI?" Mitch said.

"She owns her own business," T.J. reminded him. "Why would she want to work for the FBI?"

"Good point." Mitch nodded. "Anyway, we sat down first with his mother — the father died last year — who basically told us nothing about her son. Oh, sure, he played in the school band, he liked the beach. She showed us his room. The life-sized *Saturday Night Fever* poster — complete with Travolta, posed in that white suit — still hangs on the wall. The room has been cleaned, but nothing has been moved in all these years. It was pretty creepy, actually."

"That is really sad," Lorna said.

"It gets sadder," Regan told her. "Just as we were leaving, Sid's older brother, Bob, shows up outside. We introduce ourselves, we chat, he tells us to stick around for a few minutes, Mom is leaving for work, and we can talk."

"Did Bob have something worthwhile to share?" T.J. asked.

"Did he ever. Seems Sid had known at a very young age that he was more interested in guys than in girls. He apparently tried to come out to his family when he was thirteen, but Mom and Dad wouldn't hear of it. They told Sid it was just a phase he was going through and he'd grow out of it."

"Poor Sid." Lorna put her burger down on her plate.

"Well, poor Sid knew better, and just more or less went with it. Bob said over the next few years, Sid became actively homosexual and sought out relationships. He said that on more than one occasion, he'd had to drive into Philadelphia or Wilmington to pick up his brother, because he'd gotten himself into a jam with someone who turned out to be not so nice."

"Sounds like Sid wasn't very discriminate in his choice of partners," T.J. said.

"I think it was more inexperience than anything else," Regan told him. "I think he just hadn't learned how to tell the good guys from the bad guys."

"So maybe he hooked up with someone who was badder than he'd bargained for," Lorna thought aloud.

"That's what Bob thinks," Mitch agreed. "And in view of what we learned about the other victims, I'd say Bob was right on the money."

"Are you going to tell us?" T.J. gestured for Mitch to continue.

"Victim number two. Hugh Costello. Newark, Delaware. Age seventeen. Same deal," Mitch told him. "Only difference was, his parents were more rational. We met with both of them. They're retired now, living in a small beach community on the Delaware Bay. While they admitted that the gay lifestyle would not have been their first choice for their only son, they tried to be loving and understanding. And you have to give these folks credit, this was before the current openness about homosexuality. I think they tried really hard to be accepting, and twenty-five years ago, that must have had its difficult moments."

"They obviously loved their son very much," Lorna observed.

"It was very apparent. But like Sid's brother, Bob, they worried Hugh would fall into bad company. Apparently, he did," Mitch told them.

"And neither Bob nor Hugh's parents had any idea who this bad egg was?" asked T.J.

"None. It sounded to me as if it was a one-night thing, both times. Both times, the guy went to a club and never came home. The only difference is that the Costellos were pretty certain that the club was somewhere outside Wilmington." Mitch bit off the end of a French fry. "Same with the third victim, Tim Gossette. Disappeared after leaving the house to go to a club around Wilmington."

"I guess you already know the name of the club," T.J. said, "given your superb computer skills."

"Actually, I do. It was called the Purple Pheasant."

"Was?" T.J. asked.

"It closed about twenty years ago. But with my superb computer skills and my trusty laptop, I was able to find the name of the owner. Who, unfortunately, is not available." Mitch looked around the table, then asked, "Anyone want to take a guess?"

"Don't say he disappeared." Lorna's jaw dropped.

"About a month before the club closed. Which, incidentally, was the reason it closed down. He simply vanished. According to the newspaper archives I was able to access, the club had been very popular and appeared to be operating in the black. In spite of the fact that it was visited often by the state police and closed down more than once for serving underage boys."

"So the owner . . . what was his name?" Lorna asked.

"Lorenzo Blair," Regan told her.

"So Blair runs this club . . . which all of the victims so far had frequented. They disappear and are found buried in my woods. Then he goes missing?" Lorna bit her bottom lip. "Do you think he could have been the killer?"

"I think it's more likely he was one of the victims," T.J. replied. "No one is going to walk away from a venture that's making money. You'd sell it, but you wouldn't just walk away. Maybe we can track down a relative, see if we can get some DNA, perhaps get a match to one of the remains found back there."

"Already on it." Mitch smiled. "I have a meeting with his mother next week. First, however, I'll be meeting with Chief Walker to fill him in. Gotta keep the locals in the loop. Besides, I want to see what he's found over the past few days. He's been awfully quiet."

"Wouldn't he have told you if another body had been located?" Regan asked.

"I'd certainly expect that, yes. But I'm interested in the other things, the little things they might be digging up or putting aside. Things that might contain DNA or fingerprints."

"After all these years, you can get fingerprints and DNA?" Lorna stood and began clearing the plates. All the burgers and fries had been devoured and nothing remained but a few crumbs.

"Sometimes. Both depend on a number of factors. Exposure to the elements, temperature, that sort of thing. I spoke with the county techs the other day and they all seem to be on the ball. I just want to see if anything that's been recovered looks like something we might want to expedite to the FBI labs." Mitch then turned to Regan. "What time is your flight tomorrow?"

"It's early evening, from Baltimore, but I

need to run home and pack a few things first."

"So you're going to do your TV thing, then see if you can find Eddie Kroll?" Mitch asked.

"I'm going to hunt him down." Regan grinned. "I am so curious about this guy. I'm wondering if maybe he wasn't a friend or even a distant relative of my dad's. That would be great, to find a relative, after all this time."

"Didn't you know any of your father's family?" Lorna stood at the sink, cleaning scraps from the dishes into the trash can.

"No. I never met any of his relatives. His parents died while he was in college, and his only brother died while we were living in England," Regan told her.

"How long did you live abroad?" T.J. rose and walked across the kitchen. To Lorna, he said, "You wash, I'll dry."

"You wash, I'll put things away after I dry." She smiled. "And thanks."

"We lived in England until I was twelve. My mother was born there, and she very reluctantly left to move here. I knew all of her family, we're still close. But I never met anyone on my dad's side."

"No cousins?" T.J. asked.

"He didn't have any. Just the one brother

who died." Regan smiled wistfully. "I miss my British cousins. I wish I had someone here to feel connected to. It's just . . . odd. No grandparents, no aunts or uncles or cousins. You feel very much alone without family."

"How often do you see your English relatives?" asked Mitch.

"I usually visit twice a year, my cousins have been over at one time or another. My cousin Polly used to take her vacation — her 'holiday' — here every year, but she's married now and has small children. It's been too difficult for her to arrange a visit, between her husband's business and her having babies." Regan rested her chin in the palm of her hand and sighed. "I do miss her."

"Hey, I have about forty cousins, I'd be happy to loan you as many as you want," Mitch offered. "There is no shortage of Peytons in Maine."

"I'll remember that, if I ever get to Maine again."

"And you're always welcome here," Lorna assured her.

"I appreciate that. I really like it here." Regan looked out the kitchen window. "Maybe when I come back, we can get that garden along the back fence cleaned out. I started pulling some weeds the other afternoon, but I stopped when Mitch arrived."

"Thanks for the reminder. I do have to clean up that entire section. It's one of the places my mother wanted her ashes."

"You still have your mother's ashes?" T.J. turned to her.

She nodded. "Two more urns of them. Smallish ones. She wanted to be in three places. So far I've only managed to get to the family plot. The third spot was the pond. I've barely even been down there since I got home."

"Any particular reason?" T.J. asked.

"No." She shook her head. "I just haven't had time. Between trying to keep my business running, going back to Woodboro for the meeting yesterday, and everything else that's been going on around here, I haven't had much quiet time to myself."

"Well, maybe this will all be over soon and we'll be out of your hair," T.J. told her.

Lorna smiled weakly. She was just getting used to having them all around. Especially T.J.

"Hey, you can always fire Dawson." Mitch grinned. "Which reminds me, we're still waiting for the rundown on your meetings today. Did you find out anything important?"

"We discovered that Mike Keeler and his brother have different recollections of the nights that both the Eagan kids disappeared." T.J. finished rinsing the last plate and handed it to Lorna, then dried his hands on a towel.

"How different?" Mitch wanted to know.

"Different enough that I don't think the variations are due to the amount of time between then and now. One of them is lying."

"Any feel for which one?"

T.J. shook his head. "On the one hand, there's Fritz, who we know travels out of town a few times each month. I'd like to know where he goes, who he sees. Then there's Mike, who believes the police already have the right suspect in mind."

"He thinks Billie's guilty?" Mitch leaned back in his chair.

"Yeah. His time line is so different from his brother's — when he arrived, who was there at what time, that sort of thing. It will be interesting to see how Dustin Lafferty remembers things. We're going to be meeting with him tomorrow at his office. He owns an insurance agency in a place called Elk Run, which Lorna assures me isn't too far from here."

"Between here and Lancaster," Lorna said.

"And what about that friend of Melinda Eagan's you were going to visit?" Mitch drummed his fingers on the tabletop. "What did she have to say?"

"She said as little as possible," T.J. told him. "She claimed to barely remember Melinda. Even Lorna's attempts to jog her memory seemed to bounce off her."

"Which was really hard to believe," Lorna interjected. "Since I happen to know that Melinda spent quite a few weekends at Danielle's house that last summer and fall."

"Why would she deny knowing her?" Regan asked.

"I have no idea. Obviously I knew she was lying. And she said she sort of remembered my name. I was never a friend of hers, was never at her home, never socialized with her, but she remembered my name, not Melinda's?" Lorna shook her head. "Not even close to being credible.

"And the second we left she was on the phone to someone," Lorna said.

"Oh, right, the number you wanted the phone records for. I should have them by tomorrow, depending on how busy my buddy is back in the office."

"I can't wait to find out who she felt needed to know we were asking about Melinda." Lorna slipped the last of the dinner plates into the cupboard. "I wonder who would be that interested, after all these years."

"Well, hopefully by this time tomorrow, we'll know." Mitch stood and pushed his chair in, obviously preparing to leave. "And with any luck, we'll have IDs on the last three remains, maybe even a better idea of who killed them, and why."

Eighteen

The ride north on I-95 at nine-thirty in the morning was always an exercise in patience. As another weekend approached, the travelers who saved their vacation until late summer were in a hurry to get to their destinations. That usually meant taking the quickest route, which — north to south and back again — was I-95. Add the commuters to the mix, and you had heavy volume. Throw in a little road repair and you had yourself a backup.

T.J. moved his seat back to give his legs a little extra room. For some reason, when he was driving, the space didn't seem quite as narrow as it did when the car was sitting still. He toyed with the idea of putting the top up. Stopped on a major highway in three lanes of traffic that were going nowhere, you felt pretty much exposed to your fellow travelers with the top down. With the temperature rising steadily, and the sun blazing, you just knew all the other drivers were sitting there watching you fry.

He hunted in the console for a paper towel or a tissue to dry the sweat from his face. He found a crumpled but unused yellow napkin from a fast-food restaurant, and put it to work, blotting the area around his eyes and the back of his neck. Leaning against the headrest, he slipped his dark glasses back on and closed his eyes.

The drive to Callen wasn't more than forty minutes in light traffic. He'd told Lorna to expect him around ten. Their appointment with Dustin Lafferty was at noon, at his office in Elk Run. Lorna figured that was about an hour from her place, so they had time to spare. Or would have, if traffic got moving again.

Being stuck in the car, with nowhere to go and nothing else to do, gave him plenty of time to think about things he'd been trying not to think about for the past few days. His future. The voice-mail message on his cell phone from John Mancini. Lorna.

He figured the future was wide open. He didn't have to rush to make any decisions right away. Selling the business had provided more than enough cash to live on for a while. Money wasn't going to be a problem, unless he did something really stupid, which wasn't his style. Once the sale of his house in Baltimore went through, he'd be sitting even prettier. Until, of course, he found another place to buy, but he was in no hurry to do that, either. He could always rent something for a few months, or a year if he had to, until he decided where he wanted to go, and what he wanted to do.

Bored, he listened to the message from his former boss again, disconnected from voice mail. He didn't know how he felt about the Bureau right now. He'd loved that job. Loved being Special Agent Thomas Jefferson Dawson, loved the challenge of putting together the facts and circumstances of a crime in order to solve it. He'd been good at it — so good, they'd asked him if he was interested in being assigned to the National Center for the Analysis of Violent Crime and taking on some of the duties generally termed "profiler." T.J. had jumped at the opportunity, and over the next few years had developed analytical skills that had set him apart from most of his peers. Over time, he'd honed those skills and had become sought after more and more for consultation in the most complicated cases. He'd loved the work, loved the role he'd played in bringing down vicious criminals. He could have gone on with the Bureau until retirement, had all intention of doing exactly that. Until Lakeview, Georgia, and Teddy Kershaw . . .

The ringing of his cell phone brought him back from a place he'd just as soon not go.

"Dawson."

"T.J., it's Lorna. I have the TV on and I just saw the tie-up on I-95."

"That's me there on your screen, top down, baseball cap, dark glasses."

She laughed. "If you can get as far as Havre de Grace and exit the interstate, I'll give you directions that will save you time. Assuming traffic is still slow."

"Traffic is not slow. Traffic is at a standstill."

"Well, if it gets moving, call me back."

"I'll do that, thanks." He paused, then said, "We may need to call Lafferty and reschedule for later today, if possible. What's the latest you think we can leave your house and still make it to his office by noon?"

"Eleven-twenty, not much later than that, unless we don't mind being a few minutes late."

"I don't mind being late, but I don't know how much latitude Lafferty has in his schedule. What's he like? Is he the type to get annoyed at being postponed?"

"I have no idea. I never really knew him very well. He's a few years older than I am — six or seven, I think — and the only times I ever saw him were at the Eagans'. I don't have a clear recollection of him, really. So I don't know if he'll be put off or not."

"Well, hopefully, we won't have to worry about that. Hey, I see a little movement from the vehicle ahead of me." T.J. straightened in his seat and put the car in gear.

"Great. Well, call me back if you need directions."

"Will do. And thanks, Lorna."

The Crossfire inched along behind the Tahoe directly in front of him. The SUV being taller and wider, T.J. couldn't see over or around it, and wasn't sure how far ahead traffic had begun to crawl. It was stop and go for the next mile. He saw the sign for Havre de Grace up ahead, and thought about calling Lorna back. He'd wait until he got closer, to judge whether he needed an alternate route.

Not that he'd mind another reason to call Lorna. So far, the best thing about striking out on his own had been meeting her. The case was intriguing and complex enough to challenge him, and though he'd be hard-pressed to admit it to Mitch, T.J. was enjoying working with his old teammate again. With Lorna in that mix, T.J. almost felt as if he'd won the lottery.

He'd always liked women with brown eyes, and Lorna's were almost the exact same shade of cinnamon as her hair. She was down-to-earth and pretty, with a frequent smile and an easy laugh. She was independent and smart, and he couldn't think of one thing about her that he didn't like. In fact, he'd liked her the minute he met her. He'd never been one to mix business and pleasure — too risky to one's professional reputation — but he didn't figure this case would go on forever. In the meantime, he couldn't think of anyone he'd rather be working a case with right now. All around, it had been a very good week.

If he hadn't been thinking so much about Teddy Kershaw, the week would have been damned near perfect.

"You want to drive?" T.J. asked Lorna as she walked toward the car.

"Sure." She grinned. "I'd love to drive, thanks."

He got out of the car and dangled the keys in front of her.

"You remember the rules?"

"Yeah, yeah. No lead feet and if I get stopped for speeding, the fine is on me." She grabbed the keys and got in, tossing her handbag onto the back ledge before putting the key in the ignition and turning it on.

"Don't you love the sound of that engine?"

She laughed. "Yes, I guess I do."

"Easy, Andretti. She has a little more pickup than your SUV," he reminded her.

"Don't I know it." She was still grinning as she turned onto the road.

T.J. adjusted his seat, moving it back to make room for his legs, content to let her drive, pleased to have given her so much to smile about. She was a cautious driver — he'd discovered that the other day when he'd let her take the sports car for a short drive — but she clearly was having fun behind the wheel. He leaned back against the headrest and watched the countryside roll by.

They drove past farm after farm — from the most modern-equipped to the Amish and Mennonite homesteads — past ponds where great blue herons fed and one where a lone swan was curled upon the bank. The drive was restful, the airflow through the front seat making it too difficult to carry on a conversation. They rode mostly in silence, but neither appeared to care.

"This is it." Lorna slowed at the first red light on the outskirts of Elk Run, a small town just southeast of Lancaster. The office of the New Security Insurance Agency was located in the brick strip mall to their right. The light changed to green, and she made the turn into the parking lot. There was a space right in front of the storefront with Dustin Lafferty's name on the door, so she parked and turned off the engine.

"That was so much fun." She handed T.J. the keys. "I felt as if I were flying."

"Actually, you *were* flying there for a while." He took the keys and unhooked his seat belt. "Fortunately, no one seemed to notice except me."

"I tried to keep the speed down," she said as they got out of the car. "It's just so hard to drive slowly when you get behind that wheel."

"Well, shall we go in and see which version of the truth Mr. Lafferty has for us?" T.J. dropped the keys into his pants pocket and held the door to the office open for her.

"Sounds as if he already has one strike against him."

335

"He does. We know he must have been lying about having seen Billie and Jason arguing after he dropped Jason off that night, because we've already established he couldn't have seen into the house if he'd stayed in his car. I can't think of one good reason to lie about something like that. So yes, I'm going into this interview with a healthy bit of skepticism. Let's see what develops while we're here."

They stepped inside and were greeted by a young woman wearing a knee-length skirt and a short-sleeved sweater over her T-shirt. The air-conditioning in the room was apparently set to frigid, and Lorna wondered how the receptionist managed to avoid frostbite.

Dustin Lafferty heard them enter, and came out of his office to greet them. In his early forties, he had the beginnings of a bit of a paunch around the middle and thinning dark brown hair styled in what came dangerously close to a comb-over.

"Well, Lorna, I don't think I've seen you since you were maybe in junior high. You've changed a lot since then," Dustin told her as he shook her hand. "And you're Mr. Dawson."

"T.J."

"Right. Come on in." He waved them

into his office. "Charlotte, hold my calls, and see if you can bring some iced tea in for us."

He closed the door, not bothering to wait for her response.

"So, you want to talk about the Eagans." Dustin held a chair out for Lorna and indicated to T.J. to take the side chair. "I heard about all those bodies they're finding out there on your farm. Or should I say, The Body Farm?"

Lorna visibly winced.

Dustin addressed T.J. "You're working as a consultant for the FBI, huh?"

I am?

Before T.J. could respond, Dustin went on.

"Lorna told me all about it. I thought about joining the FBI when I was younger, but I kept putting it off. You know what the cutoff age is for new agents?"

"Last I heard, it was thirty-seven," T.J. told him.

Dustin snapped his fingers. "Damn. I missed it."

He folded his hands on the desk in front of him and looked at T.J.

"So. What do you want to know? Where do we start?"

"Let's start with Melinda Eagan," T.J.

said, jumping right into the questioning. "You were around the night she went missing, from what I understand."

"That's right. I stopped at Matt Conrad's on my way home from school."

"Do you remember what time that was?"

"Must have been around six. It was already getting dark out."

"You were just on your way home from school at six?"

"Detention." Dustin smiled. "I got a lot of that back in those days. I know you'll find this hard to believe, Agent Dawson . . ."

"Please, it's T.J. I'm not —"

". . . but I used to have a problem with my mouth. Just couldn't keep it shut."

"Really." T.J. stared at him.

"God's truth. Anyway, since I was already late getting home, I stopped at Matt's to see what the guys were doing. See if I could bum a smoke."

"Who was there when you arrived at Matt's?"

"Oh, let's see. Matt, of course. Fritz Keeler and his younger brother, Mike. They were getting ready to leave, but then Jason came back and asked if anyone had seen his sister, and none of us had, so he asked if we'd help look for her. So, sure, we did. We went all through that field. Didn't find her, though. Not that night, not any night."

"Did you look for her after that night?"

"Not really. She was just gone."

"Any thoughts on what might have happened to her?"

"Not a clue."

"Are you sure both Keeler boys were there when you arrived?"

"Absolutely. They were getting ready to leave."

"Let's jump ahead a few weeks, to the night Jason disappeared."

"Night he was *murdered,* you mean."

"We don't have any proof that he was killed that night."

"Hey, there's no way anyone would have held him for a day or something, and then killed him. Someone like Jason, if you're going to kill him, you're going to have to kill him fast. He was one tough mother." He glanced at Lorna. "Sorry, Lorna. He was one tough guy."

"You were all drinking beer at your house."

"We started out at my house, later on that night we went out to White Marsh Park."

"You, Matt, Fritz, Jason, Mike." T.J. ticked off the names.

"Mike?" Dustin frowned. "I don't remember that Mike was there, but maybe."

He thought for another minute before saying, "I don't remember about that."

"You drank for a while and then drove everyone home."

"Right. I was the only one with a license that year. I think Fritz might have already been sixteen. With Mr. Keeler being dead, Fritz could've gotten a hardship license, but his mother wouldn't let him get his license right away." He rolled his eyes. "What a piece of work she was. A miracle either of them turned out normal. If you think Fritz is normal, that is."

Lorna spoke up for the first time. "What's that supposed to mean?"

"You know." Dustin paused while his receptionist came in with a pitcher of iced tea and three glasses. The room fell very silent while she poured and distributed the drinks.

"Anything else?" she asked Dustin.

"Not right now, thanks," he told her. After she closed the door behind her, he said to Lorna, "Well, you know that Fritz is gay, right? I mean, everyone in Callen knows that, right?"

"No, I didn't know."

"Not that I care," Dustin was quick to

340

assure her. " 'Course, back then, when we were kids, none of us had any idea. But everyone knows how his mother bullied him and Mike. It never seemed to affect Mike so much, he was always such a man's man, you know? Aggressive, cocky. Big football star, wrestler. Bigger personality. He played in college, you know that? Over at West Chester. Then he got hurt — back injury? Shoulder? Don't remember. Anyway, he couldn't play anymore and he dropped out, married Sarah. Guess the rest is history, right?"

"But you think he wasn't there that night at your house?" T.J. tried to steer the conversation back on course.

"I think I would remember if he had been, but I just don't. Sorry."

"The police report says that after you dropped Jason off at home, you saw him go into the house, heard his mother yelling at him."

"I guess, if that's what it says." Dustin picked up his glass and drank.

"Well, did you see him go into the house?" T.J. pressed.

"I must have. Otherwise, why would I say . . . ?" Dustin took another drink, then set the glass on the desk. "All right, I saw him go up to the house. I saw him go around to the porch as I was pulling away. That's all I really saw."

"The statement you gave to the police says otherwise," T.J. reminded him.

"I don't remember exactly what I told the police." His face began to flush.

"Want me to remind you?"

Dustin shook his head. "No. I guess I must have exaggerated a little bit, maybe said I saw more than I did."

"Why would you do that?" Lorna asked.

"I don't know. I guess . . ." He shrugged. "I guess because it made me look important, you know? Like I was there or something. I can't explain it now. I was just a kid then. I never thought it would matter much."

He paused, then asked, "Does it matter much?"

"Only to make me wonder if you lied about anything else," T.J. told him.

"No, I swear. Everything else is the truth." Dustin looked from Lorna to T.J.

"Did it ever occur to you to go back to the police and change your statement?" Lorna asked.

"A couple of times I thought about it, but it didn't seem to matter. Jason never came back. After awhile people stopped talking about it. We all just figured he'd run away, maybe the sister, too." Dustin shrugged. "That's what I woulda done, if I'd had a mother like that. I'd have run away and never looked back."

"So what do you think?" Lorna said when they were back in the car, T.J. driving.

"I think Dustin reminds me of all the worst used-car salesmen I've ever known."

Lorna nodded. "It's the hair. Not a good look."

T.J. laughed and drove out of the parking lot and stopped at the light.

"It wasn't a complete waste of time, though. We came away with two possible suspects," he said.

"We did?" She frowned. "What suspects?"

"The Keeler boys."

"How do you figure?"

"Let's start with Mike. He's not telling the truth about where he was the night Jason disappeared. We've had three versions now, and two of them say he wasn't out with the other guys. But he tells the story as if he were. Why? Maybe because he doesn't want us to know where he really was that night."

"Maybe Fritz and Dustin just don't remember it clearly. It was a long time ago, and they were drinking."

"They seem to remember the other details well enough. And I'm not sure I understand where Mike was when Melinda went missing. He says he was at Matt's the whole time, but no one's backing him up."

"Again, it was a long time ago."

"True, but that night turned out to be an event. Something important happened. A child disappeared, they all took part in the search. You remember things like that. My grandmother has days when she can't remember the name of her next-door neighbor, but she can tell you in detail where she was and what she was doing the day President Kennedy was shot. People tend to remember the dramatic times, Lorna. Their friend's younger sister disappearing was such a moment."

"What about Fritz?"

"Well, let's take a look at him. According to Dustin, everyone in Callen knows he's gay — except you, apparently — and we've confirmed that at least three of the nine missing boys were."

"That's not much to go on."

"Agreed. But it's more than we've got on anyone else. Besides, he was around the night Jason disappeared."

"He was home by then."

"Was he? We have only his word for that. Remember, his mother was away that night. Jason had been home for a while, first arguing, then talking with his mother, before he went out that door into the yard. Billie's already told us that. Fritz would've had plenty of time to ride his bike out to the Eagans'."

"But why would he have done that? What would his motive have been?"

"I guess we'll have to ask Fritz. In the meantime, let's have Mitch run a trace, find out where Fritz has been going a couple of days every month over the past few years, and see if any bodies have popped up in his path."

"I don't see it." She shook her head. "Fritz is just too gentle a soul, T.J. I don't think he has an aggressive bone in his body."

"That's what some people said about John Wayne Gacy. And Ted Bundy." He took his phone from his pocket and speed-dialed Mitch's number. "If I learned one thing all those years I was with the Bureau, it's that there's no way of telling what goes on inside the head of another human being. The person who looks craziest might be harmless, and the person you least suspect might be a monster who is capable of things you can't even begin to imagine."

"A monster?" she said softly. "Where did that come from?"

He watched the light change, then made a left onto the two-lane road that would take them back to Callen.

"T.J.?" She reached over and touched his arm. "Where did the monster thing come from?"

"From long ago."

"Do you want to talk about it?"

He drove in silence for almost a mile before replying.

"Not today." He stared at the road straight ahead. "Maybe some other time, but not today . . ."

Nineteen

Mitch was sitting in a rocking chair on the front porch, feet crossed at the ankle and resting on the railing, when T.J. and Lorna returned to the farm.

"Hope you don't mind," he called to Lorna after she'd gotten out of the car, "but I needed a little downtime to think a few things over."

"I don't mind at all." She smiled. "*Mi* rocker *es su* rocker."

"*Muchas gracias,*" Mitch said. "Now, Dawson, tell me why, with all the super-duper spy equipment that I know you've purchased over the years, you need the FBI to get telephone information for you."

"I sold it all when I sold the business."

"You sold all your toys?" Mitch's eyebrows rose.

"Every last one of them."

"That's too bad." Mitch shook his head. "And damned poor planning on your part."

"Hey, I was retiring and the buyer made an offer, lock, stock, and barrel. My partner said to sell it all, so we did." T.J.

stood on the grass with his arms folded over his chest. "Are you going to tell me what you came up with?"

"A name, dates. A phone number. The usual."

"Are you going to make me beg?"

"Nah." Mitch opened the briefcase that sat at his feet and handed T.J. a folder. "Name, Claude Raymond Fleming."

He looked at Lorna. "That name ring a bell?"

"No." She shook her head.

"Claude Raymond lives on Michigan's Upper Peninsula. I have someone checking him out as we speak."

"Maybe it's just a coincidence?" Lorna frowned. "Maybe the call had nothing to do with Melinda after all. I guess that would have been too good to be true."

"We'll see what turns up. According to the records, it's a number Danielle hadn't called in the past four years, so that right there makes me curious. That she'd be dialing even as you're leaving. Seems as if she was telling someone something they needed to know right away, doesn't it?" Mitch turned to T.J. "So how'd it go with you today, Dawson?"

"It went." T.J. sat on the top step and leaned against the support pillar.

Lorna unlocked the front door. "I'll be back out in a few. I want to see if I have a message from any of my clients."

"Take your time," T.J. told her. "I expect we'll still be here when you're finished."

"You learn anything from . . . which one did you see today?" Mitch asked.

"Dustin Lafferty. The one who drove Jason home the night he disappeared. About the only thing I learned was that he admitted he lied about having seen Jason go into the house that night."

"Why would he have lied about that?"

"Seems he thought it would make him look important. He wanted people to think he knew something no one else knew."

Mitch nodded. "I hate it when that happens."

"And he also told us that Fritz Keeler is gay."

"Well, there's something." Mitch stopped rocking. "Gay victims, a gay perp could make sense. Local guy, just like we thought. Maybe I should have a chat with him. Tell me, what do your instincts say?"

T.J. shrugged. "I don't have any."

"That's bullshit, Dawson."

"Let's just look at the facts as we know them, okay, and leave it at that."

"In that case, I'd say it's time for me to bring in Fritz."

"Then do it."

"You don't think it's him," Mitch said flatly. "I can tell by the look on your face. Will you please tell me what you're thinking?"

"I'm thinking that it's one of three guys — Fritz, Mike, or Dustin. I'm thinking maybe you should run a trace on all three of them, see if there are any priors of any sort. But you should see if there are any registered sex offenders in the area. See if there are any other viable suspects."

"I've done all that. I've run traces on everyone remotely connected to Jason Eagan, including the chief of police, who, you might be interested in knowing, at one time had a clandestine relationship with Dustin Lafferty's mother. It ended a few years ago, but I thought I'd pass that on. None of the others have arrests for any sex crimes — not even a peeper among them — but Mike Keeler has had a few assault charges against him. Never convicted, charges were always dropped. Mostly bar fights. Walker also told me Mike had been stopped a few times for driving without a license before he turned sixteen, but it was no big deal. Apparently all the boys around here did that."

"Dustin said Mike had an aggressive streak."

Mitch lowered his feet and leaned forward in the chair to face T.J. "Knowing what you know about the players you've been talking to, I want your gut reaction, T.J. I need it. You may not trust yourself anymore, but I still do."

"That's real nice of you, Mitch," T.J said drily. "Nice try."

"Will you knock it off?" Mitch's jaw tightened. "You gonna carry that cross for the rest of your life? Everyone makes mistakes."

"Everyone's mistakes don't cost innocent people their lives," T.J. snapped.

"Sometimes they do. Look, I admit, what happened in Georgia, that was horrendous. No getting around it. And I can understand why you would want to walk away, why you'd never want to put yourself in that position again. I might look at things that way myself, for a while. But it wasn't your fault, what happened. It was Teddy Kershaw's fault those people died. I think you've repented for his sins long enough, don't you?"

"Ask those kids in Georgia whose mothers Kershaw killed, the husbands who

351

lost their wives. The parents who will never see their daughters again." T.J.'s eyes clouded. "Ask them if they think I should be let off the hook."

"You have to let it go, buddy." Mitch shook his head. "You just have to let it go."

When T.J. didn't respond, Mitch said, "So what are you going to do with the rest of your life?"

"I'll think of something."

"Sorry I took so long." Lorna opened the screen door and stepped out onto the porch. "I got tied up with emails. I've gotten behind in my work this week. I'm afraid I have a lot to catch up on."

"Well, I'll be out of your hair for a few days," T.J. told her. "There are a few things I need to take care of, too."

"If everyone is bailing on me, you can at least give me your impressions before I leave," Mitch said.

"I don't know," Lorna said. "I'm not the professional here. Ask T.J. He did almost all of the talking, anyway. Which he should have," she hastened to add, "since I'm not a detective."

"I don't have a favorite." T.J. shook his head, determined to remain uncommitted.

"Well, in that case, I think I'll start with Fritz and Mike, move on to Dustin. Not that I think they'll tell me anything they didn't tell you, but I want it all on the record."

"Were you able to find a listing for Matt Conrad?"

"No. But I did learn he's been on the West Coast for the past nine years or so," Mitch told them.

"I thought he was out near Reading?" Lorna recalled.

"That was apparently very old information. I talked to Chief Walker earlier today, just wanted him to be aware of our thoughts about the local 'boys,' and he tracked Matt through a cousin who still lives nearby," Mitch said. "If we go with our theory, that the killer has remained local to stay near his kills, I think we can cross him off the list, but I'll have someone in the San Diego office pay him a visit. I don't expect it to pan out, though. No, I'm sticking with one of the Keelers or Lafferty for now." He rocked for a moment, then said, "Maybe we want a warrant for that big old house Fritz is living in. Might be some souvenirs there."

"I don't see Fritz as your killer." The words were out of T.J.'s mouth almost before he realized he'd spoken.

"Really. Who do you see?"

"I don't see anyone in particular. He just doesn't fit . . ." T.J. stopped in mid-sentence.

"He doesn't fit the profile? Why not? He's gay, like three victims were. He was there both nights. He grew up around here, might very well have frequented the Purple Pheasant. I will definitely ask him about that. And he's stayed close to home, close to the remains, just like we figured the killer might do." Mitch finished the thought. "If he doesn't fit the profile, who does?"

"I'll see you in a few days, Lorna." T.J. stood, choosing to ignore Mitch's question. "Call me if you need anything. I'll have my cell with me."

"Thanks." She watched him walk to his car and get in. He turned the car around and waved as he drove past the porch.

"Was it something I said?" Lorna asked as his taillights disappeared at the end of the drive.

"No, it was something I said." Mitch sounded regretful. "I should learn to keep my mouth shut. Learn to take no for an answer."

"What was the question?"

"The Bureau would love to have T.J. back. He doesn't want to come. I should just shut up and let the man live his life."

"Why do you make such an issue of it? Why don't you drop it?"

"That's exactly what I should do. And I will, I guess. I just remember how good he was, how clever at picking apart people's stories and their personalities. I hate to see such talent go to waste. Especially when he loved it so much."

"He's a big boy. He'll do what's best for himself. If he loves it that much, he'll have to decide on his own to go back. If he doesn't, it means he really doesn't want the job."

"Maybe you're right." Mitch got out of the chair. "I should be going, too. I'll have a lot to do tomorrow."

"Can you let me know if anything happens?"

"Sure. Thanks for the loan of the porch."

"Anytime."

Lorna watched Mitch drive away, much as she'd watched T.J. leave. She leaned over the porch rail for a few minutes and watched the last of the season's fireflies dot the growing blackness out near the field. The heavy scent from the orchard reminded her that autumn was closing in. She was about to go inside when headlights turned into the driveway. She watched the police cruiser pull to a stop.

"Lorna," Chief Walker greeted her curtly as he got out of the car.

"Hello, Chief." She stood her ground on the porch.

"I just wanted to give you a heads-up." He stood at the end of the brick walk, hands on his hips, looking more than a little formidable. "The DA's dropping the charges against Billie Eagan. While I don't know that I totally agree, the preliminary hearing was set for Wednesday, and he doesn't feel he has enough evidence to make it through right now. Doesn't mean he can't refile, but for now Billie's off the hook. I thought you should know."

"Thank you. I appreciate that. And Billie knows this?"

"Just stopped out to tell her myself." He looked like he wanted to say more on that subject but apparently decided against it.

Instead, he asked, "Any idea where the FBI fellow went when he left here? Guess I just missed him, eh?" he said, as if to let Lorna know that he knew she was harboring the enemy.

"I didn't ask where he was going."

"Well, I guess I can call his cell phone," Walker grumbled, clearly unhappy to have to deal with Mitch in any capacity. "I have to tell you, I for one am not happy to have him around. This is my town, my investigation. Nothing would please me more than to see him leave. You can go 'head and tell him that, as you're so buddy-buddy."

"He's a friend of a friend. But maybe in the long run, it will work to your benefit, having the FBI involved."

"How do you figure that?"

"Supposing it turns out that someone local is involved. You want to be the one slapping the cuffs on?"

He started to answer, then stopped, as if mulling over what she had said.

He shrugged. "Depends on the local, I guess."

"Well, I overheard Agent Peyton tell someone on his cell phone that he's looking strongly at all the boys — men now — who were around both nights the Eagan kids disappeared." No tales out of school here. She knew Mitch had already had this conversation with Walker. "You know all those families — the Keelers, the Conrads. Oh, and the Laffertys."

She paused to let that last name sink in, then continued.

"You know, I saw that piece on the news the other day, about how Melinda's disappearance was your first big case after joining the force, and how ironic it was that the case has resurfaced now that you're chief, and how nice it would be, with you getting ready to retire this year, to have this case off the books. I was thinking how tough it must be, with a police force the size of ours, to keep the investigation going, while at the same time keeping up with all the normal duties the force is responsible for."

"It's been a bitch. What's your point?"

"Well, my point is, with the FBI working with you, they can take a lot of the heat off your department. Plus, they have resources that the Callen PD probably doesn't have, right?"

"True enough." His expression never changed even as he nodded in agreement.

"So if they can help you solve the case, it will only be to your advantage. Especially if someone from Callen turns out to be a suspect, someone whose family you know." She looked at him meaningfully to let it sink in — *Dustin Lafferty* — and he got the message. She could almost hear the explanation he'd be offering. *Now, Nancy, you know I would never have called your boy in for questioning, but the FBI . . .*

"Seems to me it's a win-win situation

for you," Lorna said.

"Seems like it's a colossal pain in the ass, all the way around. I wish to God none of this had ever happened."

"There are four — maybe more — young men who'd no doubt share that same wish, Chief."

"I'll keep you informed, Lorna," he said as he walked back to his car.

"Thanks, Chief. I'd appreciate it." She went as far as the end of the walk. "Oh, by the way, Chief? Does the name Claude Raymond Fleming mean anything to you?"

He paused in mid-stride, then turned around.

"Where'd you come up with that name?"

"I just heard it."

He scratched the back of his head. "It rings a bell, but I don't know why. Not a name I've heard recently, but it has a familiar sound."

"Was it someone local?"

"I don't recall."

"If you remember where you heard it, would you let me know?"

"Sure." He got into the car and slammed the door. It echoed across the quiet yard between the house and the trees.

She waved as he passed by and wasn't particularly surprised when he failed to wave back. She stood out in the drive for a few minutes, watching the stars fight their way through the haze of clouds, then went inside the house. In the dining room, she sat at her laptop and prepared the accounts payable and receivable reports for several clients and transmitted them via email. She'd gotten halfway through a profit-and-loss statement when she realized she was close to falling asleep at the table. She saved her work, turned off the computer, and locked up the house.

Lorna made her way upstairs, mentally compiling a list of things to do in the morning. Finish the P&L for her client, make a run to the supermarket — and oh, yes, take her mother's ashes down to the pond.

Lorna was still drying her hair with a towel when the phone rang. The clock on her bedside table read eleven-thirty. She reached across the bed to grab the receiver.

"Hello?"

"Lori? It's Rob." He cleared his throat. "Is this too late to call?"

"No, no. I just got out of the shower. It's fine, Robbie," she assured him, wondering what was up. Rob never called. "How are you? Is everything all right?"

"Sure. Fine. Listen, I keep seeing all this stuff on the news out here, about this Body Farm thing. It's our farm, right?" His voice held a hint of the incredulous. "It seems so surreal."

"Tell me about it. And yes, it's our farm, and surreal is exactly right. Law enforcement agencies — Callen PD, the county detectives, the FBI — everywhere you look, media vans parked all along the roadway. Mostly I ignore them, but I know they're there. And I've stopped watching the news. I don't want to see any more."

"Well, these guys — these dead guys — they have any idea who killed them?"

"The FBI thinks it's someone local, someone who lived here then who still lives here now. I don't suppose I'm giving away any secrets by telling you they're concentrating on the guys who were around the nights Melinda and Jason disappeared."

"Like who?"

"Like the Keelers, like Dustin Lafferty."

"Oh, good." He added somewhat hastily, "Makes sense that they'd suspect the guys who were around those nights. Yeah, that makes sense."

"It's a starting point."

"One thing the media hasn't said much

about is Melinda. Do the police believe she was killed by the same person who killed all those guys?"

"I don't think anyone really knows right now what happened to Mellie. No body's been discovered, but then again, there's a lot more to dig up in the field. And why someone who seems fixated on boys of a certain age would want to kill a nine-year-old girl, that doesn't really add up."

"Unless she saw something the killer didn't want her to see," Rob said softly.

The hair on the back of Lorna's neck rose.

"Rob, what do you think she might have seen?"

"Nothing. I mean, I don't have anything in mind. I don't know why I said that." His laugh sounded tinny, false. "It was just a thought. Anyway, the real reason I called was to apologize. I was mean to you when you called Monday. I'm sorry."

"Apology accepted. I pretty much forgot about it, to tell you the truth. I figured I woke you out of a sound sleep and chalked it up to that."

"Thanks, Lorna. You always were the best."

"Well, if not the best, then a damned close second."

He laughed, and it sounded more natural this time. "Gran used to say that all the time."

"She did."

"How are you moving along with the sale of the house?"

"I'm not." She hastened to add, "But I will be. As soon as I can. Things have been a little hectic here, and with all the notoriety surrounding the property, I don't know that this is the best time to put it on the market. We might get a better price if we wait."

"I guess a real estate person could give you a better idea of that. When you can get to it. I know you have your business to take care of, too. I guess Andrea and I are lucky that you're there to handle all of this for us. I don't think I thanked you, but I'm thanking you now."

"I appreciate that, Rob. In the meantime, if you need cash, you can always borrow from Mom's savings, then pay the account back after the property is sold."

"That would be great, Lori. I could use a little help right now. I'm starting a new job in another week, a new restaurant down near Brentwood, but in the meantime, I've got some bills backed up."

"Give me your account number and I'll

have the bank make a wire transfer."

He put the phone down while he looked for his banking information, then gave her what she'd need.

"I really appreciate this, Lori. I really do." He paused, then asked, "But you'll tell me when they make an arrest, right? You'll let me know when this is over?"

"Of course I will," she assured him. "Rob, are you sure there isn't something bothering you?"

"Positive. Look, you just keep me up-to-date with what's happening out there," he said, suddenly his old self again. "You'll send me some money, and I'll let you get some sleep. Love you, Lori."

"Love you, too, Rob." The phone went dead in her hand, and as she hung up, Lorna couldn't help but wonder what that call had *really* been about.

Twenty

For Lorna, the next several days passed in a blur of spreadsheets and profit-and-loss analyses, bank reconciliations, and conference calls. She'd managed a quick trip to her favorite Amish farm stand, where she picked up tomatoes, corn, peaches, eggs, and green beans. She bought extras of everything and packed several bags of produce to drop off at the Eagans', where they toasted Billie's status as a free woman with glasses of iced herbal tea.

For the first time in a week, she'd been grateful to have the house to herself and the time to devote to her business. Her involvement in the investigation had been engrossing, in a macabre way. For a few days, she'd gotten to be Nancy Drew. But however much she'd enjoyed her stint as an amateur detective, she had a business to run, and needed to refocus on the needs of her clients. She'd spent years building her reputation and expanding her client base. She couldn't let it go untended, as appealing as her chance to play Miss Marple had been.

And it *had* been appealing. Especially partnering, however briefly, with T.J. She smiled to herself as she poured water into the coffee pot. Now, that had been a fantasy fulfilled. Zipping around country roads in that sexy little sports car in the company of a totally hunky PI — it was the stuff of daydreams. And if she felt a little like Mrs. Walter Mitty, who could blame her?

But now it was time to return her focus to reality. She had work to do, a property to sell. A life to get back to.

She poured herself a cup of coffee and took it into the dining room, where she emailed a client to confirm a meeting he'd requested for the end of September. She paused to wonder where she'd be then. Would she still be here, in Callen, or would she have returned to Woodboro? So much depended on the speed with which the case was resolved, and how much all the publicity hurt her chances of getting a good price for the farm.

Her memo and her coffee both finished, she hit the *Send* button on her email and walked to the window. Stretching out the kinks from having sat too long in one position, she raised the window sash to let in the fresh morning breeze. A front that had

366

blown in this weekend had brought cooler air and lower humidity. She filled her lungs, and decided to take a walk outside. A little exercise in mid-morning was a good thing, she reminded herself as she grabbed her running shoes and unlocked the back door.

The view over the back field was a familiar one. Delicate Queen Anne's lace and sturdy cornflowers had turned the field into a study in white and blue, with a few wild black-eyed Susans thrown in for accent. The corn Gil Compton had planted in the far field was well over six feet tall, and Lorna wondered when the police would let him on the property with his tractor to harvest it.

She sat on the bottom step and exchanged her flip-flops for the Nikes. She'd just finished tying them when she remembered she'd brought the second of her mother's urns downstairs on Saturday to take it to the pond, but hadn't gotten there yet because of the rain. Today would be the day. She went back inside and picked up the urn, locked the door behind her, and set out for the pond.

Palmer's Pond, as locals still referred to it, had at one time been a watering hole for the cattle, sheep, and horses that the earliest Palmers had raised. When cash crops like corn and wheat became more profitable, the pond was marked strictly for swimming and fishing. Mary Beth had told Lorna of many lazy summer days spent reading a favorite book on the banks, floating along mindlessly in a rowboat, and taking a dip with her friends to cool off from the heat. As much as her mother had loved the pond, it had come as no real surprise to Lorna that Mary Beth would want some bit of herself to remain there.

Lorna tucked the urn under one arm and trudged along the edge of the field until she reached the family graveyard. She walked around the fence and down the slight incline to the pond. The rowboat was still tied up where her mother had left it two years ago, and Lorna held on to its rope and pushed it out into the shallow water to see if it leaked. When it appeared to be watertight, she pulled it back to shore, placed the urn on the bottom of the boat, and climbed in. With the single oar that rested across the seat, she pushed off from the edge, and finding one oar a difficult steer, decided to simply let the boat drift aimlessly. Once it arrived near the middle of the pond, she removed the lid from the urn and held it over the side of the boat and tilted it slightly. Ashes sprinkled out in a thin shower of gray and floated singularly and in clusters on the rippled surface.

When the canister was empty, she filled it with water, replaced the top, and dropped it into the dark water.

"As you wished, Mom," Lorna said. "Two down, one to go."

She lowered herself to the bottom of the small boat, leaned back against the wooden seat, her hands locked behind her head, and looked up to watch the clouds gather into shapes. A dog morphed into a large bird. A tree changed before her eyes into a castle with three turrets. A sailboat fashioned itself into a snake. She closed her eyes, letting the gentle motion of the boat rock her to sleep, and take her where it would.

The bang of the boat against something solid woke her, and she sat up with a start. She'd drifted across the pond and struck the last remaining pile from the old dock. She sat up and grabbed hold of the rope that hung from its side, then pulled the rowboat to shore. Once on land, she tied the small craft to the piling and got out. Her mission completed, her break over, she started up the rise to return to the house.

At the top of the rise stood Fritz Keeler.

She startled when she saw him. "Oh. Hey."

"Hey, yourself." He was smiling and holding a huge bouquet of roses. "I knew you had to be here someplace. I stopped at the house and saw your car, but no one answered the door, so I thought maybe you were out for a walk. I'd been just about everywhere else. This was my last stop."

He held out the roses. "I was afraid I'd have to take these back with me. They're going to start to wilt pretty soon, without water."

"They're lovely, Fritz. Thank you." She reached for the flowers. Their scents mixed, spicy and floral, and she inhaled deeply. "Simply beautiful. Your mother would be proud of your green thumb."

"And not much more, I'm afraid." He shoved his hands into the pockets of his jeans. "That FBI agent just left my house. He thinks I had something to do with those killings out here. I can't believe anyone would think I could . . ." He shook his head. "Anyway, he had some other agents come and they searched my house and took stuff — I don't even know what all they took, they were making a list of items."

"They had a warrant?"

"No. He asked if they could search the house and I said sure. I have nothing to hide. What's the worst they could find? The love letters my dad sent my mother from Vietnam?"

He shook his head again, almost imperceptibly this time, and looked beyond her. "I've never been suspected of any crime in my life, Lorna. The thought that anyone could believe I would hurt someone else is killing me. I don't know what to do." He tried to laugh. "So, of course, when in doubt, take flowers to a pretty lady. Take flowers to a friend."

"I am your friend, Fritz." She held out her hand, and when he took it, his own was shaking. "Let's walk back to the house, and you can tell me what happened."

"The doorbell rang and this tall guy was standing there and he asked me if I was Francis Keeler and I said I was. He introduced himself as an FBI special agent and asked if he could come in." Fritz shrugged. "What do you say? So I let him in. And he started asking me questions. A lot of questions."

"Such as?"

"Such as, did I ever hear of a gay bar outside of Wilmington called the Purple

Pheasant." His face looked ashen. "Well, so much for my efforts to remain safely in the closet, where I've been all my life."

"Fritz, you know, it's a different world than it was when we were kids. People are more accepting now —"

He held up one hand. "People in general, yes. People who are members of your own family, not necessarily."

"You mean Mike?"

Fritz nodded. "And my mother. I tried years ago — many years ago now — to talk to Mom about this, but she went absolutely insane. To be *that way* is an abomination, she said, how could I humiliate her by being *that way*. She made me promise that no one in Callen would ever know, and that I would do my best to make it go away." He laughed. "Can you imagine? 'Francis, make it go away. We will not speak of it again, but you must make it stop.' "

"I'm so sorry." Lorna placed a hand on his arm for comfort.

"Oh, that's not even the best part. My brother had come into the house and made the mistake of walking through the room at that moment, and she turned on him. 'Don't you ever be what he is, Michael. Promise me. Swear to me you will never be what he is.' "

Fritz's eyes filled with tears.

"As if *what I was* was something more horrible than she could bear." Fritz visibly shivered. "That was the single worst moment of my life."

"How old were you then?"

"Young. Fourteen, fifteen, maybe."

"And yet you stayed with her, took care of her, all those years."

"It was never discussed after that day. Never. And, she was, after all, my mother."

"I wish for your sake she'd given you the respect you gave her."

"That's very sweet, very good of you."

"What did Mike say?"

"Nothing."

"Nothing? He walks in on an argument like that and says nothing?"

"I guess he was as humiliated as I was, as my mother was. I always look back on that as a bad day for everyone, all the way around."

"Did you tell this to the FBI agent?"

"No." He shook his head. "He wasn't interested in family dynamics. He wanted to search my house, and he wanted to know about the nights the Eagan kids disappeared and where I go when I leave Callen every other week. Like in case I'm running around the country killing young gay men and burying them in the first available field or woods I can find."

"Where *do* you go?" she heard herself ask, at the same time wondering about the wisdom of permitting the authorities carte blanche to look through your belongings.

"I go to St. Louis. I have a house there, which I share with the same man I've shared it with for almost sixteen years. He has a florist business there — a family business he took over about twenty years ago — and I have my business here. So we have our separate lives and our shared life. It may not work for everyone, but it works for us."

"He never comes here?"

"Are you crazy?" Fritz laughed. "My mother would rise from the dead and raise holy hell. No, we keep it this way. I'm more comfortable, not dealing with that here in Callen. I'm afraid I'm really quite a coward, Lorna." He sighed heavily. "Though I suppose those days of anonymity are over now. I'm sure my brother will have plenty to say, once this gets out."

"I'd expect Mike to be more understanding. You're his brother."

"He had the fear of God put into him by the very best of 'em. My mother could scare the pants off anyone. Mike hasn't forgotten what she said, what she made him promise. In return, he made me promise to keep that part of my life to myself. And I always have."

"I wish I could say something that would make you feel better."

"Just you listening without censure makes me feel better, Lorna. You really are a friend."

They reached the barn, and turned the corner. In the middle of the drive were two black-and-white patrol cars, along with Chief Walker's vehicle.

"Uh-oh," Fritz whispered.

"Hey, Fritz," Chief Walker called out, then to acknowledge her presence, added, "Lorna."

"Chief Walker. Long time no see." Fritz tried to appear unconcerned that the police had apparently followed him to the farmhouse.

"I need you to come down to the station with me, Fritz," Chief Walker said. "There are a few items that were taken from your attic that we need to talk about."

Fritz frowned. "What kind of items?"

"Oh, just some things we're having a hard time identifying. You mind coming with me? I'll have someone drive your car to the station."

"All right." Fritz shrugged, trying to appear nonchalant, though Lorna suspected he was churning inside. "Don't forget to put those roses in water right away, Lorna. And an aspirin in the bottom of the vase will keep them fresh for an extra few days."

"Thanks, Fritz." She watched him walk away with the chief at his side.

"You are one lucky woman." Brad Walker stood behind her, speaking softly.

"What do you mean?" Lorna turned around to face him.

"Let's just say my heart was in my mouth when I drove past here and saw his car in the drive, and then you not answering the door. We were just about to break a window to get inside, when you came down the drive here." He took off his hat and wiped sweat from his forehead. "Thank God we got here when we did."

"Brad, none of this is making any sense."

"It would if you could see what all we took out of his attic." Brad pointed toward Fritz, who was getting into the back of the chief's car. "We've got this case locked, Lorna, no question about it. We got ourselves the killer . . ."

Twenty-one

"Mitch, I can't believe you really think Fritz killed all those boys." The police car carrying Fritz Keeler had not yet made the turn onto Callen Road before Lorna had dialed Mitch's number. "There's no way he could be guilty of this."

"Lorna, calm down." Mitch did his best to soothe her. "And it doesn't matter what I think, or, frankly, what you think. What matters is the evidence. And we found a hell of a lot of evidence in that house." He hesitated a moment before adding, "Lorna, we found a trunk filled with items. In his attic."

"What kind of items?"

"Things that I believe he took from his victims. A key ring, a couple of driver's licenses. A belt buckle. Personal items that represent souvenirs of his kills. Several of the remains found in the field had bits of masking tape clinging to the clothes. We found tape in the trunk in the Keeler attic, and I'd bet my next promotion it will match the tape we found on the victims. Plus rope, a shovel. Everything one might need to tie up and bury a —"

"God, I just can't believe it." Her voice was almost a whisper. "He brought me roses . . . he swore he had nothing to do with this."

"I doubt he'd be confessing right about now. And maybe he was looking for an ally. Maybe he figured you for a supporter."

"You met him, you talked to him. You really think he's capable of these terrible murders?"

"Like I said, it doesn't matter what I think. What matters is the evidence that was found in his house."

"Stop talking like a textbook and tell me what your gut says," she shot back. "Isn't that what you always ask T.J.? 'What does your gut say?' "

Mitch was silent for a moment, then replied, "My gut never talked to me quite the way T.J.'s talks to him. But for the record, between you and me, going only on my personal impression of the man, I never would have pegged Fritz Keeler for this."

Lorna hung up the phone and paced, trying to sort it all out. She was out of her league and she knew it. Finding such evidence in the Keeler home was pretty conclusive, and yet she couldn't reconcile what she knew of Fritz with a ruthless killer.

Though, what *had* she known of Fritz? Did she really know him at all?

All she knew at the moment was that she probably wouldn't have made a good cop. How did one keep one's personal feelings from influencing an investigation? She didn't know if she ever could.

She called T.J. and left a message on his voice mail, and then, because she couldn't think of anything else to do, she called Regan and left a message for her as well. She tried to work for a while but was too distracted. She wondered if Fritz had a lawyer, wondered if the search of his house was legal. She'd seen something on TV once about a search that had been declared unlawful because the police had looked inside dresser drawers to find evidence, and the owner of the property had testified that he had given permission for the cops to "look around," which the judge had deemed to mean items that were in plain sight. Maybe a lawyer would know.

Then again, if Fritz was in fact a killer, why would she *want* to help him?

Her cell phone rang and she jumped on it. She looked at the call number.

"T.J.," she said, relieved.

"Hey, are you all right? Your message sounded a bit jumbled. Want to run through all this for me again?"

She did.

"Does it sound right to you?" she asked after she'd related the events of the entire afternoon. "Did you think it was Fritz?"

"Well, like Mitch said, you have to look at the evidence," he said carefully. "But no. I didn't have that feeling about him. On the surface, he does seem to fit the . . ."

When he paused, Lorna said, "You can say it, T.J. He seems to fit the profile."

"I hate to fall back on that. Profiles can be misleading. You can get way too wrapped up in all that; you can miss other key information if you let yourself believe too much in your own fiction."

"What the hell does that mean?"

"It means that profiling isn't an exact science, but a lot of people think it is. A profile is only as good as the person compiling it, and it's not something that's written on stone tablets. At best, it's a guide. At worst, it can blind you to the truth."

"If you were to work up a profile on this killer, would you have come up with Fritz?"

He fell silent for a long moment.

"Maybe not." He thought for another few seconds. "Probably not."

"Why not?"

"Because I felt all along that the killer was obsessed with hiding, not just hiding his crimes, but hiding who and what he really is." He paused, then added, "If I were to guess, I think the killer picked up these boys, had sex with them, and then killed them. I think he's been repressing his homosexuality for a long time."

"Refusing to admit even to himself that he's gay."

"Exactly. I think the killer is someone who fought long and hard against his feelings, and when he finally gave in to what he wanted, he had to get rid of the evidence. He killed his partners."

"Like a black widow."

"Sort of. But he wants to keep them close to him, he doesn't want to part with them. So he keeps something of them, then buries them someplace nearby. It's enough for him to know that his victims are right there, right down the road."

"If your theory is right, then Fritz can't be the killer. Fritz hasn't repressed the fact that he's gay. He's kept it under wraps here at home, in deference to his family's wishes, but he doesn't deny it and he's had a relationship with the same man for many years. Does that sound like someone who's repressed enough to behave the way you just described?"

"No," T.J. admitted. "When did Fritz discuss this with you?"

"Earlier today. After Mitch questioned him. He brought me some roses from his garden." She bit her bottom lip, thinking, then said, "You don't think he made that up to throw me off, do you?"

"Not unless he thinks like a cop. And he might. Someone who kills over a long period of time has learned how to be cagey. Manipulative. Perhaps he's good at it. There's always the possibility that Fritz is actually a really good manipulator."

She sighed heavily. "Maybe so. Maybe I just don't know him at all."

"Look, I'm a little tied up right now, but as soon as I can break free, I'll head on up there and you and I can talk this through. I'll see you in a while."

Lorna hung up and tried to go back to work, but it was futile. Something was nagging at the back of her brain, and she couldn't keep her mind on the numbers until she remembered what it was. It had to do with her brother. And the reason why he left home as soon as he could, and never came back.

She logged off her computer and went into the kitchen, grabbed a bottle of water from the fridge, and went out the back door. Her mother always said she did some of her best thinking while she was weeding. Lorna figured it was worth a try. Besides, if she was going to scatter the last of her mother's ashes in the garden, as she'd promised, it had better be cleaned up a bit.

She found her gardening gloves on the ground near the gate, where she'd dropped them a few days earlier. She pulled them on and started to work on the nearest of the beds. She weeded through the lilies and around the herbs, all the while trying to put her finger on whatever it was that had been eluding her.

She was halfway through the mint when it came to her.

She stripped off her gloves and tucked them through the pickets on the fence, then took her phone from her pocket and dialed Rob's number. When he didn't answer, she left a message on his voice mail.

"Robbie, it's Lorna. I need you to call me as soon as you get this. It's about what happened to you, years ago, when you were . . . honey, I don't even know how old you were when it happened, but I'm pretty sure something did. I'm talking about Fritz Keeler, Rob. Please give me a call. We need to talk about it."

She hung up and slipped her cell phone into the pocket of her jeans and resumed weeding. She wondered if maybe she shouldn't have left the message; it might upset her brother too much to listen to it. Perhaps she shouldn't have said anything at all. And there was a chance she was wrong. Maybe Robbie hadn't been molested as a boy, maybe there were other reasons why he'd stayed away from home for so long, why he'd sounded relieved when she told him the police were narrowing the suspects to the individuals who'd been around both nights the Eagan kids had disappeared. Could be there was some other explanation, and she'd stuck her foot in it, big-time.

She continued to fret, and even thought of calling back and asking him to ignore the message. Right. As if he could, once he'd listened to it.

The sound of tires on the gravel out front drew her attention to the drive. She walked around the front of the house and watched an unfamiliar car park near the walk. The driver's door opened, and Mike Keeler got out.

"Hey, Mike," she called to him, and felt suddenly tongue-tied. What do you say to a man whose brother has been picked up on suspicion of being a serial killer?

"Hi, Lorna." He walked toward her. "I just heard about what happened here today, and I wanted to stop over and tell you how sorry I am that you got pulled into the middle of it. And how embarrassed I am about . . . well, you know. Everything."

"I wish I could think of something to say to you, Mike. But I can't. And I can't believe that Fritz is guilty."

"I can't believe it, either, but, well, you're his friend, and I'm his brother. Maybe we're prejudiced, you and I. And the police or the FBI must have some pretty strong evidence, to have taken him to the station in the back of a cop car like that. I heard all about it. I was at the store when they took him in, and of course, they had to drive right past the Quik Stop." He paused. "I heard they took some stuff out of the attic, but I don't know what. Did Walker mention, when he was here, what they found?"

"No, but I did hear from the FBI agent who interviewed Fritz at the house this morning. Mitch Peyton is a friend, and he knows that Fritz and I are friends. He said there were a number of items in a trunk. Things that belonged to the victims."

"Is that legal, do you think? To go into someone's house like that, and just take stuff?"

"It is, I suppose, depending if the owner gave permission for the search. There may be some specifics, some technicalities I don't know about, but I think if you give permission, they can search."

"Well, I guess that's that, then, isn't it?" Mike shook his head slowly. "My poor mother must be tossing in her grave right now." He jammed his hands in his pockets. "I can't believe this has been going on all these years and I didn't even have a clue."

"People who have something like that to hide get pretty good at keeping it hidden after awhile. Or so I'm told."

"But all these years . . . all those boys he hurt. All those families . . . God knows how many. It makes me sick just to think about it."

"It makes me sick, too." She swallowed hard. "Mike, he might have molested my brother, Rob, at some point."

"What?"

"I think the reason Rob left home as soon as he graduated from high school, and never came back, is because something happened to him here. I can't think of anything else that would have traumatized him so."

"Did he tell you that Fritz . . . ?" Mike asked slowly.

"No. I called him earlier to discuss it with him, but I had to leave a message."

"You left him voice mail asking him if my brother molested him?"

"Yeah. That might not have been a good thing, huh?" She grimaced. "I've been questioning whether I should have done it since the second I hung up. Think it was a mistake?"

"The biggest mistake you ever made."

She looked at him quizzically.

"You should have kept it to yourself, Lorna. Whatever it was you thought might have happened to your brother, you just should have left it alone."

In her pocket, her phone began to ring.

"Don't answer it," Mike told her.

She took the phone from her pocket and glanced at the number. "It's Rob."

"Don't. Answer. It." He reached for the phone and took it from her hand, tossed it into the grass.

She stared at him for a long time, as it all began to sink in.

"You," she said softly. "It was you. Not Fritz."

"Hell of a time to figure it out, when none of your law buddies are here. Sorry, Lorna, but you are now officially a liability." He took her by the arm, not forcefully, but firmly, and turned her in the direction of the barn.

Behind her, in the grass, her cell phone began to ring again.

Was it Rob calling back? T.J.? Regan?

It occurred to her that she would probably never know. There was no way Mike was going to let her live, knowing what she now knew.

"You're forgetting, Rob knows it's you, not Fritz." She struggled to break free, and he tightened his hold on her arm. "If something happens to me, he'll know, and he'll tell."

Mike's laughter was harsh and loud.

"First, they're going to have to find you. And that might take some time. Second, Rob's not telling anyone anything. Ever. I made sure of that years ago." He was still laughing as he dragged her into the barn. "Yeah, I tried out your brother. And he should have ended up like the rest of them, in the back woods. But he got away from me. Imagine that? That skinny little runt.

Well, I told him what I'd do if he ever — I mean *ever* — told anyone what I'd done. Obviously, he never did, if you're just figuring it out now."

"What did you threaten him with?"

"I told him I'd kill everyone in his family."

"I can't imagine he'd have believed you had that kind of power."

"Oh, he believed it." He laughed again. "Your father made certain of that."

"What does my father have to do with this?"

"He made me look like the most powerful man in the world." He leaned down and whispered, "He died two days later."

Lorna felt as if the wind had been knocked from her lungs.

"He died of a heart attack."

"Yeah. Pretty good timing, wouldn't you say?" Mike pushed her through the barn door and took the gun from his pocket. "Unfortunately, I can't rely on lightning striking again, so I'm going to have to make my own luck."

"You killed Jason."

"Stupid-shit Jason, yeah, I killed him." He shook his head. "Who would have thought he'd be up at that hour of the morning? And with his mother, no less?

Damned bad luck on his part, looking out the window when he did."

"He saw you with someone."

"Unfortunately, yes, he did." Mike spoke calmly, as if they were discussing the weather. "He came running out of that house, yelling at me, and what the hell else could I do? I dropped what I was carrying and let him chase me into the field, away from the house. I didn't need a witness."

"He saw you with one of your victims."

"Well, the sky didn't open and drop them into the woods, Lorna. They had to get there somehow." He rolled his eyes. "Yes, I was carrying someone. And yes, he was already dead when Jason came out the back of the house. He saw me, saw what I had from the window, and came running outside yelling something about his sister. I guess he figured I'd killed his sister, too."

"Did you?"

"No. Oh, I would have, I wanted to. She saw me the night she disappeared. She was running across the field and we all but smacked into each other. How 'bout those Eagan kids, eh? Always around at the wrong time." He shook his head. "I grabbed at her — had her, too, but she managed to get away from me and she ran like hell."

"Ran where?"

"Beats the shit out of me. Don't think I didn't try to find her. Searched for hours, but it was as if the earth opened up and swallowed her whole. I couldn't track her, and the next thing I knew, she'd officially disappeared. I didn't have a decent night's sleep, I can tell you that, until I realized she wasn't coming back."

"Then where did she go?" Lorna's brows knit together. "If you didn't kill her, where has she been all these years?"

"I don't know, and frankly, I don't care. All I know is that the gods were smiling on me that night, because wherever she went, she obviously didn't tell anyone what she saw."

"You really think the gods had anything to do with that?"

He gestured at her with the gun. "Walk. Straight back."

He was leading her to the door to the wine cellar.

"I don't understand how you got those boys out here. I mean, you couldn't very well pick them up on your bike and ride to the woods with a body over the handlebars."

"Very funny." He looked amused. "Actually, I used my mother's car. She'd be sound asleep every night by nine, I'd be out of the house and cruising down the road by ten."

"And Fritz didn't notice? He didn't care that you were taking the car and driving around without a license?"

"He was my brother, why would he tell? Besides, everyone around here drove before they had a license. It's farm country. Everyone does it. The local cops would stop me once in a while, slap me on the wrist, and that would be that. Outside of town, I was never stopped. I've always been a good driver, never gave them a reason to pull me over. Didn't speed, stopped at the stop signs, never jumped a light." He grinned. "My driving record is perfect."

"Where did Fritz think you were going, all those nights?"

"I always told him I had a hot date. I was pretty popular with the girls, maybe you remember." He smirked.

Her face flushed, recalling her own crush on him, then realized the absurdity. *He's holding a gun on me, he's going to kill me, and I'm embarrassed to remember that I used to have a crush on him.*

"You would drive to the Purple Pheasant to pick up your victims."

"It was the perfect feeding ground. They never checked ID. Actually, they welcomed the young boys. The younger the better."

"The owner. You killed him, too."

Mike nodded thoughtfully. "He was one sharp dude. He knew the guys who'd disappeared had all been in his club. It took him awhile, but eventually he realized he'd seen them all with me. If I'd been a little older, maybe I'd have been a little smarter. As it was, hey, I was fourteen, fifteen, sixteen years old. I didn't hunt often, but when I did, I hunted well."

Lorna fought the urge to throw up.

He stopped at the door to the wine cellar.

"Open it. And turn the light on."

She did as she was told.

"Down the steps," he commanded.

She started taking them slowly, trying to think of how to distract him. There was only one way in or out, and that was by the steps they now descended. She eyed the barrels that lined the room and wondered if it would be possible to use them offensively. She didn't think she could move quickly enough to roll them before he got off a shot.

Okay, Uncle Will, if you're really still

around, now would be a good time to show yourself.

"Keep moving. Back there, through that doorway."

He pointed to the tasting room.

She might have a chance after all.

"Where's the light switch?" He felt inside the doorway, first on the left side, then the right.

"It's on the opposite end of the room," she told him. "All the way back."

"Go turn it on."

"Sure." She stepped into the windowless room and tried to remember where she'd left the candles. She dropped to her knees and crouched behind one of the two upholstered chairs, and held her breath, and let the darkness swallow her whole.

"Hey, Lorna," Mike called from the doorway, and she heard him start to follow her into the room. "Turn on the lights."

She knelt still as a stone. If he wanted her, he was going to have to find her in the dark. She had the advantage of knowing where the furniture was. Her only chance was to circle around him, without him seeing her, and make it to the door. If she could get that far, she'd slip outside the room and bolt the door behind her, locking him inside.

If she could get as far as the door.

"Damn you." He kicked at something on the floor and it bounced off the wall. "Damn you . . ."

In the dark, his breathing was erratic with rage and seemed to come from all sides at once. The room wasn't large enough for her to make a clean break for the door. The most she could hope for was to draw him farther in. She moved stealthily to the left, knowing that even as her eyes grew accustomed to the dark, so did his.

"Honest to God, Lorna, I was going to make this easy for you. Shit!" He cursed loudly as he tripped over a chair. "Damn you! I'd planned one clean shot to the head. But now, I swear, when I get my hands on you, you're going to beg me for that one bullet."

A little farther to the left. Inch by inch, trying to stay within the shadow of the chairs.

"Bitch."

He shot the gun into the room and the sound momentarily paralyzed her. He fired twice more and she began to shake all over. She held both hands over her mouth to keep from crying out. She was too frightened to move now — even if she could make it to the door, her legs wouldn't support her to take her there.

It occurred to her for the first time that she wasn't going to get out of the cellar alive.

Another shot, this one closer.

"I've got plenty more, Lorna. I can stand here and shoot at you all day."

"Gonna be hard to do that with a bullet in your brain." T.J.'s voice from the doorway was steady, but there was no mistaking the intent.

"Well, hey, Mr. PI. Nice of you to stop by."

"Drop the gun, Mike. Don't make this more difficult than it needs to be."

Mike responded with a shot to the doorway.

"Sooner or later, you're going to run out. I won't," T.J. told him calmly.

"You forget, PI," Mike's breath was ragged, "I've got something you want in here."

"If you had her, you'd have killed her already. So unless you were talking to a corpse a few seconds ago, I'd say you don't have her."

"She's in here, I'm in here. You're out there." Mike laughed. "She moves, she's a dead woman. How do you figure you're going to get her out?"

"I shoot you. She walks past your body on the way to the door."

"You can't shoot what you can't see."

A shot rang out and Mike shrieked. His gun hit the floor. Lorna screamed and backed into the wall, falling off her feet. T.J. came into the room and stepped over the moaning man and picked up the gun.

"Lorna?" T.J. said softly. "Are you all right?"

"I'm over here." She struggled to get to her feet and he was there, reaching down to help her.

His arms closed around her and tightened. "Are you all right?" he repeated.

She nodded shakily.

"How could you see him? How did you know where to shoot?" she asked as he led her out of the dark room and into the light.

"Night goggles." He slipped them off over his head with one hand. "A favorite of PIs everywhere."

"I thought you told Mitch you got rid of all your toys."

"Almost all."

"Is he going to die?"

"No. But he won't be writing any letters home for a while." He handed her his cell phone. "Go outside and call Mitch.

There's no signal down here. I tried calling him when I realized you were in the wine cellar, but I couldn't get a signal."

She stumbled and he caught her.

"Maybe you'd better sit down for a minute." He turned a barrel on its side and guided her to it, but she shook her head.

"I'm fine. I'll be fine. It was just so . . . I was so . . ."

She couldn't find the words.

"Hey, I've been shot at a time or two myself. It's not fun. Maybe one of the scariest things that can happen, and if you're not used to being around guns, and you've never been shot at before, it's a pretty scary experience."

"It was so loud." She covered her ears, remembering. "I swear, I'm usually not very wimpy."

"It is loud, and when you're that close to it, yeah, it's real tough on the ears." He brushed the hair back from her face. "I don't think you're wimpy at all. I think you were damned smart to lure him in there. You gave yourself a fighting chance. If you hadn't done that, you'd be dead right now."

"If you hadn't shown up when you did, I *would* be dead right now. I didn't think I was going to get out of there alive."

"You did just fine." He wiped the tears from her cheeks, then leaned over and kissed her. "You did just fine."

She nodded. "I'll call Mitch. You keep an eye on Mike."

Lorna made it to the steps and held on to the railing while she climbed up to the barn. She walked across the wooden floor and out through the door and resisted the urge to pinch herself. Five minutes ago, she'd been certain that her life was going to end. She'd never faced that kind of challenge, never known that kind of fear. Yet she'd still managed to outsmart Mike, long enough for help to arrive.

All in all, it could have been worse.

She was alive, the bad guy lay bleeding on the tasting room floor, and the cool guy had not only saved her, but he'd kissed her as well. She leaned back against the barn door and dialed Mitch's number.

Yeah, she thought as she listened to the phone ring, all in all, it could have been a hell of a lot worse.

Twenty-two

"Lorna, how are you feeling?" Regan rushed up the front steps and dropped her bag on the porch. "Mitch told me what happened. I tried calling your cell and the house phone, but you didn't pick up."

"I'm fine, thanks. It took a few hours for the ringing in my ears to stop, but all's well now." Lorna got up from the chair where she'd been rocking, passing the time quietly while she waited for T.J. and Mitch to come back with the beer and Chesapeake crabs they'd set out for almost an hour ago.

"God, I turn my back on you for five days and you damn near get yourself killed."

"But I didn't get killed. T.J. arrived, like the posse, to save the day." She smiled and added, "My hero."

"Not bad, as heroes go." Regan took the rocker next to Lorna's.

"Ummm. Not bad at all. Thanks for the referral. Who'd have thought, the day I called you, that it would lead to all this?"

"All what?" Regan narrowed her eyes. "Lead to what? Are you holding back on me? Is something going on between you and the PI?"

Before Lorna could answer, the Crossfire pulled into the drive and stopped on a dime. Mitch and T.J. got out, laden with several bags.

"I hope you're both very hungry," T.J. called, "because we have enough crabs here to feed an army."

"Did you catch them yourselves?" Lorna stood at the top of the steps. "You've been gone for an hour. The Crab Shack is just two miles down the road."

"Well, we stopped for the beer first. Then we decided to have the crabs cooked for us, instead of cooking them here. Then we realized we didn't have enough beer, so we had to go back to the state store." T.J. grinned at Lorna. "You see how this could take some time."

"I do." Lorna laughed. "Bring it all into the kitchen and we'll get some plates."

"Plates?" Regan appeared horrified. "You don't use plates to eat Maryland crabs. You cover the table with newspaper, then paper towels, then you put the crabs right on the table."

"Don't you get newsprint on the crabs?" Lorna asked.

"Not if you use paper towels. Then,

when you're finished, you wrap up the paper, crab debris and all, and toss everything into the trash can. Preferably one with a tight lid, so the raccoons don't litter your yard with shells."

"Hey, you live on the Bay, I have to think you know what you're talking about. But I can go you one better." Mitch took a roll of paper from one of the bags. "Unprinted paper. What do you think of that, eh?"

"Where'd you find that?" Regan went down the steps to inspect the roll.

"The guy at the crab place sells it." Mitch looked pleased with himself.

"Definitely much better than newspaper," Regan agreed. "That's why you're a special agent with the FBI, right? 'Cause you're so smart?"

"You betcha." Mitch took her by the arm. "Now, let's go in and eat. The smell of those crabs had me gnawing on my hand all the way down Callen Road."

The foursome crowded into the kitchen. Lorna spread the paper thickly on the top of the table, and T.J. dumped the crabs in the middle. Mitch opened four bottles of beer and set one in front of each of the chairs. Lorna grabbed a handful of paper napkins and passed them around.

"Looks like we're all set," Lorna said.

"I'd like to propose a toast," Regan said. "To friendship."

"There's something we can all drink to."

They all did.

Mitch turned to T.J. "So, now that your last big case has been solved, what say we talk a little more about getting your name back on the government's payroll?"

"Sorry, pal. I already have plans."

"What plans?" Mitch grabbed a crab and broke it open.

"I'm thinking about going into business for myself."

"I thought you'd decided you didn't want to be a PI anymore."

"Different business." T.J. separated meat from cartilage and began to eat.

"What kind of business?" Mitch frowned.

"Well, I think I want to try my hand at a winery," T.J. told him.

"You're kidding, right?" Mitch laughed.

"Dead serious." T.J. nodded and turned to Lorna. "The place is still for sale, right?"

He'd caught her completely off guard and she stammered. "Ah . . . well, yeah. I suppose so. Did you want the whole farm?"

"I was thinking just the vineyard."

"We'd have to see if it could be subdivided." She heard herself think out loud. "And the wine cellar . . . did you want the wine cellar?"

"What's a winery without a wine cellar?" he replied.

"It's under the barn." Lorna frowned. "The barn should stay with the house."

"We'll see what we can work out."

"What do you know about wine, except that you like to drink it?" Mitch asked.

"Actually, I know quite a bit," T.J. told him.

"Since when?"

"Since I spent the weekend talking to several growers in the area. I spent hours before and after that reading up on the subject on the Internet." He turned to Lorna. "This is a good site, and you've already got the trellises set up. There are at least seven really good vineyards in the area, and several wineries. I sampled the products and was pretty impressed with what they produce. You already have the cellar, you have some barrels. It's a start."

"How do you know what kind of grapes to grow? What kind of wine to make?" Mitch persisted.

"Actually, the classic white wine grapes do very well here. And for the first few years, I'll grow and sell the grapes to some of the local wineries. Then, when I feel I'm ready, I'll move on to the next phase of making my own wine."

"You really are serious," Lorna said.

T.J. nodded. "Very serious. So if you're selling — look no further for your buyer. Of course, I'll probably need to scout up a little capital."

"I might have a few bucks to invest," Regan told him. "I don't have a lot of time to put into a new venture right now, but I will down the road. And I could design the labels for your bottles when the time comes."

"All right. My first investor." T.J. turned to Mitch. "How 'bout you? You in?"

"I might be. I'd like to look at your prospectus first."

"Well, that's where Lorna comes in." He touched her arm. "You want to make it a four-way partnership?"

"I already have a business," she reminded him.

"Exactly. We'll need a good CPA. You can be our moneyman."

"I'll consider it."

"It'll be a good way for you to work off my bill for the past ten days." T.J. grinned. "And it's a big one. My time is not cheap."

"We'll see what we can work out," she replied.

"This is great. We're going to be business partners," Regan noted. "So what do we call this vineyard?"

"Lavender Hill," Lorna said without thinking.

"What?" T.J. asked. "Where did that come from?"

"Oh. Sorry. We can come up with something, I'm sure."

"I like Lavender Hill," Regan told her.

"It's the original name of the farm. Over the years, everyone started referring to it as Palmer's farm. I found the old sign in the barn when I was a kid, and my grandmother told me about how, when her grandparents moved here, the hill out back was all wild lavender."

"Lavender Hill Wines." T.J. nodded. "I like it. Mitch?"

Mitch nodded. "Absolutely."

"So there we are. We have a business. We have a name for it." T.J. tilted his bottle. "We're in the wine business. At the very least, the grape business. Or will be, by this time next year."

"That's going to be some commute, Dawson, if you're planning on staying in Baltimore," Mitch pointed out.

"That house is sold, so I have to look for a new place, anyway. When I was driving into Callen earlier today, I saw a house for rent out on Conway Road. I wrote down the Realtor's number, so I can give him a call in the morning."

"I'm glad I didn't stay an extra day in Chicago," Regan noted. "Look what I would have missed."

"Hey, what did you find out about Eddie Kroll while you were out there?" Mitch asked.

"Not much." Regan frowned. "It's really odd. I know he existed, I have his report cards. But it seems he just vanished when he was around thirteen or so."

"Maybe he died," Lorna suggested.

"I went back through the parish records, but I couldn't find a notice of his death or that he'd transferred out of school. Midway through his freshman year in high school, he simply disappeared."

"Well, so much for that." Mitch grabbed another crab from the pile.

"No, I'm going to find out who he was. If for no other reason than to satisfy myself. Much like Lorna's quest to find her old friend. I want to know where Eddie Kroll went, and why my father had his old report cards."

"Did you hear a car?" Lorna frowned, and looked out the window.

"It's Chief Walker." Lorna excused herself. "I'll be right back."

She went through the dining room and out the front door and stood on the steps with her hands on her hips, watching the black-and-white turn around in her drive. When the car came to a stop, she walked to it.

The chief lowered the window on the passenger side and asked, "How are you doing, Lorna?"

"I'm doing fine. Thanks."

"Just wanted to stop by, see how you are. And to tell you . . . well, I just want you to know how glad I am that nothing worse happened to you. And that I'm sorry for . . . well, sorry there was bad blood there for a while."

Lorna nodded. "Apology accepted. Don't give it another thought."

"I ran into Fritz at the Quik Stop. His friend is in town, he said they'd be stopping out to see you. Seems like a nice guy, this friend of his."

"I'm sure he is."

"Mike lawyered up real fast — he's filing motions right and left. It's going to be months before the DA can get that show on the road."

"Isn't that pretty much what you'd expected?" Lorna asked. "Did anyone expect him to confess?"

"Oh, one other thing. That name you asked me about . . ."

"Claude Raymond Fleming."

"Right. I asked around, found out his sister, Joanne, lived over in Arnold. She died a few years back, cancer."

"Fleming's sister lived in Arnold?" Lorna felt a stab of recognition. Then she asked, even though she was pretty sure she knew the answer, "What was her last name?"

"Porter. Her married name was Porter. Didn't know if you still wanted the information, but thought I'd pass it on to you, all the same."

"Thanks, Chief. I'm glad you did." She stepped back from the car and waved, and he said good-bye as he drove past her. She stood in the driveway for a moment, then went back into the house.

"There's something I have to do," Lorna told her guests as she searched for her car keys. She found them on the counter, then looked for her handbag, which she found in the dining room, the strap looped over a chair. "You stay and finish your dinner, I'll be back in a little while."

T.J. had followed her into the dining room.

"Where are you going? What did Walker say that has you running out the door?"

"He told me that Claude Raymond Fleming's sister lived in Arnold. Her name was Joanne Porter." She searched her bag for her sunglasses. "As in Danielle Porter."

"Danielle's mother? So Claude Fleming is Danielle's uncle?"

"Apparently. Now, why do you suppose she would have run to the phone to call him the minute she closed the door on us?"

"Good question," he agreed. "I'll come with you."

"No, thanks. I think she's more likely to talk to me if I'm alone."

"What are you hoping to find?"

"She knows about Melinda, T.J. I'm sure she does. And I'm not going to let it go until I find out what really happened to Mellie."

Lorna parked her car alongside Danielle's double-wide and got out. She walked to the front door and knocked until it opened.

Danielle stood in the doorway. When she saw Lorna, she stepped outside and closed the door behind her.

"What now?" Danielle asked.

"I give up. What's the connection?" Lorna asked.

"I have no idea what you're talking about." Danielle turned to open the door and Lorna stuck out an arm to stop her.

"You know exactly what I'm talking about. Melinda Eagan. Where is she?"

"What does it matter, after all these years? Just leave it, and get on with your life."

"Melinda was my best friend. I need to know what happened to her. Her mother needs to know."

"Her?" Danielle scoffed. "Her mother doesn't give a shit about her and never did. Beat the crap out of Melinda and Jason every chance she got. She didn't deserve them then, and she doesn't deserve Mellie now."

"Billie's changed a lot over the years, she isn't the woman she used to be."

"That doesn't make up for what she did to them. Sorry." Danielle opened the door and stepped inside the double-wide.

"She's really a different woman. Oh, please don't close the door. Listen to me, Billie has spent the last twenty-five years regretting everything that happened between her and her kids."

"Too little, too late," Danielle said, glaring at her from the doorway. "Tell it to someone who gives a shit. A woman treats her kids that way, she deserves to lose them."

"That's not your decision to make."

"It sure as hell isn't yours." The door was all but closed.

"If you talk to Mellie, tell her . . . tell her that I never forgot her. That I never stopped missing her and that she was the best friend I ever had." The door made a little puff sound as it closed.

"And tell her she can find me easily enough, if she ever wants to," Lorna added, loud enough to be heard from inside, before she walked away.

She got into her car and backed out of the drive, tears spilling down her face, saddened to know that, after all these years, her friend was still out of reach.

The good news was that now she knew for certain Melinda was still alive.

Twenty-three

"Hey! Tall, sweaty guy!" Lorna called to T.J. from the end of the first row of trellises. When he turned around, she tossed him a bottle of water, and he caught it in one hand.

"Nice catch," she told him. She gestured toward the section he'd been weeding. "Looking good."

"These tall thorny things are murder to get out of the ground. There must be a million of them." He took the top off the bottle and drank deeply. "Thanks for the water."

"They're some kind of thistle, I think."

"They're a pain in the ass by any name." He mopped his forehead with the back of his forearm.

"You still determined to clear all this out before the frost hits?"

He nodded. "I *will* get it all cleared before the frost hits. Then, when spring comes around, I'll be ready to put in my vines."

"After having spent the winter months studying up on grapes and other related topics."

"By this time next year, I'll be conversant in all things grape. Types, soil requirements, pests — I will positively dazzle you with my knowledge."

"I'm looking forward to being dazzled."

He took off the heavy gloves he'd been wearing to weed out the worst of the overgrowth, and walked to the end of the row.

"Are you sure you won't miss the excitement of law enforcement?" She watched him approach, her hands on her hips.

"I've had about all the excitement from that quarter that one lifetime can handle, thanks."

"Even though the FBI's still after you to re-up?"

"They're wasting their time. I keep telling them that I'll never go back. I don't know what more I can say." He took another drink from the bottle.

"Maybe someday you'll trust me enough to tell me about that," she said softly.

"What do you want to know?"

"What happened to make you lose confidence in yourself?"

"Oh. That. That's an easy one," he said matter-of-factly. "Teddy Kershaw. Lakeview, Georgia."

"Who's Teddy Kershaw?"

"Was," he said with emphasis. "Who *was*

Teddy Kershaw is the question."

"Okay. Who was he?"

"He was a serial killer. I'd been asked to develop a profile for the local PD. Which I did." He stared at the ground.

"And?"

"And it was dead wrong. Well, not completely wrong. It was right, for the most part. I just got the most immediate part wrong."

"Which was?"

"I told the cops the perp had to be Caucasian. All the vics had been white — white victims, white killer. Everybody knows that serial killers only target victims within their own race." He shook his head. "How arrogant on my part, eh? Like I knew it all."

"What happened?"

"Well, when the cops got a report of a man who'd been seen hanging around the neighborhood of three of the victims, I told them not to waste their time. 'The guy described by the neighbors is African-American. Our serial killer is Caucasian.' "

He scuffed at the ground with the toe of his shoe, kicked a clod of dirt aside.

"So, armed with the gospel according to Saint Thomas Dawson, the Lakeview cops ignore the calls and keep on looking for this theoretical white killer. Three more women died before they caught Teddy. A black man. The same black man the cops had been alerted to ten days before."

T.J.'s face had gone white under his tan. "Does that answer your question?"

"How many times had you been right?"

He brushed her off. "Doesn't matter. What matters is that my know-it-all attitude cost three women their lives."

"I'm sure you didn't —"

"Didn't mean to screw up? Tell that to the families of those three women."

"T.J., I'm so sorry."

"I'll be sorry for the rest of my life. But I'll never go back to the Bureau. I don't even know why they'd want me."

"Mitch says you're really good."

"Mitch is my friend. He has to say that." He took one more drink, draining the bottle, then pitched it in the direction of the weed pile. "The bottom line is, I was responsible for the loss of innocent lives. I can't change that, no matter how many times I wish I could go back to the moment I told the cops to ignore the reports. I have to live with that. But I won't go back to the Bureau. I can find something else to do with my life." He paused. "I *have* found something else to do with my life, and I like it. I like the physical work, I like the idea of growing something good, making something people will enjoy. That the end result of my hard work will be something tangible. I like that we're doing this, the four of us."

"I don't know how much time the other two will have to devote to it after awhile. Mostly it's going to be you and me."

"Even better." He smiled. Then, changing the subject, he asked, "How long do you think you'll be in Woodboro?"

"Four days, at the most. I need to get back here as soon as possible. Remember, my brother will be coming home next week for the first time in years. I want to make sure the house is in order."

"If there's anything you want me to do while you're gone, just say the word."

"I will, thanks. It'll be interesting to see how Rob feels, now that Mike Keeler is in jail and he doesn't have that weight of secrecy around his neck. When I spoke with him the other night, he sounded really happy to be coming back. So I'd like his room freshened, that sort of thing. I can save some of the packing at my apartment for another trip, but I can't put off the meetings I've set up with my clients. I need to tell them about the change in address

417

and assure them that the service will remain the same high quality as always."

"You'll let me know if you need help packing things?"

"I should be fine on that score. My friend Bonnie will be over to help me sort through stuff and pack up the car. What furniture I don't sell, I can have brought back by a small moving van. I don't expect any problems." She sighed. "You know, when I left here, I never thought I'd want to come back to live. Then after I got home, I didn't want to leave. In spite of all the craziness — the bodies in the field, being shot at in the wine cellar, almost killed — I realized this really is my home. I don't want to leave. I don't want to live anywhere else."

"Funny, I'm starting to feel the same way." He kissed the side of her mouth.

"I know you can do better than that, Dawson."

He laughed and kissed her again, keeping her at arm's length.

"Like you said," he pointed out, "I am one tall, sweaty man. But I do clean up real good."

"Well, clean up later, because Regan and Mitch will be along any minute. They're both looking forward to working in the vineyard this weekend. I told Regan it was dirty work and there were thorns and bugs everywhere, but she said, 'Cool. I can't wait.' "

"We'll see how long she lasts."

"Don't underestimate her. She's a tough cookie. I could tell you some stories . . ."

The sound of a car door slamming near the barn drew their attention.

"I guess they're here," T.J. said. "Were they driving up together?"

"I don't . . ." Lorna watched a dark-haired woman get out of the car and look around. "That's not Regan. I'll go see."

As soon as Lorna got within fifty feet of the car, she knew exactly who her visitor was.

She stopped dead in her tracks and stared.

Melinda Eagan had grown tall and willowy, and was quite stylish in black pants and a short-sleeved white top. She had gold at her ears and on her wrists, and a gold and diamond wedding set on the ring finger of her left hand.

"Lori?" Melinda took a few tentative steps toward her.

"Mel. Oh, my God, Melinda. You really are alive." Lorna walked toward her, both hands reaching out. "You really are here."

"I'm sorry," Melinda whispered as she took Lorna's hands. "I'm so sorry for what I must have put you through all these years."

"I'm just glad you're safe. You're alive." Lorna squeezed Melinda's hands. Both women began to tear up.

Melinda smiled. "You grew up to be so pretty."

"So did you."

"I heard about everything that happened here. About Jason." Her eyes reflected her sorrow. "I wasn't surprised to hear what happened to him. I was only surprised that she hadn't done it."

"Mellie, how did you do it?" Lorna asked. "How did you manage to disappear without a trace for all those years?"

"Easier than you'd think. Once I found out about my father . . ."

"What about your father? I thought he left when you were a year old?"

"Buddy Eagan was not my father."

Lorna's jaw dropped.

"Hey, no one was more surprised than I was. I had no idea. I simply thought he didn't care about us and left, like my mother told us. When Danielle approached me at school at the end of third grade and started saying things like how she was my cousin and I didn't know who my real daddy was, I thought it was just an older girl doing something to tease one of the little kids. When she asked me if I wanted to go to her house to meet him, I got real curious, and I went, thinking it was basically her being goofy."

She crossed her arms over her chest.

"It wasn't a hoax. It seems my mother had had an affair with Claude Fleming and I was the result. She told him, but he wasn't about to go up against Buddy over it, so he left town, moved to Lancaster. I guess it began to bother him, though, knowing he had a child in Callen that he didn't even know. Years later, after he'd married and started a family, he told his wife about me. She thought he ought to know his child, so she encouraged him to find me. When he found out that Danielle and I went to the same school, he asked her to get to know me a little. Then she told me she'd heard her mother and her uncle talking about me being his daughter. The next thing I knew, I was seeing him on weekends at Danielle's house. He wanted me to meet his wife and kids, so I figured, why not. I started spending weekends in Lancaster — oh, my mother thought I was at Danielle's, but she didn't really care where I was, as long as I wasn't in her hair. Anyway, that's how I met my dad, and my stepmother."

"And your mother never knew?"

"Never had a clue. I'm sure it never occurred to her that my father would want me, or that anyone except her and Dad knew that he was my real father. She had no idea that my new friend, Danielle, was his niece. There'd been no reason for Billie to tell anyone about him, and sometimes even now I wonder if she remembered that I was his daughter. I don't know what she's like these days, but back then, she was either working or drinking. That was pretty much it."

She brightened slightly. "In contrast, my father's house was always calm and quiet and clean, and they made me feel very welcome. I had a little sister and baby brother, and there was none of the chaos I'd been living in. When my dad found out he was going to have to move to Michigan for work, he couldn't leave me behind. He and his wife talked it over, and they wanted me to go with them. They knew what had been happening at home. He wasn't about to move out of state and leave me with Billie."

"And you wanted to go?"

"Are you kidding?" Melinda laughed. "I felt like I was living two totally different lives. I couldn't wait to get away from her. I felt bad about leaving Jason behind, but I figured he was fourteen already, he'd be out of the house soon enough. Mom had made it pretty plain she wished she'd never had either of us. I didn't see where it would make much difference to her."

"And your father didn't think he should tell her he was taking you?"

"He said she didn't deserve me. That she'd never given me much of a proper home, and if she missed me at all, it was just too bad for her."

"He could have tried to get custody of you legally."

"I don't think it occurred to him to do that, things were happening too fast. He didn't have a lot of time before he had to leave for the new job, and some years later, he said that back then it was a hassle for a father to get custody. So he had simply asked me if I wanted to go, and I said yes."

"How did you do it?" Lorna asked, fascinated. "How did you pull it off without anyone knowing?"

"It was simple, really. It was my birthday, remember?"

Lorna nodded. She'd never forgotten.

"I wanted to tell you, I wanted to say good-bye. I thought about you so often, when I was in Michigan, but I knew I could never get in touch with you."

"I don't know how I could have kept that secret, Mel," Lorna admitted. "Especially from my mother."

"My stepmother figured as much, and she said I couldn't put you in that position. She was right," Melinda nodded, "but it was still hard. Anyway, about that night. I knew my brother wasn't going to walk me all the way back home, he never did. My dad was going to meet me a half mile down the road from our house, so when Jason stopped at Matt's, I just kept going. That's why it was so important to me to wear my birthday dress. It was the only thing I wanted to take with me."

A cloud passed over Melinda's face.

"Unfortunately, while I was running across the field, I bumped into Mike Keeler. Literally." She shivered. "He dropped what he was carrying and took off after me. I managed to get away. I ran and hid in our secret place."

"The wine cellar."

Melinda nodded. "It started getting cold, so I wrapped myself in one of the blankets we left there, and I waited until I

424

thought he was gone. I folded the blanket real small and took it, and I crept back through the field. I was scared to death. All my brother's friends were out there, calling me, and I was afraid they were going to do something bad to me, so I went back to the place where I'd dropped the bag that had my dress in it, then ran for my life. My dad picked me up down the road — he thought I'd changed my mind 'cause I was so late, was just about to give up on me — and we left for Michigan at dawn the next day."

"And it never occurred to you to tell someone that you saw Mike carrying a dead body? Didn't that bother you?"

"I didn't know what he was carrying. It just looked like a big sack to me. It was so dark, and the weeds were so tall, I honestly never saw it. I couldn't figure out why he was mad, or why he was trying to grab me. All I knew was that he was really angry and I had to run as fast as I could and not let him catch me. It's only been since the bodies were found here on the farm that I understood what it was he'd been carrying that night."

"You never knew about Jason?"

"Danielle told me he'd disappeared. I figured he'd either run away or my mother had killed him. I'm relieved, I guess, to find out she wasn't responsible for his death."

"Your mother has changed a lot over the years, Mel. She's not the same woman you knew."

Melinda's jaw tightened but she didn't reply.

"Look, you're the only person who knows how you feel. But I think you should know . . ." Lorna hesitated. "I guess you need to hear those things from her, not from me. Maybe someday . . ."

Melinda nodded.

"She's living in the cottage, you know. Back near the vineyard."

"She is?" Melinda was obviously surprised at the news.

"My mother let her live there, after Billie got sick. She hasn't been well for the last three years, Mel."

"And your mother?"

"We lost her about two months ago."

"I'm so sorry." Melinda squeezed Lorna's hand. "She was such a good person. When we were little, and things were especially bad at home, I used to pretend she was my mother, too. I wish I could have seen her again."

"I wish you could have, too," Lorna told her.

"Do you suppose she would want . . ." Melinda pointed in the direction of the cottage.

"I think there's nothing she'd want more."

Melinda appeared to be at war with herself. Finally, she said, "Would you mind if I left my car here? Maybe I could just walk over . . ."

"You're welcome to leave the car for as long as you want. Perhaps on your way back, you'll stop in, and we can visit a bit more."

Melinda nodded and set off toward the vineyard, her eyes focused in the direction of the cottage. Lorna watched until she was out of view.

"Phew." Lorna blew out a long breath.

" 'Phew' what?" Regan came up behind her.

"Oh. Sorry. I didn't hear you drive up," Lorna said.

"You looked like you were in a trance," Mitch told her.

Lorna nodded. "I guess in a sense I was."

"Who's that, walking across the field?" Regan asked.

"That," Lorna turned to her, "is Melinda Eagan."

"*The* Melinda Eagan?" Regan gasped. "Alive and well?"

"Alive and well, *the* Melinda Eagan."

"Where'd she come from?" Mitch frowned. "Where's she been?"

"I'll tell you over dinner," Lorna promised.

"I'm afraid I'm not going to be able to wait that long," Regan told her. "We just stopped by to tell you that Mitch is going to drop me off at the airport in Lancaster, then he'll be back to help T.J. in the vineyard."

"That explains the pretty outfit," Lorna said. "Definitely not field hand attire."

Regan laughed. "Did I tell you that while I was in Chicago, I placed a personal ad in all the newspapers in and around Sayreville, Illinois? Well, I got a call last night from someone who knew Eddie Kroll. I have an appointment to meet this woman tomorrow morning." Regan's eyes were shining. "Wait till you hear this — Eddie was one of three boys convicted of murdering one of their friends . . . he was thirteen at the time, and the youngest of the three. He went through the juvenile system and was released when he turned twenty-one."

"And then?" Lorna asked.

"And then, apparently, he dropped off the face of the earth. No one has seen or heard from him since."

"I guess that explains why your father started gathering information about him. He could have been looking into the murder for a book," Lorna suggested.

"Maybe," Regan said hesitantly. "Somehow I have the feeling there's more to it than that. I don't know why, but something tells me this was more than just another case to him."

"Well, I'm sure you'll get to the bottom of it eventually," Lorna assured her.

"With the help of my special agent." Regan poked at Mitch.

"Every beautiful woman needs her own computer geek." Mitch tugged at Regan's hand. "Come on, I want to see T.J. for a minute."

"You go on," Regan told him. "I'll catch up with you."

When Mitch was out of range, Regan asked, "So, is this a thing? You and T.J.?"

"It sure feels like a 'thing.'" Lorna grinned.

"Good." Regan hugged her, then started off to join Mitch. "Good for you."

Lorna followed her friend toward the vineyard, but paused to watch T.J.

working. From where she stood, she could see him struggling with a twisted section of vine. She knew he'd keep at it until the vine was worked free, until all the vines were worked free, and the vineyard was ready for the new plants to be set in next spring. There was such promise in that.

She smiled to herself. *Yeah, good for me . . .*

About the Author

Mariah Stewart is the bestselling author of numerous novels and several novellas. A RITA finalist for romantic suspense, she is the recipient of the Award of Excellence for contemporary romance, a RIO (Reviewers International Organization) Award honoring excellence in women's fiction, and a Reviewers' Choice Award from *Romantic Times* magazine. A three-time recipient of the Golden Leaf Award and a Lifetime Achievement Award winner from the New Jersey Romance Writers, she has been inducted into their Hall of Fame.

A native of Hightstown, New Jersey, she lives with her husband, two daughters, and two rambunctious golden retrievers amid the rolling hills of Chester County, Pennsylvania. She is a member of the Valley Forge Romance Writers, the New Jersey Romance Writers, and the Romance Writers of America.